Rachel?

The shadows cast by the overhanging trees had deepened the blue of Patrick's eyes to the color of a dusky summer sky. Looking up into those eyes, Rachel felt as if they could see beyond the flesh and bone of her substance, deep inside the place where she hoarded her innermost thoughts.

"The same things everyone wants," she replied in a whisper so faint he moved closer to catch her words.

At the first light caress of his lips against hers, Rachel closed her eyes... He kissed her gently, then the pressure grew more ardent.

Lying back on the grass, Rachel reached up to capture his face in her hands. She could feel his ragged breathing, the quivering anticipation that matched her own.

What do you want, Rachel? Patrick's question echoed in her head. Rachel let her hand linger on his face.

She wanted him....

ABOUT THE AUTHOR

Laurel Pace has been writing all her life, whether novels, short stories or poetry. Her first venture into professional writing came when she was producing commercials for an advertising agency and was called on to create copy in an emergency. She discovered that she enjoyed copywriting much more than production, and decided to make a career switch. Laurel now makes her home with her husband in Atlanta, Georgia.

Books by Laurel Pace

HARLEQUIN AMERICAN ROMANCE

192–ON WINGS OF LOVE
220–WHEN HEARTS DREAM
312–ISLAND MAGIC

HARLEQUIN INTRIGUE

112–DECEPTION BY DESIGN

Don't miss any of our special offers. Write to us at the following address for information on our newest releases.

Harlequin Reader Service
901 Fuhrmann Blvd., P.O. Box 1397, Buffalo, NY 14240.
Canadian address: P.O. Box 603,
Fort Erie, Ont. L2A 5X3

LAUREL PACE

MAY WINE, SEPTEMBER MOON

Harlequin Books

TORONTO • NEW YORK • LONDON
AMSTERDAM • PARIS • SYDNEY • HAMBURG
STOCKHOLM • ATHENS • TOKYO • MILAN

For Pam
and her memorable New England autumns

Published December 1990

ISBN 0-373-16370-3

Chapter One

Rachel Chase paused, slim fingers poised over the keyboard, and frowned at the acid-green letters that had appeared on the computer screen. Gran had sold the big heart-shaped sachets for three dollars last year, but those hadn't been trimmed with lace. Also, the fabric had gone up in price since the appearance of Heathervale Herb Farm's last catalogue. Her grandmother certainly couldn't expect to keep the farm profitable if she absorbed cost increases. Even before she had earned her M.B.A., Rachel had known that much.

In spite of these common-sense arguments, Rachel tapped the backspace key, neatly obliterating the prices. Perhaps three-fifty would be enough to charge for the large sachets. She would run another projection, based on last year's sales figures, and try to squeeze out a decent profit margin. But first of all, she would see what Gran thought.

As she swung her chair away from the computer table, Rachel chuckled. For all Gran's faith in her granddaughter's business savvy, decisions affecting the herb farm's operation still pivoted on one time-proven factor—Eleanor Haddon Chase's practical wisdom. After all, her grandmother had been running Heathervale long before Rachel had even ventured from her playpen. Rachel suspected that

Gran would have been perfectly content to continue her single-handed operation of the farm if that "infernal fracture," as she termed it, hadn't gotten in her way.

After all, it had been Gran who had taken the eighteenth-century farm she had inherited from her grandparents and coaxed its derelict fields into richly scented meadows filled with herbs and rare flowers. Even after she had been widowed, Gran stubbornly ignored the advice that she sell the burdensome farm and move to a city, where she would be less isolated. The farm was no burden, Eleanor Chase had contended, not as long as its gift shop continued to draw summer visitors and a steady mail-order business. And as far as cities were concerned, well, she had seen quite a few of them in her day and none suited her as well as little Scarborough, Connecticut.

Collecting the marked-up copy of last year's catalogue, Rachel stood up and slid her chair beneath the table. As she walked into the hall, she rose on tiptoe and zigzagged her way toward the stairs. After being back in the old house for only six months, she was surprised at how intimately familiar she had become with its many quirks and oddities. For instance, she knew exactly which of the broad floor boards creaked when stepped on and how loudly. A few let out an irascible squeak when Noodles, the cat, padded across them; others required more vigorous pressure. Right now, Rachel suspected Gran might be napping and she took care to avoid any boards with a voice.

From the top of the stairs, she could see that the door to Gran's bedroom was ajar, the room deserted. Still treading gingerly, Rachel peeked into the upstairs sitting room. Gran especially loved the view from those windows. She often puttered with her handwork up here, taking inspiration for a new gift-shop item from the luxuriant meadows below.

"Gran?" Rachel spoke softly, just in case her grandmother had dozed off in the wing chair.

Getting no answer, Rachel crept closer to the chair. She frowned when she peered over the high back and found it empty. Parts of a quilted calico wreath lay on the brocade seat, along with a pincushion and Gran's antique embroidery scissors. Rachel lifted one of the puffed squares and smiled over the meticulous stitching. Her face fell, however, when she glanced out the window.

"Oh, for heaven's sake!"

Rachel leaned on the sill only long enough to assure herself that the small figure busily weeding a patch of lemon thyme was Gran. Then she hurried downstairs and out the back door.

Before she reached the herb bed, Gran spotted her. Adjusting the ties of her big straw hat, the white-haired woman smiled sheepishly.

"With this sudden warm spell, Owen will never be able to keep up with these weeds all by himself." The curving straw brim dipped as Gran nodded toward an overall-clad man piloting a tiller through the adjoining bed.

Rachel shook her head and tried to look stern. "Gran, you know what Dr. Williams said about bending and stooping!"

Beneath the shading brim, Gran made a face. "I bend over all the time, Rachel. How do you suppose I tie my shoes? Or tickle Noodles's ears? Just because I happen to be bending over in the garden is no reason for you to go into a tailspin."

"Dr. Williams emphasized that you should use the gardening stool," Rachel reminded her. "He even went out of his way to tell me."

"Pah!" Gran defiantly anchored her three-pronged hand spade in the dark earth. But as she joined her granddaughter on the flagstone path, her gray eyes sparkled with mischief. "You know what I think about young Dr. Williams? I think he fancies you. He keeps dreaming up things that might go wrong with me so he can see you. Not such a bad idea, either, I would say. Since you and that young fellow back in Boston have agreed to see some other people, here's your chance to keep your part of the bargain."

"Oh, Gran!" Rachel rolled her eyes to the cloudless blue sky. "Richard and I just need some time away from each other to think clearly about things."

"So think about Dr. Williams," Gran retorted.

Rachel shook her head in good-humored exasperation. "Will you never give up?"

"Of course, I will—after we've found the right young man for you. What don't you like about Dr. Williams, anyway? He's intelligent, handsome, well-mannered, successful. I'll admit he doesn't have the best sense of humor, but if I had an army of sick people staggering past me every day of the week, I don't suppose I would, either. No, the way I look at it, Dr. Williams is quite a nice man."

Still shaking her head, Rachel laughed. "He's very nice, Gran. And all the good things you've said about him are true. He's just..." She hesitated, trying to find the right words to explain why Corbett Williams would never mean more to her than an amiable partner for an occasional dinner date during her sojourn at Heathervale.

"Not Mr. Right." Gran helpfully filled the blank.

"No, he isn't," Rachel agreed, relieved that Gran had seen her point so readily.

"Well, then we'll simply have to keep looking," Gran declared.

Rachel gave her grandmother's still-erect shoulders a quick hug. "I love the way you say *we*. Tell me, has anyone ever suggested that you might be just the tiniest bit meddle-some?''

"Thousands of times," Gran assured her blithely. "That's where you get it, dear. Minding other people's business is in the Haddon genes, I'm convinced. It's just a fact of life that we're both going to have to cope with. You're going to bug me about my health, and I'm going to needle you about your love life." She gave Rachel's hand a loving pat. "But look on the bright side. That's what I do. After all, if you hadn't been so meddlesome, you wouldn't have come back to Heathervale when I broke my hip."

"I was motivated by perfectly legitimate concerns!" Rachel defended herself. "The doctors expected you to have a long convalescence. You need me."

"A lot of young people in your position would have hired a nurse and been done with it," Gran countered. "Running a modest little herb farm isn't usually the number-one job preference of Harvard Business School graduates, you know. You'd just gotten that promotion, could finally start to reap the benefits of so much hard work. And what did you do? Put it all on hold to baby a foolish old lady back onto her feet."

"You may not follow doctor's orders the way you should, but you are *not* a foolish old lady. Besides, I didn't exactly abandon my career. Marquette Brothers has granted me a very generous leave of absence."

"So you can work twice as hard here at the farm!" Gran's hearty laugh belied her eighty years. "Honestly, if you hadn't taken over managing the place after I had this silly accident, I don't know what I would have done. Thanks to you, dear, I'll even be able to keep my schedule for opening the dining room this fall."

Rachel gently steadied her grandmother's elbow. "Serving both lunch and tea will be a big undertaking, even if you weren't recovering from an injury. I hope you haven't bitten off more than you can chew with this expansion plan.''

"Of course I haven't. A historic house like Heathervale should be open to visitors. By serving lunches and teas, I'll not only give tourists a taste of authentic colonial dining, I'll also encourage interest in herbal cookery. Besides, other herb farms do it. And trying new things is what keeps me from turning into a bothersome old prune. You've said so yourself.''

"I don't recall using those exact words," Rachel hedged.

"You know what I mean." Gran pulled her arm free of her granddaughter's hand in a sudden assertion of independence.

Rachel nodded in concession. Lately, however, she had begun to question the wisdom of letting her aging grandmother launch such an ambitious undertaking. Still, she realized any reservations based on Eleanor Chase's physical fitness would be dismissed with a huff. "I suppose I'm letting my conservative business instincts get in the way. But bringing the kitchen up to commercial standards *is* an expensive project, you know.''

"That's why I'm going to lease the fallow acreage to the camp for the summer," Gran told her in the resolute tone of a scoutmaster urging his troop onward. "The way I have things worked out, the rental income will offset some of the interest expense on the money I'm borrowing to spruce up the kitchen. And this fall, I'll be earning enough from the lunches to make up the difference.''

We hope, Rachel thought, but she only gave Gran a fond smile and another hug. "Speaking of the lease, aren't you meeting with Milton Weber this afternoon to discuss the details?''

Gran halted on the low stoop at the rear of the house and dug in her smock's breast pocket. Pulling out a handsome lady's pocket watch, she snapped open the engraved lid and frowned over the dial. "Dear me, I didn't realize how late it was. I told Milton I'd stop by the camp at four." She glanced from her grubby hands to her mud-caked canvas espadrilles. "That doesn't give me any time to make myself presentable. Why don't you meet with him, Rachel?"

Rachel supported Gran's arm as the elderly woman began to kick off her shoes. "You know Milton much better than I do, Gran. I think he'd probably prefer discussing things with you."

Before her granddaughter could interpose, Gran stooped to pick up the shoes. She held them clear of the stoop and slapped the soles together smartly, dislodging a hail of dirt clods into the shrubbery. "Now, Rachel, I know Milton seems like a gruff old fogy," she began, smiling gently as if she were reassuring a child that no monsters lived under her bed, "but that's a result of his being a school principal for so many years. Inside—" she dropped the shoes to thump the bib of her smock with her small fist "—he's the softest touch in the world. Why else would he come out of retirement to run a camp for underprivileged children? No one need be afraid of Milton Weber. I can vouch for that."

"It isn't that I'm afraid of him," Rachel protested. "I think he might be more receptive to some of your stipulations if he heard them from you personally. You know, you are placing a lot of restrictions in the lease, all those clauses about keeping the noise down and the campers on their side of the fence. And then there's the insurance business concerning the pond."

Gran scooted the espadrilles to one side of the stoop with her stockinged toe and opened the door. "You know, Rachel, I think you might be right about my slowing down a bit. All that weeding has really worn me out. I feel ripe for one of those naps you're always recommending." As she stepped over the threshold, she steadied herself on the door frame—so shakily, Rachel almost suspected she was doing it for show.

Whatever the case, she could tell that her grandmother's mind was made up and any arguments about meeting with Milton Weber would fall on deaf ears. "Okay, I'll drive over to the camp at four, but don't be surprised if he balks at some of your requests."

Gran's weary expression vanished instantly. "You're a dear! If you like, I'll look over that draft of the new catalogue while you're out. Before I fall asleep, that is," she took pains to add.

"Thanks, Gran." Rachel handed her grandmother the marked-up catalogue. But as she watched the trim figure jog up the stairs, she had the peculiar feeling of one who'd been had.

Whatever the case, she would simply have to cross her fingers and hope for the best at the meeting with Milton Weber. As one of Scarborough's lifelong residents, Milton remembered Rachel from the summers she had spent at Heathervale between terms at boarding school. Although he always addressed her as Miss Chase and tipped his cap when they met, Rachel was certain his mind's eye still saw a freckle-faced little girl with a mouth full of braces. Come to think of it, he had called her Miss Chase and nicked the bill of his cap to her even when she was a kid.

Although Rachel normally wore little makeup, she took time to brush a thin coat of mascara onto her long lashes and apply some rosy lipstick. She had long endured the curse of pale blond hair, with its tendency to make a grown woman look like Alice in Wonderland if she let it grow more than a few inches. Rachel paused at her dressing table long enough to sweep her shoulder-length mane into a neat

French twist. Businesslike but accommodating, she decided after briefly appraising the mirror's image.

A retired principal would certainly frown on tardiness. Rachel checked her watch, then grabbed the portfolio containing the contract Gran had drawn up and headed for her car. Normally, she would have been tempted to hike through the wooded property separating Heathervale from the camp, but she had no desire to arrive at this appointment with muddy feet and twigs tangled in her hair.

As Rachel turned the silver Volvo wagon off the main road onto a narrow gravel trail, she squinted through the trees. Under its earlier incarnation as Camp Onoconohee, the camp had been a thriving enterprise. Rachel could remember the boisterous sounds of active children filtering through the trees during her vacation visits to Heathervale. At night, she had often knelt by her bedroom window and picked out the bright campfires in the distance. In the intervening years, however, Onoconohee had fallen from glory, unable to compete with bigger camps that boasted pro tennis coaches and real lakes. In recent times, the camp had managed to survive as a site for company picnics and retreats held by civic organizations—patrons that didn't object to its Spartan cabins and less-than-manicured playing fields. If Milton Weber's youth program had not been so desperate for an inexpensive location, Rachel felt sure that Onoconohee would probably have continued its slide into oblivion.

Rachel slowed the car when the trees opened onto a clearing dotted with squat log cabins and screen-enclosed buildings. One thing she would say for Milton and his volunteers: they must be a courageous bunch. As she looked at the dingy, weathered buildings, the work Gran had planned for Heathervale's kitchen and dining room suddenly seemed inconsequential. Practically every feature of the camp, from the weed-choked tennis courts to the ramshackle canoe racks, appeared in need of extensive repairs.

A crooked sign with the words Camp Headquarters carved into it directed Rachel to the most promising-looking of the cabins. She tested the sagging front steps with one foot before trusting them with her weight and then rapped on the ripped screen door.

''Mr. Weber?''

When Milton's level voice failed to respond from the shadows, Rachel shielded her eyes with one hand and peered through the rusted screen. That the office was now in use was evident. A typewriter of the same questionable vintage as the building had been placed on the desk, right beneath an old-fashioned goosenecked lamp. On either side of the venerable machine, a collection of papers, folders and disposable coffee cups attested to work in progress. Milton, however, was nowhere in sight.

Rachel backed down the steps and frowned. Surely he hadn't forgotten the appointment. A glance at her watch assured her that she was not at fault. Turning, she decided to follow the sound of a power saw issuing from one of the screened buildings. Maybe she would find Milton overseeing repairs.

By the time Rachel reached the building, the saw's high-pitched buzz ceased. The driving cadence of a hammer now reverberated through the pines.

''All right, let's prop this baby up and see if it fits.'' A man's voice, husky from exertion, was giving orders. The muttered curse that followed a brief silence assured Rachel that the speaker definitely was not Milton. ''I need to shave a hair off the edge,'' the man concluded wearily.

As the saw whined into action once more, Rachel rose on her toes to peek through the ragged screen. Inside the long room, two men were bent over sawhorses. While one of them, a college-age fellow with lank blond hair, held the beam steady, his companion carefully guided the saw along the piece of wood. Beneath his damp gray T-shirt, the prominent muscles of his back tensed, then relaxed as he completed the pass. When he cut the motor of the saw, he smoothed the freshly trimmed edge with his hand and then straightened himself.

"That oughta do it!" Smiling broadly, the man loosened the red bandanna knotted sweat-band fashion around his head and mopped his face with it. "Let's try to fit it again."

Before the men could shoulder the beam, Rachel seized her chance to ask about Milton. "Excuse me!" She scratched lightly on the screen to attract their attention.

Both men turned, obviously startled to discover someone watching them at their work.

Rachel gestured apologetically. "I hate to interrupt you, but has either of you seen Mr. Weber? I was supposed to meet him here at four."

"Then you must be Mrs. Chase." The man in the gray T-shirt walked to the screen. Removing the bandanna once more, he ran his fingers through his curly brown hair and smiled down at her.

Rachel's eyes traveled up the sturdy columns of his blue denim legs and then caught herself. "No, actually I'm her granddaughter. Gran is recovering from an injury and she wanted me to handle this for her."

Before Rachel could continue, the man strode across the room and swung open the squeaky door. Avoiding the untrustworthy steps, he jumped clear of the porch. "I want to apologize, Miss Chase. I'm afraid I got so involved with installing those shelves, I lost track of the time. My name's Patrick Morrissey. I'm Milton's assistant." He proffered his hand and then hastily withdrew it. Grinning sheepishly, he wiped his palm on one knee of his jeans before grasping Rachel's outstretched hand.

"Rachel Chase." As she traded handshakes with Patrick Morrissey, Rachel was struck by the intense blue of his eyes. They reminded her of the periwinkles that lined many of Heathervale's stone paths, bright with dew in the early-morning sun. Those eyes contrasted pleasingly with his high color and craggy features, like precious stones in the rough, she thought.

"Milton had some business to take care of in Hartford today, but he asked me to look over the contract on the forty acres Mrs. Chase will be leasing to Camp Onoconohee."

Rachel chuckled, eliciting a puzzled look from Patrick. "I didn't know you had kept the camp's old name," she explained. "But I'm glad."

"Why is that?"

Rachel shrugged, a little surprised that he would ask. "Oh, I don't know. Sentimental reasons, I guess. You see, I used to spend my summer vacations with my grandmother, back when the camp was in its heyday. The kids always seemed to have a really good time here. Although, I suppose, by today's standards, old Onoconohee was pretty primitive. No computers, no tennis pros, no water skiing."

Patrick shook his head emphatically. "The campers coming here this summer aren't going to pout over the lack of frills. Most of them will just be happy to get out of a crowded inner-city neighborhood, come to a place where they can breathe fresh air, walk on real grass and enjoy some sports and outdoor activities."

"So these are youngsters who would probably never have a chance to go to camp if it weren't for a program like the one Mr. Weber's developed?" Rachel remarked.

Patrick nodded, but a certain wariness had crept into the dazzling blue eyes. "That's not going to be a problem, is it?

I mean, just because these kids come from less-than-ritzy neighborhoods doesn't make them juvenile delinquents. A few of them have had some problems, but no more than you'd find among any group of young people anywhere.''

"Of course there's no problem," Rachel quickly assured him. "Gran and I think the camp is a wonderful idea." Patrick obviously took a personal interest in the camp and its goals. She could only hope that he wouldn't react too strongly to some of the restrictions in the contract. With that thought in mind, she decided to ease into that ticklish topic. "My grandmother does have a few stipulations about how the Heathervale land can be used, just ordinary precautions."

To her relief, Patrick's appealing face didn't show the faintest trace of distrust. "I understand. While you're here, why don't you have a look at the site plan? Then you can see exactly what we have in mind."

"I'd love to see the plan." Rachel fell in step with Patrick as they headed back to the office cabin. She let him swing the screen door open for her, beckoning her into the messy little room.

"Careful. I'm afraid our volunteer repair crews haven't made it to these steps yet." His fingers clasped her elbow with the strong, sure grasp of a man accustomed to working with his hands. It was a helpful gesture and nothing more, but the tangible masculinity of his touch seemed to awaken all of Rachel's nerve endings. As if he sensed the furor he had set off among the tiny synapses beneath her skin, he quickly picked up the conversation. "We have a crew of students coming out from the university this weekend, so I expect to make big progress. Okay, let's see where I put that site plan."

Furrows creased Patrick's ruddy brow as he shuffled through several large scrolls propped behind the desk.

Rachel decided to use the time to dig the contract out of her portfolio. She needed to have it handy, ready for her to present at the right moment.

"Here we go." Patrick unfurled a blueprint on the desk, anchoring it firmly with both large hands. "Here's the office. These'll be dorms. This big building is the cafeteria. That's the craft cabin and library, where Trip and I were putting in the shelves just now. Over here we'll have a baseball diamond. Stable. Tennis courts. Archery range. Space for volleyball and soccer."

Rachel's eyes followed Patrick's finger as it pointed to the various bluelined diagrams. "So you're keeping most of the original plan?"

Patrick nodded. "Onoconohee is on a fairly tight budget and that precludes any new construction. We figured the most practical approach was to fix up the facilities we already had. So far, that's worked out well."

Rachel fingered the folded contract. "Well, I'm glad you've been able to salvage a lot of old Onoconohee. You mentioned the stable. Is the camp actually going to have horses again?"

"Sure is. Believe it or not, a riding academy in Weymouth is donating a few of their animals for the summer. That Milton is a genius when it comes to drumming up support for the camp. He presents things to people so that they can't say no. But, you know, I really believe that anyone who understands this project would want to get behind it. If you could see those kids..." He hesitated, his strongly featured face suddenly a palette of emotion. "Some of them have been in foster care or come from broken homes. Most are poor. When they see pictures of the camp, horses, simple stuff like canoes and outdoor grills, well, their faces just light up. Once someone's seen those little faces, he'd give us the shirt off his back. I'm convinced."

"I'm sure you're right," Rachel concurred, not without a trace of self-consciousness. Silently, she thanked heaven that Gran had already settled the financial details of the lease with Milton. Already, a certain reluctance kept the contract tightly folded in her hand, and it had nothing to do with Patrick Morrissey's personal appeal. Capable businesswoman that she was, Rachel could stand firm, even when her adversary was a charming Tom Berenger lookalike. Listening to Patrick's moving description of Onoconohee's campers, however, she had started to feel like a Grinch bent on dampening the fun of deserving children.

"Uh, about the horses," Rachel began, taking a deep breath. "I suppose you plan to use Heathervale land for trail rides?"

"If Mrs. Chase doesn't mind." Patrick gave Rachel such an accommodating smile she couldn't have brought herself to say yes even if Gran did have objections. "We'll see that the trails are kept clean. And we'll keep clear of the fences."

"Fine." Rachel unfolded the contract and hastily scanned it. "Uh, let's see. We've talked about the horses. 'Maintenance of fences.' Just remind everyone to use the gates, okay?"

"No problem."

"'Noise.'" Rachel pursed her lips and then shrugged. "Well, Gran said that was never a problem with the picnickers and weekend campers who have been using the camp for the past few years, and some of them have had live bands. I see no reason why it should cause any difficulties now. The trees make a nice buffer." She swallowed, reining in the impulse to talk as fast as possible, to get past any sticky wickets with a minimum of fanfare. "Heathervale does have a lot of tourists in the summer and Gran likes to offer them a tranquil atmosphere. You understand?" she felt obliged to add. Rachel glanced up at him, just to see how she was doing.

Patrick gave her another of his easy-going smiles. "Sure. We'll keep the hootin' and hollerin' close to home."

"About campfires . . ."

Patrick looked almost insulted. "We'd never dream of allowing fires *anywhere* outside our own grilling pits."

"No, of course not," Rachel quickly concurred. She skimmed the remaining points about litter and trespassing and security deposits. "I don't really see anything else we need to discuss except the pond."

"We'll keep it clean. No one will go near it without supervision. And we'll do a bang-up job on the dock we build."

"A dock?" Rachel repeated weakly. A vision of Gran's alarmed face rose in her mind.

"Just a place to tie up a few flat-bottomed boats."

"Boats?" She watched her mental image of Gran gasp.

Patrick nodded. "Water-safety instruction is a key element in Onoconohee's summer program. For a lot of these kids, this will be the first time they've had a chance to learn to swim."

"The first time?" Rachel blinked. For a moment, she could say nothing as her head whirled with images of flailing nonswimmers and overturned boats disturbing the calm of Heathervale's shady green pond. If ever there were an accident—or two or three—waiting to happen, it was in the scenario Patrick Morrissey had just painted for her. Exactly the sort of thing Gran wanted to avoid. Just the sort of thing she expected Rachel to make clear.

For a split second, Rachel longed to have the stern-faced Milton standing across the desk from her, anyone but warmhearted, likable Patrick Morrissey. "I don't know if Gran's insurance company will buy the idea of your using the pond for swimming and boating lessons," she finally managed to get out.

Now it was Patrick's turn to blink. "But what's a camp without a lake?"

Not much of a camp, Rachel thought. "Gran has to abide by the terms of the farm's insurance policy." Recognizing the deflated look in Patrick's eyes, she was grateful to be able to shove the blame onto an absent meany, but it did little to ease her guilt.

"Look, I understand your grandmother's position, but we've got to work something out. Everyone is expecting a water-safety program: I've already lined up certified instructors. And even if I were willing to scotch the program, that would just make the pond more attractive to the kids. If they were forbidden to use it, you can bet that a few of them would find a way to take a dip on the sly. Without swimming lessons, we'd really be asking for trouble."

Rachel frowned. Other than filling the pond in, she could think of no alternative to the arguments Patrick had presented. "Then we've got a problem," she said, falling back on the phrase she had heard so often in business negotiations.

"Maybe it isn't as big as we think." Patrick's sinewy face relaxed into a smile and he nudged her arm lightly. "Why don't we have a look at the pond? It isn't very big, and if we could figure out a practical way to oversee the whole body of water, we might be able to satisfy Heathervale's insurance contract by putting a trained lifeguard on duty."

"Another volunteer?" Rachel grinned, relieved to have the tension eased.

Patrick broke into a hearty laugh. "Leave that to Milton!" Turning, he led the way out of the office.

Outside, the sky had faded to the hazy pink chrome of a late-spring dusk. As they followed the footpath to Heathervale's property line, the light played hide-and-seek among the tall trees, gliding across them only to disappear into the shadows. When they reached the fence, Rachel nimbly scaled the post-and-rail barricade.

"But the campers still have to use the gate," she reminded Patrick teasingly over her shoulder.

Now on familiar turf, Rachel plunged through the tangled undergrowth. She had walked these woods so often, both as a child and lately as a grown woman, she could find the pond as readily as if she carried a compass. When she caught sight of the dark green pool, she waited for Patrick to catch up with her.

"Look!" Patrick whispered hoarsely, and clutched at her elbow.

But Rachel had already spotted the white-tailed deer drinking from the pond. Both of them stood in silence for a moment, responding to the mesmeric quality of the graceful animal poised at the water's edge. They were standing close together now, so close that Rachel could sense the contour of Patrick's body behind her, feel its warmth that contrasted vividly with the forest's damp chill. Just as insidious was the utterly irrational temptation to lean back against the source of that inviting, sensual heat.

Suddenly, the deer lifted its dripping muzzle from the water. Its limbs stiffened and its nostrils quivered for a split second. Then it bolted into the forest. Taking a cue from the deer, Rachel pushed aside a low branch and blazed a trail to the pond's shore. In the opening, her head felt clearer, her mind more in control of things.

"It isn't a very big pond. Our problem is its irregular shape. There isn't any single vantage point from which a lifeguard could watch the whole thing." She frowned, surveying the deceptively peaceful body of water that, at some point in the past thirty minutes, had become "*our* problem."

Digging his hands into his pockets, Patrick strolled a few feet along the bank. Then he turned abruptly to Rachel and gave her a look of amused defiance. "Who says we can have only one lifeguard?"

Rachel grinned. "Certainly not I."

Patrick returned the smile. "So we get two lifeguards. Or three. Or four, if that insurance man of your grandmother's wants to be a stickler. Hell, with volunteers, we can have as many as we like! We'll put up elevated chairs for them, if that's all right with you."

Rachel lifted both hands in acquiescence. "Anything for safety's sake."

When Patrick folded his arms across his chest, he looked supremely pleased. "So we have a deal? Onoconohee can have its water-safety program on your pond?"

If I can talk Gran into it. Rachel hesitated, grappling with that single yet still-formidable obstacle. Then she gave him a resolute nod. "It's a deal." Someway, somehow she would make Gran see her point. She had given Patrick her word and now had no choice.

Rachel offered her hand to seal the agreement and then stopped short. Giving him a sly grin, she carefully brushed her dusty hand against her twill slacks before closing it over his. But as they locked in a hearty handshake, something told Rachel that she was getting far more than she had bargained for.

Chapter Two

Rachel eased the front door closed behind her, grimacing at the irksome squeak of the hinges. She paused in the shadowy hall and peered warily up the stairs. Gran was one of those blessed souls who enjoyed blissful deep slumber yet awakened at the slightest irregular noise, and Rachel knew she was pressing her luck. Still, she crossed her fingers and wished that, just this once, her grandmother would sleep through her arrival. Maybe by the time she had put dinner together, she would have thought of a tactful way to tell Gran she had capitulated on the pond.

Any hopes Rachel had of slipping the subject of Onoconohee's water-safety program onto the table, somewhere between the pickles and the carrot sticks, evaporated the second she opened the kitchen door.

"There you are!" Wiping her hands on a red-and-white-checked dishcloth, Gran spun around from the sink. "I was beginning to wonder what was taking you so long."

"Is it that late?" Rachel's attempt at smiling and sounding offhand reminded her of her single, futile attempt at auditioning for a high-school play.

Gran shrugged and turned back to the hard-cooked egg slices she was arranging on a platter of chicken salad. "No, but Milton is usually in such a hurry to get on with busi-

ness. After a bit of the frowning and grumbling he feels ob-
ligated to put on, I would have expected him to wrap things
up and speed you on your way.''

Rachel snatched up a handful of cherry tomatoes from
the colander and began to garnish the salad. "Milton had to
go to Hartford. I ended up talking with his assistant.''

"Mr. Morrissey?'' Gran's small fingers picked at a sprig
of parsley, delicately tucking it into place.

Rachel nodded. She frowned over the salad as if it were a
chess board and she were contemplating a life-and-death
move. Before she could think of where to place the next tomato, much less how to explain her dilemma with the pond,
Gran picked up the conversation.

"Well, from what Milton has told me, he's a very capable young man. I'm sure you can rely on anything he says.
Right there, dear.'' Gran helpfully pointed to a bare spot
between a celery chunk and a ripe olive. She nodded en-
couragement as Rachel feebly dropped the tomato into
place. Then she picked up the platter and led the way to the
door. Armed with a basket of wheat crackers, Rachel followed her grandmother into the dining room.

"They want to use the pond for swimming and boating
lessons,'' Rachel mumbled as she slid into her chair at the
big oak table.

Gran chuckled as she scooped up a hefty serving of
chicken salad and held it poised over one of the plates.
"Milton has been making noises about swimming and ca-
noeing for his campers ever since he approached me about
using the property.''

Rachel intercepted her plate before Gran could heap a
lumberjack's portion onto it. "They've got a good point.
From the sound of things, this is a rare chance for most of
these kids to learn basic water safety. Besides having fun,
they would be acquiring some very valuable skills." To her

surprise, she had adopted not only Patrick's choice of words but a trace of his persuasive tone, as well.

"I quite agree." Gran inspected the basket of crackers before depositing three wafers onto her plate. "It's really unfortunate that the insurance people have made such a bugaboo out of the issue."

"Maybe there's a way to get around their objections. I mean, if the camp provided lifeguards to oversee the entire pond, enough trained attendants to keep an eye on every single camper, surely the insurance company wouldn't make a fuss." Rachel nudged a bite of chicken with her fork, staring at the plate.

"Oh, I don't know, dear. Milton has forever tried to convince me to let him use that pond, but—" Gran abruptly broke off. Propping her fork on the edge of her plate, she leaned across the table. "Rachel, is there something wrong?"

Rachel swallowed and forced herself to look up at her grandmother. "I told Patrick Morrissey we'd consider..." She cleared her throat, determined to get the worst of it behind her. "I told him we'd let them use the pond if they could provide enough lifeguards to cover the whole pond."

For a second, Gran only blinked. To Rachel's relief, however, she didn't look all that surprised. Then again, she didn't look all that delighted, either. "Well, that is quite a serious commitment." She pressed her lips together, blotting them deliberately with her napkin.

Rachel pushed the plate to one side and leaned across the table. "Oh, Gran, I'm sorry if I've gotten you out on a limb," she began. She glanced at the vacant chair next to her, wishing that Patrick Morrissey were sitting in it, ready to put his support—and considerable charm—behind her argument.

"This does complicate matters a bit." Gran looked as stern as her perennially merry gray eyes would permit. Then she heaved a resolute sigh. "But you've given your word and I suppose we'll have to abide by it."

Rachel felt a relieved sigh of her own wheeze from her chest. "You won't regret it, Gran, I promise. Besides, I'm convinced that the camp's management will make safety their number-one priority."

Gran folded her napkin, her little fingers pressing a precise crease in the pale blue linen. "I've known Milton Weber for years and I can vouch that there's no man in New England more trustworthy than he. I'm sure this young Morrissey is a reliable sort," she went on, her voice a shade less effusive. "Otherwise, Milton would never have hired him as his assistant. Still, where Heathervale's liability is concerned, we cannot afford to rely on other people's good intentions. You'll have to make sure they carry through on their promises, Rachel."

"Me?" Rachel sat back in her chair, taken by surprise.

Gran's healthy pink face suddenly contorted into a mild grimace. She shifted in her chair, easing the weight from her injured hip. "You certainly don't expect *me* to hobble around that overgrown pond, nagging people about life-jackets and safety buoys and such."

"No, of course not," Rachel hastily assured her.

"When one can be held responsible for mishaps, one must never assume that a job is being done right." Gran held herself erect, punctuating this incontrovertible fact with a brisk nod of her head. "I know it will be a time-consuming task for you, Rachel, but we've simply no choice."

"I'll do my best, Gran," Rachel agreed meekly, but in spite of herself, she couldn't help smiling.

"To look at you, I'd almost believe we were ready for the first onslaught of campers." Patrick grinned as he rounded the desk, giving the sneakered feet propped on its edge a playful jostle.

"Chill out, Patrick. Everything *is* under control, thanks in no small part, I might add, to my lightning efficiency." Trip Barton slouched deeper into the orange canvas director's chair and smiled lazily up at his companion. "The bunk beds are all shored up. The canoes are racked and ready to go. The cafeteria pantry is stocked with provisions. And do not forget that it was I, C. Theodore Barton III—" he roused himself from his languor enough to tap his chest lightly "—who managed to muster five—count 'em, folks—*five* volunteer lifeguards after you wheedled the herb-farm ladies into letting us use their pond."

"You're doing a great job, Trip, and you've earned a rest," Patrick conceded. As the still-vivid memory of one of those herb-farm ladies drifted through his mind, he smiled. Ordinarily, he would have been relieved to have circumvented a problem for the camp. In this case, however, Rachel Chase's role in the matter had taken precedence over mere nuts-and-bolts details. Since Patrick's first glimpse of her face, fair and lovely as a Renaissance angel's as she peered through the dingy screen, her image seemed to have found a permanent spot in his thoughts. At the oddest moments, he would flash on a remnant of that encounter with Rachel—the smell of her floral perfume, sweet yet secretive; the sound of her low, clear voice; the smooth texture of her skin when they chanced to touch.

Patrick caught himself and quickly drew a curtain on his daydreams. He leaned over the desk, pulling a folder from beneath the heels of Trip's grimy athletic shoes. "There's still a lot to be done though. And we do need one more lifeguard."

Pulling himself out of the director's chair, Trip dismissed Patrick's concerns with an amiable shrug. "Trust me, Kemosabe. I'll find one." He eyed Patrick thoughtfully. "You know, I bet you could qualify. Since you're a police officer, you probably know CPR and all sorts of good stuff like that."

"Yeah." Patrick leaned back from the desk and yanked open one of the stubborn drawers. He took his time locating the counselors' applications, long enough for Trip's quicksilver attention to refocus on something besides Patrick's career in law enforcement.

Since his arrival at Camp Onoconohee, Patrick had made a point of giving his co-workers only the sketchiest information about his background. Everyone knew he had been a cop on the Hartford force for ten years. They all thought that burnout on the beat had prompted him to take three months' paid leave to work at the camp. Only Milton Weber knew the whole story, and for now Patrick preferred to keep it that way.

"How about you, Mr. Weber? Interested in earning your lifeguard's badge?" As the white-haired camp director entered the office, Trip scuffled out of his chair to greet him.

Milton carefully closed the screen door behind him. "Goodness, Trip, are we *that* desperate?"

Both Trip and Patrick broke into laughter at the look of comic horror Milton gave them.

"Not desperate by a longshot," Patrick assured his boss.

"I should know by now that I can rely on you fellows," Milton praised them.

Something about the retired school principal's presence always caused Trip to straighten his shoulders automatically. "I've already scrounged up materials for the guard stands. When our helpers get here this afternoon, I thought we'd start working on them," the lanky college student volunteered.

Milton considered the matter for a moment. "Why don't you hold off on the stands for a bit?" he suggested. When Trip's youthful face fell, Milton quickly added, "The stable must come first. We'll be in a fine pickle if the riding-academy folks arrive with the horses and we've no place to put them."

Trip nodded agreeably, but Patrick continued to watch Milton from behind the desk. Despite the older man's resolutely cheerful tone—or precisely because of it—he sensed that something was bothering Milton. As soon as Trip had been dispatched to repair box stalls, Patrick decided to sound Milton out.

"I guess everything went all right at that meeting with the Department of Human Resources? No big problems on the horizon?" It wasn't a particularly subtle question, but then Patrick never had been one to finesse things, no matter how hard he tried. His instincts were always geared to get right to the point. Well, that approach had worked pretty well with Rachel Chase. A plain-spoken man like Milton would probably appreciate the same straightforwardness.

"Oh, no. Human Resources is delighted with the programs we've developed for Camp Onoconohee...." Milton hesitated, blinking as if he were trying to dislodge a foreign object from his eye. Then he reluctantly pulled an envelope from his jacket's breast pocket. Dropping the letter onto the desk, he stepped back and folded his hands in front of him. "I suppose you ought to read this."

Patrick immediately recognized the imposing letterhead of one of the key philanthropic foundations backing Camp Onoconohee. He shot an uncertain glance up at Milton, but he could already feel the ponderous weight sinking to the pit of his stomach. To judge from the camp director's grim expression, the news contained in the letter could not be good.

And it wasn't. Patrick read through the letter twice before he had actually convinced himself that the foundation was only offering half the funding the camp had requested. There were several apologetic paragraphs about cutbacks and reallocations, sugared over with bright promises for future years. Nothing, however, could cushion the harsh blow of the bottom line: Camp Onoconohee would not be receiving a sizeable chunk of money.

Patrick angrily clamped the letter to the desk with his fist. "How can they do this to us?" Although he already knew the answer to that question, he needed to vent his frustration.

"Money is tight these days," Milton remarked in his characteristically laconic fashion. Turning, he pulled the director's chair closer to the desk and then slowly seated himself. Although he never complained and rarely admitted fatigue, his lined face looked very weary. Organizing the camp from the ground up would have challenged a far younger man than Milton, Patrick reflected. To have a critical contribution suddenly snatched away from his hard-won project must have been a personal blow.

"Can't we appeal their decision?" Patrick suggested, but Milton was already shaking his head.

"I phoned the foundation director as soon as I received their letter. You see, Patrick, it isn't a question of caprice or favoritism. The foundation simply does not have the money available this year. They've had to cut back on all their endowments. And I'm afraid we will have to take similar action here. Camp Onoconohee must tighten its belt."

"But how? We're already operating on a shoestring!" Catching the disappointment in Milton's eyes, Patrick swallowed hard. With a crisis facing them, this was no time to howl and protest like a spoiled child. The camp needed realistic, clear-sighted thinkers right now who could tackle a tough problem and solve it. "I suppose there's always another corner we can cut. Any suggestions?"

Milton stared in silence at his folded hands for a few seconds. "We can't eliminate any counselors without jeopardizing the children's safety. Nor can we cut back on basic amenities like utilities and food. We'll have to take a look at some of the luxuries."

Patrick was wondering where in the Spartan camp Milton hoped to find anything resembling a luxury. "The horses, maybe? They're expensive to feed."

"Porter's Feed and Seed has already pledged enough free grain and hay for three months."

"We could scotch the outing to Mystic."

Milton's faded blue eyes flared. "Oh, no, we won't! Not after I've browbeat the Department of Human Resources into providing buses!"

Chastened, Patrick sank behind the desk.

"No," Milton went on in a more even tone. "I was thinking about the extra land."

"You mean the acreage we're planning to lease from Rachel Chase? I mean, from Heathervale Farm," Patrick hastily corrected himself.

Milton nodded, much too decisively to suit Patrick. "It's the one thing we're paying rather dearly for."

"But what about the water-safety program?" Without warning, his most cherished program had been put on the firing line. In his desperation to save it, Patrick had to struggle to keep from sputtering. "Swimming is one of the most vital skills Onoconohee is offering. Most of these kids will probably never sit astride a horse again in their lives, but a lot of them will continue to swim. Why, our swim lessons might even save one of them from drowning some day!"

"I agree with you, Patrick, but we may not be able to afford a water-safety program this year."

"Do you think there's any room for negotiation with Heathervale Farm?" Patrick asked hopefully.

Milton shifted in the director's chair, his well-disciplined spine obviously at odds with its sagging contours. "Eleanor Chase is a most generous and kindhearted woman. However, I don't believe she is in a position to lower the rent on that acreage. You see, she is having some work done on her house this summer, to make it more of a tourist attraction. Eleanor is too proud to tell me outright, but I know she is counting on the rental income to defray some expenses."

"Then Mrs. Chase needs to rent out that tract of land as much as we need to use it!" Patrick declared, giving the stained desk blotter a triumphant thump with his knuckles.

Milton heaved a sigh. "Ah, yes, which brings us to another sticky issue, breaking the news to Eleanor that we want to renege on our agreement. I've known Eleanor Chase for most of my life, but I'll confess I don't relish the prospect of bearing bad tidings to her." He let out another protracted breath. "Especially in this case."

"I'll do it."

Milton looked up and blinked at Patrick. Then he smiled gently and shook his head. "You're a crackerjack troubleshooter, Patrick, but I can't slough this task onto you. I made a commitment for Camp Onoconohee that we now cannot honor. It is my responsibility to face the consequences."

Patrick moved quickly to thwart Milton's argument. "Please don't talk as if you were shirking your duty. I'm sure when Mrs. Chase understands the circumstances behind our dilemma, there will be no hard feelings. And it will seem less personal coming from me." Milton was softening, Patrick could tell. All Milton needed was a gentle push and he would cave in. "Come on, Milton. It's not every day I volunteer to be the bad guy." Patrick grinned, giving his friend just the right psychological shove.

Milton looked both reluctant and relieved. "Perhaps if you showed Eleanor the letter from the foundation," he suggested.

Patrick's grin only widened. "That's exactly what I plan to do."

ACTUALLY, PATRICK WAS UNSURE just what he had in mind. He would never have admitted as much to his elder colleague, of course. And he certainly had no intention of telling Milton that he planned to approach not Eleanor Chase, but her granddaughter, Rachel. Even when he picked up the phone the following morning and dialed the herb farm's number, he would have been hard pressed to outline a precise plan of action. All Patrick knew was that Heathervale Farm and Camp Onoconohee now had a mutual problem—one that he needed to discuss with Rachel Chase.

"Hello?" The chipper voice that answered instantly conjured up a vision of the indomitable widow whom Milton had often described to Patrick.

"Good morning. Uh, am I speaking with Mrs. Chase?"

"Yes, this is she. May I help you?" To judge from her quick response, Eleanor Chase didn't put much stock in dallying around on the phone.

"This is Patrick Morrissey. From the camp," he added.

"Of course, I know who you are!" Mrs. Chase's chuckle was a shade more lusty than he would have expected from an eighty-year-old blue blood. "Milton has told me *all* about you. What can I do for you today, Patrick?"

"Actually, I was calling for Rachel."

"Oh, really!"

Did she sound taken aback? Amused? Perhaps even pleased? Patrick couldn't decide, but he forced himself to get on with business. "I need to talk with her about the property." He gulped the unspoken words *we were planning to lease.*

"Certainly! Rachel explained to me how you two worked everything out concerning the pond. I want to tell you, I'm absolutely delighted! But I'm afraid Rachel isn't in right now."

"She isn't?" For some absurd reason, Patrick felt like an overinflated balloon that someone had just punctured.

"No. She left a few minutes before you phoned. She needed to run a few errands in town."

Blind instinct inspired his next move. "Well, I was planning to drive into town. Maybe I'll run into her." *Especially if you'll tell me where she was going,* he added to himself.

Fortunately, Rachel's grandmother required no further prodding. "Oh, I'm sure you will. Scarborough is so tiny. Rachel was planning to stop by the bank, the drugstore and the grocery. You can probably catch up with her before she gets to the A&P. If you hurry, that is."

Was he imagining it or was Eleanor Chase actually egging him on? "Thank you, Mrs. Chase."

"Eleanor. Please call me Eleanor."

"Eleanor," Patrick docilely repeated before bidding her goodbye.

Mindful of Eleanor's admonition, Patrick rushed out of the camp office and jumped into his car. Trip's crew could always use another box of ten-penny nails, and the office's coffee supply was running low. He had perfectly valid reasons to make a shopping run. Besides, his veteran cop's instinct told him that a face-to-face conversation with Rachel would be far more effective than talking with her on the phone. And a heck of a lot more satisfying personally.

When he reached the Scarborough business district, Patrick shifted down into second gear. For once he was thankful for the unsynchronized stoplights that gave him ample time to scan the parking slots for Rachel's Volvo. If it had not been for one of those tediously erratic lights, he would not have seen her coming out of Copeland's Pharmacy. With reflexes trained from years of responding to emergency radio calls, Patrick wheeled the car into a parking space and braked with a lurch.

He was halfway across the street before Rachel spotted him. She looked startled, but then she broke into a smile. God, she was beautiful when she smiled! Her whole face seemed to radiate warmth and kindness and good humor. When she stepped out from beneath the drugstore's awning, her long hair captured the sun's rays in a flow of spun gold. And her eyes, those amazingly large, deep-set gray eyes.

Patrick jumped when a horn tooted, abruptly putting an end to his reverie. Seeing him scramble for the curb, Rachel laughed.

"We have traffic, even in Scarborough," she reminded him as he joined her in front of the drugstore.

"Yeah. It's easy to forget." Patrick dug his fingers through his unruly hair and grinned. "Out at the camp, I only have the squirrels and chipmunks to contend with, and they never honk. Maybe I ought to come into town more often, just to keep myself on my toes."

Rachel shook her head, releasing a fan of gold dust over her shoulders as the fine strands settled back into place. "I tell myself that, but except for the occasional movie or some shopping, I never seem to find a worthwhile excuse to leave the farm. Gran says I really prefer living in the eighteenth century."

"Well, modern life does have a few advantages." Hands buried in his pockets, Patrick glanced up the street. Detectives were good at sizing up a situation and he quickly found what he was looking for. "For instance, I imagine Kohler's Bakery dishes up better stuff than I do out at the camp." Nodding in the direction of the small shop, he glanced toward Rachel.

She seemed to be having trouble controlling her smile. "Do you bake?"

"No," Patrick confessed. "I heat up things that come in plastic bags and aluminum trays. But I bet Kohler's can beat the freezer-chest people hands down."

Rachel giggled. "You sound like a man who's looking for an excuse to indulge himself in some of the world's best apple strudel."

Patrick cocked an eyebrow. "It's that good, huh?"

"It's worth coming into Scarborough for."

"You're making a strong case. Tell you what. Since we're both in town, let's make the most of it and get a couple of slices. If Kohler's doesn't have coffee, we could probably—"

"They serve coffee and tea," Rachel interrupted to assure him. To his delight, she dropped her keys into her handbag and turned toward the bakery.

"So how are things going at the camp?" she asked, as they paused in front of the bake shop's inviting window.

Patrick swallowed, not taking his eyes off the trays of crullers and cinnamon rolls. "Oh, pretty well. We're finished with the dorms."

"You know, walking to the pond with you the other afternoon reminded me of how much I enjoyed it when I was a kid. It's kind of exciting to be sharing such a special place now with these children. Please let me know when you start work on the dock and the lifeguard stands." Her smile looked slightly embarrassed. "I mean if you don't mind, I'd love to witness some of our little pond's transformation."

Looking at her lovely reflection in the bakery window, Patrick experienced a gnawing seizure of guilt. "All this window shopping is making me hungry. Let's go inside."

As soon as they had ordered and gotten decently settled at a table, he would tell her about the lost funding. After all, that was why he had cruised Scarborough's main street and tracked her down in the first place. Or was it? Watching Rachel seated across from him, her high cheekbones flushed the faintest shade of tea rose, her gray eyes sparkling, made him suddenly uncomfortable. If the truth be known, he had been waiting for an excuse to see Rachel Chase again, and Camp Onoconohee's latest problem had seemed as good as any. Now, however, he felt as reluctant as Milton to break the bad news.

For the moment, Rachel was too concerned with arranging her packages beneath the tiny café table to notice his discomfiture. "Doesn't this look marvelous?" She eyed the wedge of apple strudel appreciatively before breaking off a bite with her fork. "Just think. If we hadn't bumped into each other just now, you might have spent the whole summer here without ever discovering Kohler's!"

Patrick picked up his fork and then laid it down again. "Rachel, I didn't exactly run into you by chance just now."

"You didn't?" She looked up from the pastry in surprise.

Patrick shook his head. "No. I phoned the farm and your grandmother told me I could probably find you in town."

"Well!" Rachel blotted her lips with the paper napkin, obviously unprepared for the revelation.

Thank God, she seemed more flattered than put off. But Patrick refused to indulge that heartening feeling right now. "There's a problem with Camp Onoconohee renting your grandmother's land. I need to talk with you about it."

Rachel replaced the napkin in her lap and her expression cooled. Was she disappointed that he had not engineered their meeting for social purposes? Damn it, he had! If the idiot lease were the only issue, he could just as well have discussed it with Eleanor Chase on the phone. But he had wanted to spend some time with Rachel, even if the circumstances were less than perfect. As he met the unyielding gray gaze across the table, Patrick had a hard time envisioning less-ideal circumstances.

"What's the problem?" Rachel prompted. She took a sip of coffee without taking her eyes off him.

While Patrick filled her in on the camp's various funding sources, he dug the foundation's letter out of his pocket and handed it to Rachel. "We thought we had this money in the bag, but apparently we didn't. I guess Don't Count Your Chickens Before They Hatch isn't such a bad motto, after all. Milton and I have thought of every way we could possibly manage renting the extra land, but I don't see how the camp can afford it this year. I know this probably leaves your grandmother in a bind..." Patrick broke off. Somehow when he had rehearsed his presentation in his mind, it had not sounded nearly as bleak as it did just now. "I'm sorry," he added lamely.

Rachel's pale brow furrowed as she stared down at the letter. "I am, too. I understand the realities of the business world, but it doesn't seem fair that a few inches of calculator tape can deny those kids an important part of their camping experience."

"That's exactly the way I feel." Patrick raised his eyebrows, a little startled at the unexpected empathy Rachel was showing.

"And you're sure there's no way you could juggle the money? We could afford to stagger the payments," Rachel offered.

"Onoconohee has money for half a month's rent, period. Two weeks isn't enough time to teach anyone to swim. And you know as well as I that if we encouraged the kids to use the Heathervale woodland for two weeks, we'd have a rough time suddenly declaring it off limits." When Rachel only continued to frown and bite her lip, he went on. "We'll forfeit our deposit, of course. I hope that will be satisfactory."

The clear eyes flared with such ferocity that Patrick drew back in his chair. "It certainly will not! Do you honestly think my grandmother would squeeze money out of a financially strapped camp for underprivileged children?"

"No, but the forfeiture clause of the contract..."

Rachel thrust out her chin, effectively silencing him. "As far as I'm concerned, we don't have a forfeiture yet. There's simply got to be a way to work this out. We managed to find a solution to the lifeguard problem, you know." She shook the fork at him gently before spearing a chunk of apple.

Despite the seeming hopelessness of the situation, Rachel's can-do attitude was hard to resist. "Believe me, I've racked my brain. I've even considered wacky stuff like putting an Onoconohee-sponsored lemonade stand out on the highway," Patrick confessed.

Rachel chewed thoughtfully and then swallowed. "That's an idea."

Patrick gave a rueful chuckle. "Only problem is we'd have to charge about twenty-five dollars a glass to make it work."

Rachel shot him an impatient but tolerant look as she pushed her empty plate aside. "I'm not talking about selling lemonade, Patrick, but the *concept* has possibilities. Think for a moment about the way charities fill their cash boxes. They have bazaars, raffles, even circuses. Why not have the camp stage a fund-raiser?"

"Well, I don't see why we couldn't," Patrick replied slowly. Clasping one hand behind his neck, he smiled and shook his head. "Just when I thought I had my hands full juggling lifeguard schedules and free horse food, I've got a whole new ball game to deal with. I'm game for a fund-raiser, if I can just figure out where to start."

"Let the campers do it." When Patrick did a dubious double take, Rachel leaned over her coffee cup, the better to make her point. "The trick is to choose a theme that will be fun for them, something that you can incorporate into the camp's overall program."

"You mentioned a circus. What about a country fair?" Patrick could feel his enthusiasm growing, not least of all because of Rachel's infectious interest.

Rachel propped her chin on the back of her hand and thought for a minute. "I remember the local Jaycees held a medieval festival once, during a summer vacation I spent with Gran. They had crafts, music, costumed players, even a jousting tournament."

"Jousting! And I thought you were the one who was so concerned about insurance liability!" Patrick could not resist the temptation to tease her a bit.

The corners of Rachel's mouth twitched as she tried to look serious. "I was using the Jaycees' festival as an example of an interesting theme. Onoconohee might want to do something like the Gay Nineties or New England Colonial times."

"Colonial! That's it!" In his excitement, Patrick smacked the table, sending his fork clattering to the floor. As he stooped to retrieve it, he went on in a more controlled tone. "The colonial theme would fit right in with the camp's location. After all, we're right next door to a genuine eighteenth-century farm, aren't we?"

Rachel nodded enthusiastically. "And the campers would learn a lot from the experience. You could make candies, soap, organize a fife-and-drum corps, all sorts of wonderful things. I could even lend a hand with some authentic herbal dyeing techniques." She sat back in her chair and beamed with pride. "Mr. Morrissey, I think we've just solved Problem Number Two for Camp Onoconohee."

"Assuming it makes money." To Patrick, the idea still seemed too good to be true. Then, too, he felt bound to play devil's advocate, if only to keep a rein on his own anticipation of further involvement with Rachel.

"It will," she assured him.

"But when?" Patrick sobered. "You know, assuming we do pull this thing off, we still won't realize any profit from it until late in the summer."

For a moment, Rachel fixed him with a pair of the most determined eyes he had ever seen. Then she picked up her napkin and carefully folded it. Reaching into the handbag draped over the back of her chair, she pulled out a ball-point pen and wrote three words on the napkin. When she shoved the napkin across the table to him, she looked immensely pleased with herself. "Problem Number Three solved."

"'I.O.U.,'" Patrick read the letters, along with the amount of the rent for the forty acres and Rachel's name.

"All you have to do is sign it," she prompted him.

Her generosity was so overwhelming, Patrick was uncertain what to say. "Are you sure?" he finally managed to get out.

Rachel's face broke into one of her glowing smiles that could dispel rain clouds and doubts with equal aplomb. "As sure as I am that Camp Onoconohee's Colonial Fair is going to be a terrific success."

Chapter Three

No matter how many planting seasons Rachel witnessed as a child, the springtime ritual had never failed to delight her senses. In truth, she probably spent far more time now than was necessary inspecting the tilled beds, poring over the seedlings for the first sign of buds. Even on a day as busy as this one had been, she could not resist the appeal of a late-afternoon stroll through the meadow Owen had finished planting.

Pausing on one of the stepping stones, Rachel stooped to savor the rich, sweet fragrance of newly-turned earth. Purslane was one of the last herbs her grandmother put out, usually in early June when the danger of a late frost had safely passed. Right now, the purslane bed was a dark square of neatly combed rows, but in a few weeks, it would be covered with yellow flowers clustered among fat green leaves. A twinge of anticipation pricked at Rachel as she straightened herself to scan the broad fields that stretched to the rear of the big saltbox farmhouse.

That would be Owen ambling out of the largest barn. His red flannel shirt stood out like a bright flame against the muted landscape as he sauntered toward his ancient truck. Owen never hurried, even when he was on his way home after a day's work, but he was industrious and reliable, two traits that more than compensated for his plodding pace. Smiling, Rachel waved to him. Owen returned the gesture through the truck's open window and then churned the engine to life. Only when its aged dyspeptic chug had disappeared down the drive did Rachel hear the spirited whistling in the woods behind her.

Turning, she glimpsed a figure passing through the trees. When a shaft of sun caught the whistler's curly brown head, Rachel recognized Patrick Morrissey. He had apparently spotted her, too, for he halted and threw up his hand.

"Ho, there!"

"Out for your afternoon constitutional?" Rachel smiled as she waited for him beside the stone wall separating the woodland from Heathervale's cultivated fields.

Patrick tore at the twigs that had anchored themselves in his hair, all the while thrashing his way through the thick undergrowth. Just before he reached the wall, he paused to wrench free the last twig. Then he tugged the neck of his T-shirt and grinned.

"Actually I was performing my task for the afternoon," he informed her. "I wanted to check the fences to be sure they're secure before the campers arrive."

Rachel patted the gray stone surface. "You don't need to worry about this wall. It's been here for a good two hundred years and will probably hold for another two hundred or so."

Patrick whistled appreciatively. "Now that's the kind of lore that makes the chairman of a Colonial Fair sit up and take notice. Any more tidbits you'd like to share?"

Smiling primly, Rachel stepped back and clasped her hands behind her. The mischievous light dancing in Patrick's eyes clearly said that he was flirting with her. And to her surprise, she felt the urge to flirt right back. "Oh, there are all sorts of interesting things about herbs, growing and

drying them, making teas and dyes and tonics from them."
She shook her head. "Too bad you don't have your notepad with you."

Patrick tapped his forehead. "I keep my notes right here.
Where do we begin?" He was still grinning, but Rachel
could see that he was at least half-serious.

"I could always give you a tour of the farm, whenever
you have the time." *Like right now,* Rachel thought. Although she habitually ordered her busy life with calendar in
hand, the engaging look on Patrick's face was enough to
persuade her to dispense with such rigidities for now.

"Is that an invitation?" Patrick asked. When she nodded, he agilely swung himself over the stone wall.

For a moment, he simply smiled down at her. Common
sense told Rachel what she should now do and say. *Welcome to Heathervale, an authentic eighteenth-century herb
farm!* she should announce in the quasi-giddy voice of a
Disneyland guide. They would both laugh, setting an ap-
propriately light tone. Then she would launch into the brisk,
information-packed narrative that Gran used during her
guided tours of the farm. But Rachel only continued to look
up into Patrick's Irish-blue eyes, vainly waiting for common sense to kick in. It took a blue jay's obstreperous
squawk from one of the branches overhead to prod her back
to reality.

"I suppose we can start with purslane," she began,
clearing her throat. "As you can see, we've recently planted
this bed."

"Purslane?" Patrick rolled the word around on his
tongue as if it were an unfamiliar and not entirely edible
food.

"It isn't a very well-known herb these days, although
people used to brew a tonic from it. Gran recommends
adding the fresh leaves to salads and omelettes. Don't

worry," Rachel assured him. "Heathervale grows lots of common herbs like sage and mint and thyme, too."

"I'm afraid I won't recognize even the ordinary varieties if they aren't packaged and labeled on a supermarket shelf." Patrick shook his head and chuckled. As Rachel headed for the next cultivated plot, he followed her along the stone path.

"The comfrey is just starting to come up, but this woodruff is already pretty thick. Instead of starting from seeds, Gran cultivates it by dividing old plants in the fall," Rachel explained. She paused, propping one foot on the cross tie delineating the edge of the bed, and pointed to the small creeperlike plants. Catching Patrick's nonplussed expression, she grinned. "I bet you're familiar with something we make with woodruff."

He shrugged good-naturedly. "Beats me if I am."

"Have you ever heard of May wine?"

"Sure. That's the concoction that the really florid Valentine's cards rave on about, isn't it? Along with sweet kisses, of course," Patrick added with a devilish hint in his voice.

Rachel kept her attention focused on the bed of woodruff. "May wine's claim to sweetness is not merely poetic license, thanks to these little plants. Gran and I like to add a bit of dried woodruff to apple juice, too. It's really delicious—if you have much of a sweet tooth, that is."

"I'll have to try it sometime," Patrick told her with studied seriousness. As they continued along the walk, he turned, walking sideways to take in the verdant prospect of Heathervale Farm. "Funny, but I feel as if I jumped a time barrier when I crossed that wall. This *is* a different world on your side of the fence."

"I guess that's one feature that attracts visitors to the farm," Rachel agreed. "Of course, some people are truly interested in the herbs, but most, I suspect, are hungry for a taste of a way of life that was closer to the earth, more natural than modern society.''

''Is that what keeps you interested in the farm—besides your grandmother, I mean—that nostalgia?'' Patrick took a stride long enough to bring him even with her on the path.

Rachel pursed her lips and thought for a second. It had been a long time since she had been called upon to explain her ties to Heathervale Farm. She had always relied on the convincing formula of country retreat and grandmotherly need, but somehow Patrick Morrissey seemed to merit a more accurate explanation.

''Heathervale will always be a part of me,'' Rachel said at length. ''You see, I spent a lot of my childhood here on the farm. My parents traveled a great deal with their work, so I usually spent holidays from boarding school with Gran.''

''You went to a boarding school?'' To judge from the way Patrick phrased the question, he might as well have said reform school.

''From grade one on. Lots of teenagers go to prep school,'' Rachel countered, feeling a little defensive. ''I started boarding earlier than most kids because of . . . of my situation.''

Glancing over at him, she studied the slightly crooked profile, the frank, open expression, the direct eyes. Patrick Morrissey was probably the product of a family so normal and well-adjusted that the Cleavers would pale by comparison. To him, parents who raced from Bangkok to Leningrad on photographic assignments, seeing their daughter only when their hectic schedule permitted, would seem as alien as the rare herbs bordering the footpath. For now, she had no desire to explain her irregular childhood to him.

Fortunately, Patrick appeared willing to move the conversation on to less troublesome topics. "So you learned all about herbs from your grandmother and by the time you got to college, you knew exactly what you wanted to do with your life?"

Rachel chuckled softly. "What kid knows what he wants, just starting college? But, no, I didn't major in botany or agriculture. I took my degree in economics and then went on for an M.B.A. If Gran hadn't tried to prune the apple trees herself and taken a bad fall, I'd be in Boston right now, tending balance sheets instead of herb beds. When Gran broke her hip, I took a leave of absence from my job to look after her and keep the farm running smoothly." She shrugged and smiled. "So here I am, home until Gran can completely manage on her own again."

"You don't seem too unhappy about the career interruption."

"Oh, not in the least," Rachel assured him without hesitation. "Gran means the world to me and the farm is . . ."

"Your home," Patrick coaxed her. "That's the word you used a moment ago."

Rachel paused, surprised by his observation. She had been unaware that she had referred to the farm as home, but that was exactly what Heathervale meant to her—a home in the truest sense. "Yes, I suppose so," she confessed, her voice suddenly soft. "What about you?"

"What about me?"

"You don't work at the camp year around," Rachel explained, although she sensed that Patrick knew exactly what she had been getting at. "What do you do during the other nine months? Teach?"

"No," he replied slowly. "I'm a cop."

"A policeman?" That came out sounding so incredulous, Rachel hoped she had not offended him.

"By any other name. I've been on the Hartford force for over ten years." Patrick's blue eyes narrowed as if he were trying to see beyond the tree-scattered horizon.

"This must be a big switch, being out here in the country building bunks and organizing fairs." Rachel hated to make such a lame comment, but she was still having trouble readjusting her mental image of Patrick. Of all the careers this easy-going, good-humored man could have practiced, law enforcement seemed the most remote possibility.

"It's a switch, all right, which is exactly what I needed." When he swallowed, the sinews of his neck tightened into taut cords beneath the ruddy skin. "Burnout is a serious problem among cops," he added, giving her a cautious sideways glance.

"I can imagine—" Rachel began, but Patrick quickly seized the chance to change the subject.

"So! Where do we go from here? Is this the center of Heathervale's little universe?"

They had reached the point where the garden's many paths converged, right at the foot of the bronze sundial's pedestal.

"Let's take a look at one of the farm's factories." Without waiting for Patrick to reply, Rachel turned down the path leading to a small clapboard outbuilding.

"This is a far cry from any factory I've ever seen." Patrick regarded the rustic building skeptically.

"I use the term loosely," Rachel teased as she shoved open the door. "But it is where we make our natural dyes." Her face fell at the moment she spotted the small, smock-clad woman bent over one of the worktables. "Gran! You told me you were going to take a nap!"

Gran gave the dried sorrel leaves she was crumbling into a large wooden bowl another stir before turning. "I wasn't sleepy," she explained testily. When she caught sight of

Patrick, her pink porcelain face broke into a wide smile. "Besides, making dye is a much more interesting way to pass an afternoon, don't you agree? My granddaughter keeps trying to make an invalid out of me," she added, giving him a conspiratorial look.

Before Gran could get carried away, Rachel hastened to handle introductions. "This is Patrick Morrissey from Camp Onoconohee, Gran. I was giving him a tour of the farm."

"Patrick, how nice that we finally meet face-to-face!" Gran shook his timidly extended hand as if it were an old-fashioned pump handle.

"It's nice to see you, too, Mrs. Chase."

Gran wagged her finger in admonition. "Now, now! What did I tell you? The name is Eleanor."

Patrick smiled and nodded apologetically. "Eleanor."

"So what have you seen of Heathervale? Has Rachel shown you the house?" Gran demanded, her proprietorial instincts now in full throttle.

"Not yet, Gran," Rachel interposed in an effort to regain control. Given Gran's propensity for meddling in her personal life, the presence of an attractive man in their midst offered truly endless potential for mischief. The sooner she got Patrick out of the dyeing barn, the better. "I was going to show him the drying shed and then give him a quick tour of the house."

"Not too quick, I hope!" Gran jiggled the bowl of dried sorrel, her bright gaze still fixed on the two young people. "While you're in the house, Rachel, be a dear and check the pork roast in the oven. Come to think of it, that roast is terribly large. Would you care to stay and help us eat it, Patrick?"

"That's very kind of you, Mrs....Eleanor." The hesitant look he gave Rachel suggested that he was unsure how she felt about her grandmother's invitation.

Gran might be an incorrigible matchmaker, but Rachel saw no point in cutting off her own nose to spite her face. "We'd love to have you, if you don't have anything else planned," she assured him.

"Frozen pizza keeps," Patrick quipped with a grin. "But I don't want to impose."

"Nonsense!" Gran scoffed. "Now run along, both of you, and let me set this dye to steep." She turned back to the worktable and switched on an electric kettle before reaching for a large bundle of flax.

Once they were outside again, Rachel shook her head, winning a low laugh from Patrick.

"I'll bet your grandmother is a none-too-patient convalescent," he remarked.

"To put it mildly! Of course, her refusal to take it easy is probably the main reason she's made such a remarkable recovery. *No one* is going to tell my grandmother to use a cane and sit quietly in the house. Sometimes, I don't know what's best for her. On the one hand, she does need to slow down a bit at her age. But then again, she's so lively and energetic, it seems a shame to rein her in."

"I'd let her enjoy life," Patrick advised. "Which is what you're doing, by all appearances."

Rachel made a face. "With a strong-willed woman like Gran, do I have any choice?"

And, thank God, she sometimes didn't, Rachel reflected as she showed Patrick through the drying barn. Watching him duck to avoid the bound sheaves of herbs dangling from the beams, she was grateful that their chance encounter that afternoon had been skillfully extended into the evening, courtesy of Gran's unabashed intervention. Up until today, her contact with Patrick had been all too brief. That he was attractive, any woman who came within focusing range of him could determine; as for his less-apparent traits, Rachel had spent enough time with him to recognize his ready wit and likeable disposition. But there was much, much more she wanted to know about Patrick Morrissey. Tonight would be a start.

That he might feel the same way about her occurred to Rachel as she was leading him through the rambling salt-box farmhouse. Accustomed as she had grown to tourists since her return to Heathervale, Rachel took care to point out the historically interesting features of the house. Patrick listened politely as she talked about the carved mantels, hand-turned moldings and various period furnishings, but his interest piqued when she mentioned personal things like Christmas celebrations in the high-ceilinged parlor or popping corn over the huge open fireplace.

When they reached the kitchen, Rachel dutifully took a peek at the pork loin and found it roasted to a perfect caramel brown. While she opened home-canned applesauce and thawed a frozen batch of Gran's whole wheat rolls, Patrick took charge of tossing the salad and setting the dining room table. By the time Gran wandered into the kitchen, they had a complete meal ready to serve.

Gran was in her element, presiding over a dinner that included a guest so obviously to her liking. Her still-sharp eyes sparkled like the crystal water goblets as she complimented Patrick on his carving and urged him to take yet another helping of the herbed stuffing. Although they often entertained friends from the community, Rachel could not recall Gran ever making such a fuss over Reverend Baker or the Copelands. If she had not understood her grandmother's motives so well, she would have suspected that Gran was setting her own cap for Patrick, Rachel mused, indulging in a little private smile as they cleared away the dishes after dinner.

"Go on, Rachel, and leave the straightening up to me!" Gran scolded, seizing the empty platter her granddaughter held. "Don't you know it's rude to leave a guest sitting alone in the parlor while you stew about in the kitchen?"

Shaking her head, Rachel relinquished the platter rather than engage in a tug-of-war. "Why don't *you* leave things and join us?"

"I will in a moment," Gran replied, none too convincingly. "Why don't you see if Patrick would like coffee?"

Rachel could not argue with this last suggestion and she obediently trooped out of the kitchen. When she reached the parlor, however, she found Patrick standing by the window, jacket in hand.

"Don't tell me you have to go so soon?" In her disappointment, Rachel sounded almost as dismayed as Gran would have.

If anything, Patrick looked even more reluctant to conclude the evening. "I wish I didn't, but I have to be in Hartford early tomorrow morning for a meeting at the Department of Human Resources. Unfortunately, they're expecting me to deliver a small mountain of paperwork, which I still haven't completed. But I really did enjoy this afternoon, the tour, dinner...." He hesitated, shifting his jacket to his other arm before adding, "Everything."

"We'll have to do it again," Rachel said. Good Lord! she thought. How long had it been since she had said that to a man—even Richard—and meant it?

"I hope so." Patrick's voice was unusually soft, his rugged face tempered by a tender expression. Or was it just the combined effect of the muted glow of the wall sconces and her own willing imagination?

Gran appeared in the doorway, eyeing Rachel as if she had been derelict in her duty. "Now what about that coffee?"

"Patrick has to go home to prepare for an early meeting tomorrow," Rachel explained. To her relief, Gran nodded sympathetically, apparently deeming it an acceptable excuse.

Patrick extended another round of thank-yous as the two women escorted him to the porch. When he started down the steps, however, Gran looked alarmed.

"You can't mean to walk through the woods to the camp at this hour!" she exclaimed.

Patrick glanced up at the fading sky. "It's still pretty light." He chuckled. "Believe me, I'm accustomed to tromping around outdoors in the middle of the night, whenever the raccoons decide to raid the camp's trash barrels."

"Well, at least take a lantern with you," Gran conceded sternly.

"That's probably a good idea," Rachel put in. Before Patrick could protest, she hurried to the garage and fetched one of their kerosene lanterns. She held the glass flue up while he lighted the wick.

Patrick smiled as he snuffed the match. When he took the lantern, his hand briefly grazed hers. It was the closest thing they had come to touching that evening, a casual brush that with anyone else would have probably gone unnoticed. But not with Patrick.

"Good night!" Patrick called from the yard. He lifted the lantern and waved.

Waving in return, Rachel stepped back onto the stoop. Gran had already tactfully disappeared into the house, leaving her alone to watch the dark silhouette moving down the footpath.

Rachel's eyes followed the lantern's yellow beacon until it reached the far boundary of the meadow. The hazy yellow sphere rose and then dropped, a sure sign that Patrick had crossed the stone wall. On an impulse, she retreated into the farmhouse and jogged upstairs. The thick lace curtains had already expelled most of the evening's remaining light from her bedroom, but Rachel didn't bother to flick on her bedside lamp. Instead, she walked to the window and parted the curtain. Kneeling beside the open window, her hands folded on the sill, she gazed out at the night settling over the forest, just as she had so many years ago. She watched the dot of light move through the trees, growing fainter and fainter until it was only a yellow pinprick. Resting her chin on her hands, she smiled to herself as she whispered, "Good night, Patrick."

HEATHERVALE FARM MIGHT BELONG to an earlier century than Camp Onoconohee, but the Department of Human Resources was light-years removed from both places. Only after Patrick had negotiated his way to a half dozen different offices, dropping off applications here, picking up permits there, had he begun to truly appreciate the appeal of a simpler life.

Of course, the lure of Heathervale Farm was impossible to separate from his fascination with Rachel Chase. Even while he was mired in the gunmetal-gray swamp of the state bureaucracy, his mind kept drifting back to the belllike quality of her voice, her gentle-yet-knowing smile, all the countless little charms that added up to Rachel. Somehow thinking about her made the morning's tedious duties seem less onerous.

Only when Patrick had left the state offices and was driving across Hartford did Rachel's magic spell begin to diminish. For his next destination revived memories that

even her enchantment could not dispel. Patrick couldn't remember how many times he had pulled into the hospital
parking lot in the past three months, how often he had rid-
den the elevator to the fifth floor and walked down the impersonal, disinfectant-scented corridor to Alvaro Ruiz's
silent room. But he was certain of one thing. If he repeated
that awful ritual for the rest of his life, nothing would ever
dull its pain or the conflict it aroused within him.

Burnout is a serious problem among cops. Patrick's tight
lips pulled into a grim smile as he recalled the facile explanation for his leave that he had thrown at Rachel. Getting
shot up was a serious problem, too, but never in a million
years would he have had the nerve to say that—especially
since *he* had not been the one who had been shot. Oh, sure,
he had a good enough scar on his right shoulder, along with
an abiding stiffness in the joint, but when two hoodlums
spray a narrow alley with their AK-47s, only an angel could
avoid getting hit. But his own wound was nothing compared to what Alvaro suffered.

Outside the closed hospital room door, Patrick paused.
He swallowed hard, trying to contain the deluge of emotion that always threatened to engulf him at that moment.
If only someone hadn't caught scent of their sting operation! If only they had waited for the backup! If only he had
set things up differently! If only Alvaro had not been in
front! The self-recriminations echoed through Patrick's
head, filling it with an explosive throbbing.

"Good afternoon, Lieutenant Morrissey." The head
nurse, a trim woman with a friendly manner, stopped to
chat with him.

Patrick choked back his anguish to greet the nurse.
"Good afternoon, Mrs. Clark. How...how's he doing?"
he asked, although he already knew the answer.

The nurse shook her head slowly. "The same. Still no signs of recognition, no voluntary movement. But with comatose patients, you never can tell. The doctors are encouraged that Mr. Ruiz is breathing easily without a respirator. That's something to be grateful for."

Patrick nodded, although he found little consolation in the nurse's report. "I won't be long," he told her, opening the door slightly.

"Take as long as you like."

As long as you like. As if what he liked or wanted counted for anything, Patrick reflected bitterly. If he had his way, a drug dealer's bullet would never have left a good man like Al Ruiz suspended in a coma. Sometimes, Patrick even thought he would choose to change places with Al, if given the chance. Sometimes, it seemed a whole lot easier than living in the conscious world, hemmed in on all sides by remorse and self-doubt.

Patrick haltingly walked to the side of the bed. Al seemed not to have moved since he had seen him last, over two weeks ago. He lay unnaturally still, his arms outstretched at his sides, his face pointed straight up to the empty ceiling. Looking down at his friend and partner of eight years, Patrick found it hard to believe that the once-vital man would not suddenly sit up, cuff him on the shoulder and suggest they go out for a well-earned beer. Al had been so vigorous, a top-notch detective with enough energy left at the end of the day to vanquish Patrick on the handball court. He had loved his wife with the same intensity, had never tired of talking about the nursery they had prepared, all the video equipment they had bought in anticipation of their first baby's arrival. Now it seemed doubtful that Al would ever see that child.

Patrick flexed his hands around the bed's side rail, struggling with his own sense of powerlessness. If only there were something he could do to change things. But he was no magician, no miracle worker, just a cop who didn't even have much faith in himself anymore.

Patrick studied the statuelike profile for a moment. Then he leaned over the rail to make Alvaro the only vow he had left to offer. "I'll get them, Al, I promise you, if it's the last thing I do."

Chapter Four

"I do believe nothing smells more lovely than new tarragon." Gran wrinkled her nose happily over the flat bed of spindly green seedlings. "If only it weren't so *temperamental!*" Shaking her head, she caressed one of the drooping plants with her finger.

"That's because you coddle them in this greenhouse all spring." Rachel laughed as she stooped to retrieve Noodles from the bed of spearmint plants he had chosen for his midmorning nap. The fluffy gray-and-white cat gave her a brief, insulted glance before springing onto the potting table. After a languid stretch, he settled himself in the sun beside the watering can and began to purr. "Admit it, Gran. Where plants are concerned, you're a hopeless soft touch."

"Where plants and summer camps for needy children are concerned," Gran corrected her gently. She chuckled, brushing a fleck of peat moss from the tip of her nose. "I must say, Rachel, I found your little I.O.U. very clever. And just the right tactic for handling Milton."

"What do you mean?" Rachel scooped a measure of lime into a pail of soil and gave the mixture a brisk stir.

Gran's eyes danced as they surveyed the lush flats of sweet basil. "For all his virtues, Milton Weber is a proud man. If we'd offered to rewrite the contract, something formal like that, we'd have hurt that pride. But when he saw the crumpled napkin you'd scribbled on, I'm sure he couldn't do anything but laugh. The next time I see young Morrissey, I'll demand a full account of Milton's reaction to your note." Her smile reminded Rachel of a mischievous youngster concocting an elaborate practical joke.

The sound of a car droning up the drive redirected Rachel's attention. Leaning over the potting table, she smeared a peephole on the steam-fogged greenhouse window in time to see Patrick climb out of a paneled station wagon. "It looks as if you're about to get your chance." Her smile broadened, an inevitable reaction to the sight of the tall, well-built figure ambling around the car.

Wiping her hands on a soiled rag, Gran hurried to share her granddaughter's vantage point. When she glimpsed a silvery head, topped by a familiar snap-brim cap, emerging from the other side of the wagon, she pulled back in dismay. "Good gracious, what on earth is Milton Weber doing here?"

"Maybe he wants you to countersign the napkin before he has it notarized," Rachel suggested, giving her grandmother's arm a teasing nudge.

Gran ignored the joke. "I do wish people would phone first," she grumbled. "Why, this place is a perfect mess! To look at the house you'd think we do our potting *there*. And I'm certain we've nothing to offer them but banana bread that's so stale the sparrows would probably turn up their noses at it." Gran fidgeted with one of the tousled white curls peeking from beneath the edge of her head scarf.

"Relax, Gran," Rachel counseled her. "I'm sure Milton and Patrick didn't drive over here expecting a catered tea party."

Gran frowned at her hands, picking at the stubborn line of potting soil lodged beneath one thumbnail. "Do go welcome them, Rachel, and just give me a little time to straighten things up.''

"Gran, nobody expects a greenhouse to be as neat as a pin...." Rachel began, but one look at the spare little woman busily stacking empty pots told her to save her breath.

"Anyone home?" Patrick's rich baritone rose in anticipation from the garden path.

Leaving Gran to her self-imposed task, Rachel headed for the door. She felt Noodles streak between her ankles as he fled the tidying up frenzy that had interrupted his slumber. "Good morning!" Rachel hailed the visitors from the garden gate.

When Patrick turned, the clear morning light caught him full in the face, throwing its appealingly rugged angles into relief. He broke into a smile that rivaled the June sun in brilliance. Perhaps in some dark corner of the world there lived a gloomy soul sour enough to resist that infectious grin, but Rachel had her doubts.

Milton had just caught up with Patrick on the path. When he spotted Rachel, he automatically nicked the brim of his cap. "I hope we didn't choose a bad time to drop by, Miss Chase," the older man apologized.

"Oh, no, not at all!" Rachel assured him, skillfully side-stepping to block the entrance to the greenhouse. "Gran will be right out as soon as she finishes transplanting some tarragon seedlings. Tarragon is a very temperamental plant," she added lamely, wondering why even the whitest of lies always sound so clumsy. To her relief, she was spared any further stalling by Gran's sudden appearance.

"Good morning, Milton! Patrick!" Gran patted Rachel's shoulder as she breezed out of the greenhouse. "How nice of you to pay us a visit."

Rachel bit her lip to control the spasmodic twitching that the sight of her grandmother had set off. A good deal of Gran's neatening up had apparently been directed toward herself. The mud-streaked smock had disappeared, along with the faded head scarf. Gran's snow-white hair looked suspiciously fluffy, and if Rachel had not known better, she would have sworn that her grandmother's rosy cheeks owed their glow to a deft pinch.

"We won't keep you from your work, Mrs. Chase. I mean, Eleanor," Patrick quickly corrected himself, with a wink on the side to Rachel. "We were wondering if you might have a few books on colonial life and the early uses of herbs that we could borrow. The first group of campers arrived yesterday and they're all eager to get started on our Colonial Fair."

"We have dozens of books you may use. In fact, if there is anything we can do to help with the fair, just let us know. But tell me. Did I hear correctly? The campers are *already* here?" Gran gave Milton a smile that was both surprised and appreciative. "They've been so quiet, I would never have guessed. Surely you haven't confined them to their cabins, have you, Milton?" Her grin was almost coy and seemed to erase twenty years from her still-handsome face.

Milton shook his head, obviously trying not to look too pleased with himself. "I can assure you, Eleanor. They'll have plenty of fun without raising an unholy ruckus." With his hands folded behind his back, he looked as if it were all he could do to keep from rocking back on his heels like an exultant schoolboy.

"I suspect you may hear a few Indian war cries this afternoon," Patrick put in. When he smiled down at Gran, Rachel noticed the dark dimples drilled into his lean face. "We're going to give everyone an orientation around the pond. With lifeguards on hand, of course." Over Gran's

shoulder, his eyes twinkled as his gaze meshed with
Rachel's.

"Of course!" Gran impatiently brushed aside his disclaimer with a wave of her small hand. "But now, about
those books. I've so many I hardly know where to begin.
Perhaps you'd like to have some tea or coffee while I rummage through the library." Gran glanced at Rachel, tele-
graphing her marching orders to head for the kitchen.

"That's very hospitable of you, Eleanor, but I'm afraid
we're expected back at the camp shortly," Milton told them,
not without a trace of genuine regret. "If we could just have
a look at your collection of books..."

Gran's face fell, and Rachel felt her own disappointment
dimming her smile. To her credit, her grandmother quickly
recovered herself. "You'd despair of ever finding anything," she supplied for Milton with a chuckle. "Trust me.
I know exactly what you need. I'll select some books for you
and we'll bring them over to you later."

Patrick and Milton chorused their appreciation as Gran
herded them along the garden path to the drive. Now that a
social visit had been ruled out, Rachel could tell Gran was
anxious to get on with the business of raiding her well-
stocked library. Indeed, she seemed almost as eager to dispatch the two guests as she had been to welcome them only
minutes earlier.

For her part, Rachel was pinched by a sudden and unexpected wistfulness as she watched Patrick slide behind the
wheel of the Ford station wagon and switch on the ignition. He had a tantalizing way of surfacing in her life, just
long enough to prime her interest, all too briefly to satisfy
it. Adding to her sense of frustration was the knowledge that
a mere forty acres of woodland stood between them.

"To think those children were going to descend on the
pond this afternoon and we hadn't the foggiest notion they

had even arrived." Although the station wagon had long since turned onto the road, Gran lowered her voice to a dismayed whisper. "Thank goodness, you've an excuse to check on the situation this afternoon."

Rachel whirled around to face Gran. "I do?"

Gran gave her the sort of pained look that Mr. Percy had fostered whenever Rachel threatened to doze off in his tenth-grade geometry class. "When you deliver the books, you can casually wander by the pond to make sure things are functioning as we would wish."

Rachel frowned at the vision of herself tromping through the forest with an armload of ponderous coffee-table books clamped to her chest. "I agree it's important to monitor the pond, but we don't want to be too obvious. Besides, I'd feel a little foolish if they thought I'd engineered a chance to spy on them." *And even more foolish if Patrick Morrissey suspected I'd dreamed up such a silly ruse to trail him around the pond,* she added to herself, feeling embarrassed precisely because the thought *had* crossed her mind.

For better or for worse, Gran shared none of her reservations. "It isn't spying, Rachel. You're simply giving Milton and Patrick a helping hand without telling them. Now run along. While you change into something presentable, I'll get the books together," she announced on her way back to the house.

True to her word, Gran had assembled eight weighty volumes by the time Rachel had showered and slipped into a salmon-pink polo shirt and matching shorts. One look at the stack of books and Rachel realized that any marginally sane person would deliver them to the camp in a car instead of lugging them across forty acres of woodland. Still, Gran was adamant that she get a look at the pond, and the only way she could be sure of doing that—short of announcing an official inspection—was to make the trek on foot.

Thanks to her unwieldy burden, Rachel had broken into a sweat before she reached the garden sun dial. By the time she scaled the stone wall, the books' edges had lined her arms with red grooves and her shoulders ached. As she thrashed through the scratchy undergrowth, she wondered what on earth had possessed her to wear sandals and shorts.

Shaking her straggling hair out of her eyes, she glanced up at two squirrels chasing each other around the trunk of an oak. When the squirrels spotted her, they stood stock still, apparently captivated by the utterly ridiculous-looking human being trudging through their territory.

"Oh, go on and mind your own business!" Rachel said as she scowled at the squirrels, but her sense of humor was already getting the best of her. Clutching the books weakly to her chest, she surrendered to what Gran had always termed a "fit of the giggles." She was laughing so hard, she almost tripped over a young girl sitting with her back propped against a tree.

"Excuse me." Under the circumstances, Rachel knew her apology must sound as silly as the figure she cut. She clamped her lips together, trying to muster a straight face.

For a moment, the girl just stared at her. *Good Lord, this kid must think she's run into a loony. Who else would be wandering around the woods toting a small library of books, talking to squirrels and giggling uncontrollably?*

"You must be an Onoconohee camper." Rachel put on a sober, adult smile, trying to assure the girl that at least she was not a dangerous loony.

"Yeah."

As the girl climbed to her feet, Rachel could see that she was older than her first guess, perhaps fifteen or sixteen. The extra-large T-shirt and baggy camp shorts she wore emphasized the still-gawky angles of an adolescent body in transition. Exaggerated, spiky hair and heavy rings of eyeliner only underscored the girl's ongoing war with nature's sluggish pace. *A late bloomer,* Rachel thought, feeling a sudden pang of empathy.

"By the way, I'm Rachel Chase. My grandmother and I live right next door to the camp." Rachel jerked her head toward the farm's boundary as she resumed her way along the overgrown footpath.

The girl only nodded, but she fell in step beside Rachel.

"What's your name?"

The girl gave her a suspicious sideways look and for a second, Rachel wondered if she would answer. "Jody," she finally mumbled grudgingly.

The sounds of high-spirited young voices in the distance now rivaled the chirping of the forest's birds. "Sounds like everyone is having a good time down at the pond," Rachel commented, grasping for a lure to draw the teenager out of her surly silence. She glanced over at the girl, but Jody kept her ludicrously made-up eyes trained on the path ahead.

At the clearing, Rachel halted to take in the scene before her. True to his word, Patrick had erected lifeguard stands on three sides of the pond; buoys, rescue equipment and life jackets were prominently displayed on every dock. Swimsuit-clad counselors, armed with whistles, were perched atop each stand, overseeing the flocks of youngsters clustered around the water's edge. Rachel scanned the uneven sea of heads, trying to pick Patrick out of the crowd. They spotted each other at the same time.

"I brought you the books Gran promised," Rachel announced as soon as he was within earshot.

Patrick quickly scooped the heavy tomes out of her arms. "This is quite a load," he remarked.

Rachel chafed her numb arms. "Tell me! But it's such a nice day, I couldn't resist the temptation to walk. And I wanted to see what you've been up to at the pond," she added in a burst of honesty. "This is quite an improvement." She gestured toward the neatly mown banks that only a week earlier had been overgrown with briars and poison ivy.

"We aim to please, ma'am," Patrick grinned, revealing the dimples hiding in his ruddy cheeks. His eyes were twinkling with humor, but for a split second, a more complex emotion flashed through their blue depths, silvery and elusive as the quick-moving trout that darted beneath the pond's surface.

An unexpected warmth suffused Rachel's face, heightened by the contrast of the cool breeze blowing off the water. "When do you start giving swimming lessons?" she asked, grateful for the steadying bulwark of a mundane topic.

"Bright and early tomorrow. Today we're dividing the campers into age and ability groups. Right, Jody?" Patrick turned to include their teenage companion, whom, Rachel realized with a twinge of guilt, she had almost forgotten.

"I guess." Jody's tone was as flat as the still, green expanse of water.

"Jody's a senior member of the Colonial Fair steering committee," Patrick went on, pointedly ignoring the girl's sullen response. "Maybe you'd like to take these books Rachel is lending us to the committee meeting, to give you guys some ideas." His resolute smile firmly in place, Patrick thrust the books into Jody's arms.

"If you say so." Jody shifted the heavy books enough to manage an indifferent shrug. Without another word, she turned and started down the path leading back to the campground.

"Please don't worry about the books," Patrick told Rachel in a low voice. "I'll see that they're returned to your grandmother in mint condition."

"It wasn't the books I was thinking about." Rachel's eyes continued to follow the slight, slouching figure weaving between the trees. "It looks to me as if you've got one very reluctant camper on your hands."

"You mean Jody?" Patrick shook his head and smiled. "That's what she'd like for everyone to think. But you should have seen her when we were signing kids up at the community center in her neighborhood. Oh, sure she did her tough act, to start with. That was before I let her know that our space was limited and we couldn't include everyone this year. Then she came around. Fast."

"You mean she dropped her cool long enough to act excited about something?" Rachel lengthened her strides to match Patrick's rangy gait as they strolled along the pond's shore.

"Don't get me wrong. She didn't exactly jump up and down. Fortunately for her, her younger sister had already been selected for the ten-to-twelve-year-old group. Jody insisted her mother wanted her to come along, to keep tabs on her sister. But I'll warrant few of those kids cutting loose and playing down by the pond are happier to be here than Jody Marshall. Too bad she's afraid to show it most of the time."

"Maybe she won't be by the end of the summer," Rachel commented, glancing up at Patrick.

The indigo-blue eyes narrowed, scanning the horizon beyond the tranquil pond. "I hope so. Jody's been in some scrapes, a few truancies and the like, nothing serious, but enough to get a social worker on her case. Seems the family has had problems since the father died four years ago. The mother is sort of floundering around in desperation, has gone through a succession of boyfriends."

"And Jody really resents it?" Rachel interposed.

Patrick nodded. "She needs something solid to hold on to. That's one reason Milton and I picked her to be on the Colonial Fair steering committee, to give her a chance to feel she's needed, work with other youngsters and really experience a sense of accomplishment. If she learns a little bit about herself in the process, well, that will be more important than a lifetime of tennis and swimming lessons." Patrick fell silent for a few minutes, kicking idly at the acorns and leaves littering the footpath.

He really cares about these youngsters, believes in them, Rachel thought. A warm feeling surged through her, drawn to the surface by something even more appealing than his affable manner and charmingly irregular good looks. As a police officer, Patrick had surely seen people at their very worst; she had little trouble imagining how easily a person in his position could lose faith in the human spirit. Yet, Rachel was struck by how jaded many of her business associates would seem compared to Patrick.

They had reached the fence separating the campground from Heathervale's tract of land. "Speaking of the fair, how are your plans coming along?" Rachel asked as Patrick swung the rustic wooden gate open.

Patrick grinned, pulling the gate closed behind them. "Maybe you ought to ask the steering committee. It's the kids' project, you know."

That the Colonial Fair was, at the very least, the subject of spirited debate among the campers became apparent as Patrick and Rachel approached Onoconohee's stables. Near the row of stalls, a redwood picnic table had been set up beneath a shady elm. Eight young people were gathered around the table, seated on camp stools and bales of straw commandeered from the barn. Rachel recognized Jody's quick voice vying for the attention of her companions.

"*Nobody's* going to think a bunch of cutoff jeans are knee pants, Raymond. And you can forget about using nightgowns for long dresses, too." Jody planted her knuckles on either side of one of Gran's books that lay open on the table.

Her adversary, a chunky preteen with bristling red hair, frowned from behind his thick glasses. "Why not?"

The camper seated next to him, a tiny black girl wearing an Onoconohee baseball cap, gave Raymond a scarcely tolerant glance. "Because I'll bet most of the girls don't even have a nightgown, dodo. We wear pajamas or sleep shirts. Besides, Jody's right. A nightgown's not going to look like anything but a nightgown." She slid a book in front of the boy and jabbed an illustration with her finger. "Ever see a nightgown like that? Yeah, right." Slapping the book shut, she turned to the other committee members. "What we need are real costumes, like the clothes in these pictures."

"Maybe we could make 'em," a doll-faced little girl, the youngest of the group, piped up.

"You mean like *sew*?" Raymond's round face contorted in distaste.

"You can stick yours together with Krazy Glue, Ray," another boy suggested, setting off a fit of snickering among the committee's male contingent.

"First, we've got to have something to sew and glue together. And that means buying stuff." Jody's frank pronouncement cut through the guffawing and the assembly fell silent.

The small girl who had originally tabled the notion of making costumes ventured another suggestion. "I'll bet there's a store in town that sells material and sewing things."

"Oh, sure, but you got any ideas about how we're gonna pay for all this stuff?" Jody asked.

Chastened, the little girl slumped back onto the bale of straw.

"What *are* we going to do, Patrick?" The girl with the baseball cap swivelled on her camp stool to face the adults.

Rachel watched the muscles of Patrick's lean neck tighten as he swallowed hard. "Well, Tanya, we do have a budget for supplies...." he began, but Rachel could see he was thrashing about for a reasonable response. Jody's unflinching gaze wasn't making matters any easier for him.

"You know, you may not want to use modern fabrics for your costumes," Rachel put in. A look of relief washed over Patrick's sun-burnished face as the eight pairs of eyes shifted to her. "I think part of the fun with the fair is to make it as authentic as possible. The early colonists wouldn't have bought material for clothing from stores. They would have spun the fiber, woven the cloth and colored it with natural dyes made from native plants."

"You think we could do all that by the middle of July?" Jody looked skeptical but game.

Rachel smiled, heartened by this first glimpse behind the girl's habitual mask of feigned boredom. "Well, maybe you could cheat a little and skip the first two steps. I'll bet Madison's Cloth Town would be delighted to donate a few bolts of cheap unbleached muslin, and Gran and I could show you how to make the dyes. Are you interested?"

Murmured approval circulated the table. It was Jody who finally spoke for the group. "Sure! When can we start?"

"Whenever you want to," Rachel replied. After all, Gran had said they would be willing to do anything to help with the fair, hadn't she? Rachel crossed her fingers inside the pocket of her shorts and hoped that offer would extend to squiring a dozen or so exuberant kids through Heathervale's dyeing barn. "First, you'll need to hustle together some volunteers, people to make the dyes and dip the cloth."

"We've already got a bunch of kids who want to work on costumes. Could we get started this afternoon?" Jody countered. Despite the owlish eye makeup, the girl's head-on gaze reminded Rachel of some of the more promising candidates in her MBA class.

"Well, Patrick, what do you say?" Rachel turned to him and grinned.

Patrick threw up both hands in a gesture of submission. "Anything that's fine with your grandmother and the steering committee is fine with me."

That the steering committee was raring to go was obvious; Gran, however, might require some sounding out on the matter. Still, with Jody and her crew in high gear, Rachel hesitated to curb their enthusiasm. Fortunately, a practical compromise quickly suggested itself. "Since you're going to be overseeing the project, maybe the eight of you should come over to the farm this afternoon. That way, Gran and I could explain the dyeing process to you before you start assigning tasks to the costume makers."

Was it her imagination, or did Jody's hard little face actually reflect a spark of delight? Rachel watched her survey the approving nods of the co-workers before turning back to Rachel and Patrick. "Okay" was all Jody said, but this time, she smiled.

All they needed was for someone to whistle a march, Rachel mused as she led the eight youngsters through the woods and across Heathervale's herb fields. Glancing back at the uneven row of heads following her single file, with Patrick bringing up the rear, she was carried back to the weekend hikes of her boarding school days. Rachel wasn't sure how she compared to their leader, Miss Pritchard, with her sturdy brogans and charging pathfinder's gait, but the similarity made her smile all the same.

Rachel pulled the little company to a halt at the gate to the yard. Unexpected as the appearance of a full detachment of campers would be, she hoped to corner Gran, take her to one side and explain the situation before unleashing the kids on the dyeing barn. Her grandmother would have long since finished transplanting the tarragon seedlings and moved on to another chore. Rachel scanned the outbuildings, trying to second-guess Gran's plans for the afternoon.

"Gracious me! What a host of young visitors!"

Rachel wheeled to find Gran, trowel and mulch bag in hand, pulled up short behind them.

"Oh, hi, Gran! Gang, this is my grandmother, Eleanor Chase." Rachel lapsed into the sort of hand-in-the-cookie-jar smile she never had quite managed to outgrow.

To her relief, Gran was beaming as she sidled past Patrick, dispensing a motherly pat to his shoulder on the way. "I hope you're giving our new neighbors a thorough tour of the farm, Rachel."

"We're not doing a tour, Mrs. Chase. We're going to learn to make dye," Tanya explained helpfully.

"Oh." Gran hesitated and regarded the young people thoughtfully.

Rachel rushed to allay any fears her grandmother might have. "I was going to show them around the dyeing barn and explain a few techniques, just to get them started."

"I'll make sure we don't disturb anything, Eleanor," Patrick volunteered in his most winningly boyish fashion.

Gran's face broke into the smile she reserved solely for Patrick when he called her by her first name. "Nonsense, my boy! No one ever brewed proper dye without making a royal mess in the process." She cast a stern eye at Rachel. "And I certainly hope you intend to show these young folks how to do it right. In fact, perhaps it wouldn't be a bad idea if I took over from here. You know a good deal about dyeing, Rachel, but I have been at this a lot longer than you have," she added gently.

"Well, sure, Gran, if you want to." Suddenly feeling very useless, Rachel stepped back to allow her grandmother through the gate.

"You know me, dear. There's nothing I love better than sharing nature's secrets with city folk." Gran blessed the flock of campers with the knowing-yet-sweet smile of a storybook fairy godmother. She latched the gate, neatly fastening Patrick and Rachel on the other side. "I fear I may be a bit low on supplies. Why don't you two run along and gather some things for us."

Gran snatched up a basket hanging on one of the fence posts and handed it across the gate to Patrick. "We'll need some elderberries, if you can find any, and lots of marigold leaves. Come to think of it, you might as well pick a few of the blooms as well." She glanced over her shoulder to the enthralled campers. "Marigold blossoms make such a heavenly shade of yellow! And do nip a handful of leaves from the clematis growing along the wall. And don't forget oak bark. Yes, we'll need oak bark for brown and green and purple."

"Can you remember all that?" Patrick whispered to Rachel as he followed her back down the garden path.

Rachel giggled. "Trust me. Gran can make dye from just about anything we bring her."

Patrick feigned a relieved sigh. "That's good to know, since I'm sure I wouldn't know an elderberry bush from a clump of poison ivy."

"Yes, you would, because elderberries grow on a tree, not a bush," Rachel assured him with a playfully smug grin.

"Don't count on it," Patrick warned her, but Rachel could tell he was as pleased with their little assignment as she.

For all Rachel's long-standing jokes about her grandmother's tireless matchmaking, she silently thanked her for orchestrating the joint plant-gathering expedition with Patrick. Ordinarily, the only thing one could count on from anything that even smacked of a deliberate pairing off was self-consciousness and awkward conversation. The afternoon's excursion, however, was blissfully free of both.

As the two of them wandered through the gardens, stooping to admire and occasionally pluck the bounty of Heathervale's cultivated beds, Rachel and Patrick chatted as naturally as if they had known each other all their lives. Occasionally, they would fall silent, intent on their labors, but the quiet intervals, too, held a special enjoyment.

Comfortable. Rachel's mind settled on the word like a long-overlooked gem, freshly rediscovered in a jewelry box. Patrick's masculine appeal was as intense as ever, but *comfortable* was the word she would have chosen to describe the way she felt with him that afternoon—comfortable enough to relax, to share with him her joy in nature, to be herself without any thought to the impression she was making.

Even after she had known Richard for three years, he never quite seemed able—or willing—to put aside his competitive edge and simply appreciate every moment for what it was. As she picked her way through the woodland with Patrick, pausing to chip slivers of bark from selected trees, she was struck by how remote Richard's image appeared in her mind. She felt almost guilty at the ease with which her thoughts floated past him. But then with Patrick, she certainly had a very real distraction in the present.

He, too, seemed to be thoroughly enjoying himself. His mock-serious attempts to identify new plants kept them both laughing, but they were surprised at how quickly they managed to fill the basket with a varied selection of leaves, bark and berries.

"Mission accomplished." Patrick lifted the overflowing basket in salutation as he and Rachel walked into the dyeing barn. His self-congratulation was cut short, however, by Jody and Tanya, who grabbed the basket and began to inspect its contents with the critical eyes of newly-trained experts.

Jody held up a bunch of elderberries, Patrick's prize find of the day. "Some of these berries are still green, Mrs. Chase. Will they work okay?"

Before Gran could respond, Patrick lodged a complaint. "Hey, wait a minute! Here we've been toiling in the hot fields all afternoon and you want to give us grief over a few green berries." He tried to look offended.

"To make dye, they need to be ripe," Tanya informed him coolly. "Don't they, Mrs. Chase?"

Gran shot a quicksilver wink to Rachel and Patrick. "I'm sure a few green berries in the batch won't matter a whit. But now that we have our plants, you all know what to do with them?"

Eight voices assured her that they most definitely did. Soon the airy barn was filled with the sound of young people chopping leaves, mashing berries and grinding bark with mortar and pestle. After the plant material had been placed in pails of water to soak overnight, the youngsters dutifully tidied up the work tables before Patrick could even remind them.

"So I'll plan to see you all tomorrow morning at ten o'clock sharp. That is, unless the camp has something else scheduled for you." Gran turned to Patrick for approval as they were walking out into the yard.

"Ten sounds fine," he assured her. Checking his watch, he let out a low whistle. "Speaking of schedules, I'm afraid if we don't double-time it back to camp, there won't be much supper left for us."

A collective groan rose from the committee, winning a chuckle from Gran.

"We all really appreciate your help, Eleanor." Patrick turned to Gran as he herded the campers through the garden gate.

Gran put on her most gracious smile. She leaned her elbows on the fence, nodding and chatting with her young protégés as they filed past. Once through the gate, the campers broke into a jog, apparently spurred by the threat of a less-than-adequate supper. Patrick, however, hung back, lingering at the gate with his hands in his pockets.

"I haven't forgotten to thank you, too, Rachel." He pulled one hand halfway out of the pocket and then hesitated as if he wanted to say—or do—something more, but was unsure just what.

Although Gran tactfully remained by her post at the fence, Rachel instinctively dropped her voice. "I had a good time. A really good time," she added, but there was so much more she wanted to say. *You make me feel good, Patrick Morrissey. You make the sun seem brighter, the wildflowers sweeter, the world a happier place. Why do you always have to leave so soon? Will you never stay around long enough for me to find the nerve to say these things to you?*

But Rachel's questions remained unanswered, her words unspoken. For now, at least, she had no choice but to watch as Patrick waved and then turned to lope down the path after his young charges.

"YO, PAT! WANT ME TO lock up the office for the night?" Trip Barton's hearty young voice carried across the crisp night air.

Patrick shielded his eyes as Trip's flashlight beam drifted across his face, but he kept his seat on the recreation room steps. "Not yet. There are a few things I ought to look over before I turn in tonight. But thanks."

"Sure thing." The flashlight's yellow sphere cut a figure eight through the dark air, pursuing the fireflies that flickered like random sparks. "Pow! Gotcha!" Trip suddenly dropped his voice. "Guess I'd better cool it with the firefly Pac-Man game or I'll wake Milton."

Patrick chuckled softly. "He's already turned in?"

Trip's shadowy silhouette nodded. "I dropped by the cabin to pick up my guitar around nine, and he was sleeping like a baby. He deserves it, though; he really put in a full day with the orientation. Come to think of it, that bunk's starting to seem pretty attractive to me, too."

Patrick listened to Trip's stifled yawn. In spite of himself, Patrick had to clamp a hand over his own gaping mouth. "It's been a long one for all of us."

"Yeah, and don't forget reveille is at six tomorrow. Ugh! Think I'll leave the stargazing to you and hit the sack. G'night!" Trip waved the flashlight in a parting salute.

"'Night!" Patrick propped his elbows on the step behind him and leaned back. *Stargazing.* He smiled in the dark at the dreamy, old-fashioned—and, yes, romantic—connotation of the word. When was the last time he had actually looked up at the velvety canopy of an early-summer sky and picked out the diamond-studded constellations embroidered across it? Certainly never once during the long years he had worked a police detective's night beat. The only lights that mattered on those nights had been flashing blue ones. And, anyway, the city sky was too hazy to reveal more than a chunk of cloudy moon to any audience below.

It was amazing how much you could see out here in the country. As Patrick's eye swept the glittering arc overhead, it formed a personal constellation of its own. How easy it was to imagine Rachel's beautiful face against the twinkling background. Like the distant stars, her radiance shone from within, burned so bright it could bridge any distance, touch the most remote places. She had touched him with her gentle smile, her generosity, her warmth.

Alone, with only the secretive night sounds of the encroaching forest around him, Patrick imagined he could capture one of the tiny stars in his hand, feel its sparkling shards shimmer through his fingers. And if that were possible, could he not reach out and touch her face as well? Patrick closed his eyes, shutting out everything but the thought of her cool, translucent cheek beneath his palm.

When he finally rose, he moved quietly, careful not to disturb the night's precious magic. Even the office looked strangely mellow, its hard edges blurred by the desk lamp's fuzzy yellow light. Patrick adjusted the shades and then glanced over the desk. The work could wait until tomorrow, he decided.

He was reaching for the light switch when his eye fell on a folded pink telephone message skewered on the spindle. *Patrick M.* He immediately recognized Milton's flowing script. Someone must have called him while he was over at Heathervale and had left a message with Milton. Pulling the slip of paper off the spindle, Patrick unfolded it and held it beneath the desk lamp.

"Thursday June 15, 5:22 p.m.," Milton had noted precisely at the top of the message. "Detective Arnold Nordstrom phoned. Re: Court hearing Wednesday, July 12.

Message: Smell a plea bargain in the wind. Your testimony is all we've got. Don't let us down.''

Patrick punched the desk lamp's button, and darkness fell over the room. He sat on the edge of the desk for a long moment, just listening to the ringing in his ears. Then he crumpled the note in his hand and flung it into the waste basket.

Chapter Five

"Take care, Owen, or you'll bump one of the legs off! Mind the bottom step!" Gran stood at the end of the front walk and beckoned reassuringly.

"Can't see a blasted thing," Owen muttered from somewhere behind the bulky cabinet sewing machine he was trundling out of the house.

Rachel hoisted the Volvo wagon's rear hatch and then rushed to help guide the weaving Owen along the drive. He blew out a noisy sigh as he lowered his burden into the back of the wagon and then shoved it into place.

Rachel quickly rearranged the boxes of dyed muslin displaced by the machine and then slammed the hatch. "Thank you so much, Owen."

Owen mopped the back of his leathery neck with a wrinkled kerchief. "Just hope you've got someone strong waitin' at the other end."

"Between Patrick and those strapping young counselors, I don't expect you'll have any problems." Gran's breezy tone suggested that she found Owen's grunting and panting more than a little suspect. Chuckling, she turned to Rachel. "Jody and Tanya are so excited about having a sewing machine to make costumes, I imagine *they'll* have it out of the car before you can wink. When I told them they could have my old machine for the summer, the folks in Hartford probably heard them whoop. All the same, I think you'd better insist they leave the heavy lifting to Patrick.''

Rachel smiled, but somehow the mention of Patrick's name aroused a peculiar feeling in her, something akin to a persistent itch deep down inside where you couldn't scratch it. As she drove to the camp, she pondered the six-foot-two-inch, periwinkle-blue-eyed source of that itch.

She was attracted to Patrick, of course, and he seemed to like her. No, he *did* like her; there was no point in being coy with herself on that issue. Why, then, did they never manage to spend more than a few hours together?

Although she would never have breathed a word to Gran, Rachel had been heartily disappointed when Patrick had not accompanied the costume committee back to the farm on any of their numerous dyeing sessions, something Milton Weber had managed twice. Okay, Patrick did have a job to perform, but he didn't devote himself to the camp twenty-four hours a day. Even an ambitious climber like Richard had made time for an occasional dinner date. When a man and a woman like each other, they want to spend time together. At least that was what her logical, business-trained mind told her.

Unfortunately, she reminded herself, human beings rarely behaved with the neat predictability of balance sheets or financial reports. Perhaps Patrick was holding himself back because he knew they would be going their separate ways at the end of the summer. And they would be. Maybe she should rein in her feelings, too. These sobering truths settled into her thoughts like a flock of roosting vultures.

Rachel's efforts to sort out her conflicting emotions came to an abrupt halt as soon as she pulled into the campground parking area. The sight of Patrick jogging toward the car, grinning and waving like a carefree kid, had the effect on her of a chocolate sundae placed before a dieter. Only the steeliest will could have resisted, and Rachel realized that she neither had nor wanted a will that strong.

"Wow!" Patrick eyed the station wagon's bounteous load before leaning through the open window. "All of that's for us?"

Rachel pulled back slightly from the window, enough to put his hovering face and her own divided emotions into perspective. "Everything you see," she told him. *Well, almost.* "Now that the muslin the kids have dyed has set and dried, they can actually start designing their costumes and putting them together."

"Your grandmother doesn't know it yet, but the campers want to give her an honorary key to their colonial village on the day of the fair." Patrick stepped back just enough to let Rachel climb out of the car. He followed her as she walked to the rear of the wagon and unlocked the hatch.

"She'll be absolutely delighted." Rachel watched Patrick effortlessly unload the sewing machine, with none of Owen's histrionics. She pulled out a box of dyed muslin and fell in step behind him.

"You deserve something, too, you know," Patrick told her over his shoulder.

"Uhm." Falling back on Owen's tact, Rachel mumbled behind the big box.

"Any particular item on your wish list?" Patrick scooted open the recreation room's screen door with his toe and held it for her.

Rachel maneuvered the awkward carton through the door, narrowly scraping her hip against his knee in the process. "Just don't put me in the pillory or the ducking stool, all right?" The box landed with a muffled thud as she dropped it onto the table.

"No problem there. If I remember correctly, those punishments were reserved for scolds and scarlet women." Patrick laughed, a little too innocently. "I'll pass your request on to the committee, though," he promised. "Better yet, you can tell them yourself today, that is, if you accept our invitation to join us on the bike trip."

"Bike trip?" Repetition was a tried-and-true method of buying time to think, and Rachel had no intention of jumping at the opportunity to be with Patrick without considering the consequences.

"Don't worry. We're not planning on covering any great distance. A lot of the younger kids are coming along and we'll keep an easy pace."

Rachel pawed through the folded lengths of muslin, admiring the soft, natural colors. "I haven't been on a bike in years."

"You think I have?" His deep laugh filled the room, enveloping her like a warm, seductive cloud. "C'mon. It'll be fun. We're going to stop at that old mill, have a picnic lunch, play Frisbee or whatever."

"I don't know, Patrick. Gran has a kitchen full of carpenters over at the farm . . ." Rachel's voice trailed off into an irresolute murmur.

"Take it from me. Trip and I spent a whole month building stuff around here, and I can tell you from experience that the best thing you can do when a bunch of guys start hammering and nailing is to give them the widest berth possible." He gave her a playful nudge, his knuckles gently caressing her shoulder. "I'll even see that you get one of the good bikes."

"With trainer wheels and a padded seat?" Rachel looked up into his teasing blue eyes.

"Anything you say, Miss Chase. Should I interpret that agreeable smile as a yes?" His finger chucked her lightly

beneath the chin. Any inclination it may have had to linger
was cut short as the screen door slammed behind them.

"Hi, Rachel!" Jody greeted her, grinning around the edge
of the carton she carried. "I got this out of the car for you."
As she eased the box onto the floor, she turned to the small
girl who had trailed her through the door. "Hands off,
Mutt! No messing stuff up!" The younger girl reluctantly
stepped back from the box of muslin she had been inspecting and grinned up at Rachel.

"She's my little sister," Jody explained in an aside to
Rachel. "Her name's Melanie, but everyone calls her Mutt.
For reasons that are obvious." She rolled her amber eyes
that, Rachel noticed, were now mercifully free of the
clownish eyeliner.

"Rachel is going to join us on our bike trip today," Patrick announced.

Rachel opened her mouth, ready to remind him that he
was jumping the gun, but quickly thought better of it. As
the two girls chorused their noisy approval, Patrick gave
Rachel a look that clearly said "checkmate."

As it turned out, the "good bike" Patrick had promised
Rachel proved to be a squeaky balloon-wheeler, complete
with basket and old-fashioned headlight. As she wobbled
over the campground's dirt road, backpedaling to keep in
line with the troupe of campers, a wave of nostalgia welled
up in her. How many times as a little girl had she rolled such
a bicycle out of Gran's garage and filled the basket with
peanut-butter sandwiches wrapped in wax paper and a couple of her favorite books? At such times, she seemed to
outdistance the clouds hovering over her childhood, pedal-
ing hard with the sweet summer air lifting her braids out
behind her.

For safety's sake, the group maintained a tight column on
the highway, with one of the counselors in the lead and

Patrick bringing up the rear. After they had turned off the main thoroughfare onto a little-traveled road, Patrick pedaled up behind Rachel. "See, no matter how old you get, you never forget how to ride a bike."

Rachel shot him a withering look over her shoulder. "Who's talking about getting old?"

Patrick pulled alongside her, hugging the shoulder of the road. "My legs probably will tonight."

Rachel had never considered herself a suggestible person, but she couldn't help glancing down at the prominent muscles surging beneath the faded jeans that encased his thighs. "At least we don't have any bad hills between here and the mill," she assured him.

"You know this route pretty well, then?"

"I used to bike these off roads during the summers when I was a kid. I'm surprised at how little the countryside has changed."

Jody had nosed her bike through the pack to catch up with Rachel. "You grew up around here?" she asked.

Rachel smiled and nodded. "Sort of. I always spent summers with Gran. See that big gray barn back through the trees?" She loosened her two-handed grip on the handlebars long enough to point. "I always loved its weather vane, the little rooster crowing up at the sky."

Jody craned for a glimpse of the weather vane twirling in the breeze. "That's neat. I like your grandmother," she added. "I bet you had a lot of fun staying with her, didn't you?"

"Yes, I did."

"Our granna lives in Asbury Park. Dad used to take us down to visit her, and we'd all go on the rides and stuff. But we don't see her much anymore, not since he died." A frown creased Jody's pale, freckle-spattered face. "Mom's never got the time. That's what she says, anyway. Someday I'm gonna buy a car and then I'll go wherever I want to."

"And you'll take me with you," Mutt piped from behind them, her short legs pumping to overtake them.

"Oh, sure!" Jody pulled the classic expression of an exasperated older sister.

Rachel exchanged an amused glance with Patrick, but the dull echo of Jody's brief revelation about her family continued to haunt her. Although she had known the girl only briefly, Rachel guessed that Jody Marshall's home life was anything but smooth sailing. At least the camp experience seemed to be helping her to loosen up, Rachel reflected later as they were laying out the picnic lunch in the shadow of the derelict mill.

"Glad you came?" Patrick crouched beside Rachel. He rested one hand lightly on her shoulder as he reached for the jar of mustard she had just pulled out of a day pack.

When Rachel looked back at him, her chin grazed his hand and she did nothing to avoid it. "Very. Although I feel a bit guilty, leaving Gran to contend with the carpenters all by herself." She intercepted the mustard pot before Patrick could replace the cap and spooned a dollop onto a slice of rye bread.

Patrick smiled down at the neat circles of tomato he was arranging on his sandwich. "I'm sure we wouldn't have any trouble convincing Milton to include her in the outing he's planning next week."

Rachel opened her mouth to take a bite from her sandwich and then she froze, salami-and-swiss-on-rye poised in midair. "You don't mean . . ."

Patrick nodded as he dusted the tomato slices with alfalfa sprouts. "Uh-huh."

Rachel replaced the untasted sandwich on her paper plate and squirmed around to face Patrick. "*Milton* is interested in Gran?"

"Yes. And why not?" Patrick clapped the remaining slice of bread onto his handiwork and then took a hefty bite out of the sandwich.

"Well, I mean . . ."

"He's too young for her? So he's seventy-six and she's eighty. So what? They both act about twenty-five most of the time." Patrick eyed the sandwich critically, poking an errant pickle slice back into place.

Rachel frowned in exasperation. "No, of course I'm not talking about their age difference. It's just that I—I guess I hadn't imagined Milton taking that kind of interest in Gran. That's all."

Patrick shrugged, chewing slowly. "I'm not all that surprised. After all, your grandmother is still a very attractive woman, vivacious, fun to be with. Milton has a lot to offer, too. Do you think she might share some of his feelings?"

Rachel crunched a potato chip thoughtfully. "Well, now that you mention it, she did do a bit of primping when you two stopped by the farm last week." She chuckled, shaking her head. "Huh! And who would have thought?"

"Just because some people have a few years on the rest of us doesn't make their hearts immune to those kinds of emotions." Balancing his plate on his knee, Patrick leaned back against the crumbling stone wall bordering the mill brook. "It can hit anyone. At anytime. Anywhere."

"Yes, I suppose so." For some reason, Rachel suddenly felt compelled to busy herself with wrapping cold cuts and assembling containers of condiments. She jumped when Patrick gently tapped her shoulder.

"It doesn't look as if anyone is in too big of a hurry to get back to camp." He nodded toward the campers tossing a

Frisbee around the clearing. "C'mon. Let's go for a walk." He took Rachel's hand and pulled her to her feet.

As they set off along the narrow footpath skirting the mill, Patrick tightened his grip, steadying her over the rough trail. When the terrain leveled into a soft mat of leaves, he loosened his hold. Rachel wove her fingers through his and he smiled down at her.

"This is beautiful, isn't it? So quiet and peaceful." Patrick's voice was hushed, as if they had just entered a cathedral. "Out here, you can almost imagine there's no hate or meanness in the world."

Rachel nodded, letting her head rest against his shoulder for a moment. Back in the clearing, she would never have trusted herself with such a gesture. Now, however, as they walked among the close trees, soothed by the hallowed serenity of the forest around them, it seemed the natural thing to do.

"You know, Jody has taken quite a liking to you," Patrick remarked, his toe digging a shallow furrow through the leafy carpet. Something in his diffident tone hinted that he was talking about someone other than Jody, as well.

"She's a very nice girl, once you manage to lure her out of that protective shell. Believe me, it's never easy losing a parent...."

Rachel broke off and Patrick felt her small hand anxiously curl inside his. "You had to give up one of yours?" he asked gently.

"My dad." Rachel kept her eyes on the trail, not looking at him. "He was a photojournalist, he and Mother both. They were a team. I knew they were on assignment, in Australia, I thought. I'll never forget Gran's coming to school to get me. It was raining that afternoon, so gray and ugly. The headmistress was very nervous when she brought me downstairs, and the moment I saw Gran, I knew something awful had happened."

Patrick felt his throat tighten. Up until now, he had carefully considered every overture of intimacy with Rachel, had been mindful to weigh the consequences and not ask for too much too soon. Now, however, he encircled her shoulders with his arm.

"That was the first time anyone told me he had been in Vietnam. He got caught in a firefight." Her voice faltered and she paused. Patrick watched the slender sinews of her neck draw tight beneath the fine-textured skin as she struggled to maintain her composure. "No one had told me," she repeated, as if she still had not quite come to grips with her sense of betrayal. "Of course, Mother and Dad had simply wanted to shield me from worry, but I didn't understand that at the time. Now I can see how really angry I was afterward, angry at being kept in the dark, angry at Dad for leaving me, angry with myself for not being able to do anything about it." When she looked up at Patrick, he could see the tears beading on her long lashes. "I know it's irrational and unfair, but I still ask myself why we couldn't have had a nice, safe, normal family like most of my schoolmates." She bit her lip hard, her teeth drawing a taut white line in the rosy flesh.

If he had tried to speak, Patrick knew whatever he could say would have sounded clumsy and lame and inept. Instead, he followed instinct and enfolded her in his arms. Holding her snug against his chest, he swayed, rocking her, his hands gently stroking her back as if she were an injured child.

"Tell me about your family," she whispered against his chest.

"My dad was a cop until he retired last year. Hartford Mounted Patrol for thirty-eight years. All the kids on his beat knew him and his horses, and he knew all of them and their families. Watched a lot of 'em learn to walk, start school, marry and raise kids of their own. He still visits his last horse. Sam's out to pasture now, but Dad takes him an apple every now and then for old times' sake. Mom was just a great mom, which was enough for her and us, too. Nobody makes better corned beef and cabbage, and don't ever play canasta with her unless you want your socks beaten off.''

He felt Rachel begin to relax in his arms. ''Go on. They sound wonderful.''

Patrick sighed, treasuring the pressure of her face against his chest as it rose and fell. ''I have a twin brother, Peter, who played hockey in high school and makes corned beef that's almost as good as Mom's. He's a cop now, in the same neighborhood Dad used to patrol.''

''And all the kids know him and his horse, just like your dad,'' Rachel chimed in, as if she were filling in the familiar parts of a favorite bedtime story.

Patrick smiled down at the silky blond head resting against his shoulder. ''I'm afraid they don't have horses anymore, but, yes, everyone knows Pete.''

''That's too bad, about the horses, I mean. I guess you're following in your dad's footsteps, too?''

Patrick swallowed. ''I work a different precinct,'' he said at length.

They've never issued vice-squad detectives horses, just .38s and bullet-proof vests. He felt himself recoil at the ugly image intruding on the pleasant scenario he had just painted for her. If Rachel knew what his line of police work really entailed, would she feel so protected and safe inside his embrace? His arms tightened around her, as if he feared she would suddenly pull away from him.

Rachel took a step back, but only to slide her arm around his waist. As they turned and started back down the path to the mill, she smiled up at him. "I love horses, but I suppose I can forgive you for not having one."

But can you forgive me for not telling you everything about me? Her face looked so open and honest and beautiful that, for a moment, Patrick felt horribly deceitful. He had led her to believe that he was like Dad and Peter, and he wasn't. But how could he tell her that his life had been defined by danger? How could he explain the nightmares that still wrenched him from his sleep, bathed in sweat with his hand fumbling for a phantom weapon? And how could he ever tell her about Al and the role he had played in that tragedy?

Patrick could find no answer to those questions. But one thing was clear to him. Rachel's childhood had been shattered by violence that still haunted her. She craved a life that was solid, secure, free from fear, and he wanted to help create that life for her. Even if it meant keeping her in the dark about his own past.

Chapter Six

Bracing a hand on the hood of her car, Rachel clasped one ankle and flexed her leg into a V behind her. "Ouch!" Her face screwed into a grimace as a burning sensation oozed through the overtaxed muscles. Funny, but she never remembered her legs feeling this rubbery and tired after any of her childhood bicycling jaunts. Patrick had said you never lost your feel for a bike, no matter how old you got. What he had neglected to mention was how the bike made *you* feel.

Rachel was stiffly stretching the other leg, preparing to submit it to the same treatment as its partner, when she spotted her grandmother, basket in hand, coming out of the potting shed.

Slipping the basket handle over her wrist, Gran paused at the gate to applaud lightly. "I always said you would have made a lovely ballet dancer," she remarked, shooing Noodles through the gate in front of her before turning to latch it.

Rachel gave her tender calf muscles a testy squeeze. "Please, Gran! I am anything but lovely when I'm in pain. And I'm sure ballet is a hundred times more strenuous than a leisurely bicycle ride."

"So you decided to join Patrick and his youngsters on their outing to the mill?" Gran looked supremely pleased as she led the way into the house.

Rachel sidled up the two stoop steps, trying not to limp. "Yes, but how did you know about the trip?"

"One of my little candlemakers told me all about it."

Rachel smiled. In the past two weeks, Gran's conversation had become increasingly sprinkled with references to the various groups of campers whom she was teaching colonial household crafts. Not a day passed without a troop of young people filing into one of Heathervale's outbuildings, eager to make soap, dip candles and fashion wreaths from dried flowers and herbs. At first, Rachel had worried about the extra demands made on her grandmother. As usual, however, Gran would hear none of her concerns.

"With those carpenters making such a mess in the kitchen, it's a mercy I have something to keep me out of the house," she had insisted.

As they entered the house, Rachel began to see the wisdom of Gran's logic on that count. In spite of the vinyl sheet tacked over the kitchen door, sawdust had seeped into the dining room, blanketing every surface with a thin yellow frost. The refrigerator, displaced from its kitchen niche, stood purring next to the china hutch. Equally incongruous-looking was the microwave perched on the antique sideboard.

Gran absently swept a few stray wood shavings from the dining table as she made her way to the fridge. "I suppose we'll have to make do with something frozen again," she remarked, tugging a wrapped casserole from the well-stocked freezer. "Oh, by the way, some mail came for you today. I put it on the hall table."

"Thanks." Rachel was busy slapping yellow powder off two of the dining chairs with a dishcloth, but something in

Gran's exaggeratedly casual tone made her look up. Scarcely a day passed that Rachel didn't receive a few pieces of mail—charge-card bills, notes from friends, a catalogue or a book-club notice—and Gran always left them on the hall table. Why, then, had she gone out of her way to announce something that they both by now took for granted?

Rachel's suspicions were confirmed when they were eating dinner. As Gran was spooning a second helping of turkey tetrazzini onto her plate, she casually remarked, "I think you got a letter from Richard."

"A letter? That's amazing!" Blotting her lips, Rachel chuckled behind her napkin. "And I always thought I would never get anything in writing from him unless you installed a fax machine here at the farm." She had only intended to poke gentle fun at Richard's fast-track way of doing things, but her wisecrack had come out sounding more like a putdown. "Of course, he's very good about calling, even since the bank's been flying him down to Brazil so often," she quickly added.

That her initial reaction had been closer to the mark proved to be the case, however, when Rachel finally retrieved her mail after dinner. One brief squeeze of the padded brown envelope told her that Richard had sent not a letter but a cassette tape. For some inexplicable reason, she felt disappointed, like a child who has opened a Christmas package and discovered pajamas instead of a Nintendo game. It *was* a clever idea and very practical for someone constantly on the go, she had to remind herself on her way upstairs later that evening. And the sort of thing Patrick Morrissey would never do in a thousand years.

Rachel pushed the comparisons that thought invited out of her mind as she changed into a nightgown and then slipped the tape into the radio-cassette player on her bedside table. Punching the Play button, she kicked off her slippers, flopped back on the bed and waited to hear what Richard had to say.

The tape hiss was followed by the sound of a throat being cleared. When Richard said "Hello, Rachel," he sounded as if he were addressing a banquet hall full of Rotarians.

"Hi, Richard! What's new?" Rachel's eyes drifted up to the ceiling, tracing the imaginary animal figures formed by the plaster.

"I'm in Rio right now, sitting on a hotel balcony with a cold Tanqueray, feet up, taking it easy." He laughed into the recorder. "Don't get the wrong idea, though."

"Oh, I'd never do that," Rachel interposed with a smile, imagining his clean-cut, tanned face among the fanciful designs on the ceiling.

"I'm still working on the Monteiro deal. By the time this reaches you, I'll be stateside again, and..." Richard paused and the faint cacophony of traffic from the street below the hotel balcony filled the break. "I should have a thirty-million-dollar line of credit lined up for Monteiro. I know this is big news, but I'd appreciate it if you'd keep it to yourself, just until everything is signed and sealed."

Rachel glanced at Noodles, who had just sprung onto the foot of the bed, and pressed her finger to her lips, swearing him to secrecy. Folding her arm beneath her head, she listened while Richard launched into a fairly detailed account of his hand in the coup. He had approached Monteiro long before she had come to Heathervale, had been wooing the prominent Brazilian firm for months now, and Rachel knew that finally consolidating the deal was a high-water mark in his career. Still, she found her mind drifting as his faceless voice assailed her with percentage points, spreads and interest projections. She was tired from the bike ride, too tired to be bombarded with a volley of figures, she told herself.

At the thought of the day's outing, her mind wandered back to the old mill, to the quiet, isolated trail she had followed, hand-in-hand with Patrick. Guilt pricked her when the tape snapped off and she realized she had no idea what Richard had been talking about for the past ten minutes.

Taking care not to disturb the snoring Noodles, Rachel rolled onto her stomach and briefly pressed the Rewind button.

"…Jointly with Citibank. But I can bring you up to date on *that* mess the next time I see you. Looks like I've about filled this side of the tape, blowing my own horn, as usual." His laugh was frank and unapologetic, the humor of a self-assured man confident that his small conceits will be forgiven.

Well, Richard was entitled to crow a bit. He had worked incredibly hard to forge a relationship between Monteiro and his bank. Anyone who understood the stress, the long hours, the feints and false starts connected with such a sophisticated business deal—and she certainly did—could not begrudge him a little self-congratulation. Promising herself that she would replay the first side of the tape when she was more alert, Rachel flipped over the cassette.

"So, are the quaint pleasures of a bucolic existence still agreeing with you?" he asked the moment she depressed the Play button.

"Yes, as a matter of fact, they are," Rachel began, but before she could elaborate, Richard moved on to a litany of the racquetball matches, Sunday brunches and gallery openings that had filled the blanks between his business trips to Brazil.

"Saw Talbot Reeves at the Heart Fund Charity Ball. Tal sends his best. You know, everyone says the same thing. Nothing seems complete without you. When you took off for the boondocks, you left a great big gaping hole in our group. Everybody is anxious for you to come back home where you belong." Richard sang the words in a plaintive mockery of a pop tune.

"I belong here right now," Rachel told him defensively.

Richard didn't wait for her to elaborate. "By the way, Martha did a fantastic job chairing the Charity Ball. It was *the* fundraiser this year."

"We, too, have our fundraisers here in Scarborough," Rachel reminded him. She cut an annoyed glance at the cassette player when Richard blithely refused to interrupt his narrative of a recent weekend at someone's Cape Cod bungalow. Soon, however, his quick wit got the better of her and she giggled over his droll comments about mutual acquaintances who had been among the guests.

"Amanda and Chris were there, too. Amanda's cousin came down on Sunday. I immediately smelled a blind date, but they were civilized about it. We all went out on their boat, had a good time pretending we were on our way to the America's Cup. Sarah—that's the cousin's name—turned out to be a nice kid. Believe me, the operative word here is *kid*. Young, young, *young*. I imagine you're spared this excruciating fix-up business down there with your grandmother."

"Oh, Richard, if you only knew Gran!" Rachel shook her head.

"And you know the worst thing about people your friends introduce you to? They're never awful. Just inappropriate."

"Sometimes they aren't," Rachel interjected. She closed her eyes, visualized Patrick and immediately opened them again.

"Take Sarah. A really bright, attractive girl—whom I had almost nothing in common with. She told me she's working on a masters in environmental science. Okay, I can handle that. But guess what? She's planning on becoming a park ranger. Sort of a back-to-nature cop.''

At the word *cop,* Rachel stiffened.

"I mean, I'm sure it's a terrific profession, but there just wasn't much overlap in our worlds. Not like what we had.'' His pause was heavy with anticipation. "Is it okay if I say *have?*''

Richard cleared his throat again, and for the first time since she had switched on the tape, Rachel sat up in the bed.

"She wasn't you, Rachel. Uh...oh, why the hell did I ever think making a cassette would be easy? I guess what I'm trying to say is that I miss you. A lot.'' A hesitant sigh rasped from the cassette player. "Well, before I make a bigger ass of myself than I already have, I suppose I ought to wrap things up. But I do think about you a lot.'' When he broke off, Rachel held her breath.

What would he say next? "I still care about you''? "I still have some wonderful, warm feelings for you''? Or maybe even "I still love you''?

She let out a great, wheezing draught of air as he concluded with a simple "Listen, I'll talk with you soon. Take care.'' Rachel listened to the tape's empty lisp, waiting until it snapped off automatically.

Thank God, he had made no rash emotional revelations at the very end. The last thing she needed at this point was to be faced with a profession of love when her own feelings were in such total disarray. Of course, she still *liked* Richard. His energy was infectious. He had a wicked sense of humor and could always make her laugh. They had shared some fun times together. But whatever it was that had brought their relationship to a crisis and precipitated their decision to see other people remained unresolved.

What *had* come between them? Rachel repeated the by now rhetorical question to herself. Of course, they had their subtle differences, their petty conflicts, the minor friction that afflicted any friendship. *Friendship.* Her mind focused on the word. There it was. Richard was a good friend and for that reason, she would always reserve a fond place for him in her heart. But she needed something more to make a serious commitment.

I want to feel more than what I feel with a friend. I want something deep and strong and passionate, something I can't quite control, something I can't fake. Love. After all, when it was right between a man and a woman, that was the way it was supposed to feel, wasn't it? Heady. Exhilarating. A little unnerving. The way she felt with . . .

Rachel caught herself. To think about being in love with Patrick was ridiculous. Why, she had only known him for a few weeks. She was infatuated, perhaps. Patrick gave her a rush, but what woman wouldn't respond to those melting blue eyes? Besides, everyone knew that real love took time to ripen and grow.

And what if I am falling in love with Patrick? a tiny voice whispered through her protests. How prudent would it be to plunge, heart and soul, into what, in the final analysis, was only a summer romance? Neither she nor Patrick belonged in Scarborough. In a couple of months, they would return to their respective worlds. He would go back to being a policeman in Hartford, she an investment banker in Boston. They would resume old friendships, pick up the rhythm of lives put temporarily on hold, gradually lose touch with each other. To argue that in rare instances such romances flourished only underscored the odds against them. And then she wasn't even sure how Patrick felt about her.

Sitting on the side of the bed, sober, steady, logical Rachel Chase convinced her mind to accept these painful truths. But as she switched off the bedside lamp, she realized that her heart would take a lot more persuasion.

ELBOWS PLANTED SOLIDLY on the desk, Rachel placed both
hands over her ears and tried to concentrate on the pile of
order forms in front of her. With the carpenters' distracting racket reverberating through her head, she was probably shipping Savory Seasoning For Soups and Stews to
Lavender Bath Bar customers and vice versa. She had no
idea how long the phone had been ringing before she finally distinguished its jingle from the power saw's whine.

"Heathervale Farm!" Rachel realized she was shouting
into the phone and immediately lowered her voice.
"Hello?"

"Good afternoon, Miss Chase." Milton Weber sounded
slightly taken aback by the forceful greeting he had received, but was quick to recover himself. "How are you today?"

"Just fine, Mr. Weber. It's a bit noisy around here, but
the carpenters are making good progress with the kitchen."

"I'm glad to hear that." Milton hesitated. "Uh, is your
grandmother in?" he asked in a voice that was almost timid.

"Yes. Can you hold on for a moment, please?" Rachel
smiled into the receiver before laying it on the desk. She put
on a deadpan expression, however, as she leaned over the
back of the wing chair to tap Gran's arm lightly.

Dropping her needlework, Gran lifted one of the fuzzy
red earmuffs clamped over her ears and blinked quizzi-
cally.

"Telephone." Rachel gestured toward the desk.

Milton's hat-in-hand manner had suggested that this call
might be a degree more social than usual. If the elderly
gentleman intended to take a first, tentative step in court-
ing Gran, Rachel wanted to give him every advantage.
Abandoning the mail-order forms, she quietly slipped out
of the room and closed the door behind her. She was only
midway up the stairs, however, when the door flew open.

Earmuffs looped around her neck like a pilot's headset, Gran thrust her head into the hall.

"We're invited to a hot-dog roast this evening," she called up the stairs. "Patrick had to go to Hartford and unfortunately, he probably won't make it back in time. At any rate, the whole mob of campers will be there and they want us to attend."

Rachel turned and trotted back downstairs. "That's nice." The remark sounded so artificial she immediately tempered it with a smile. She told herself her disappointment was adolescent, foolish and completely out of proportion to the situation. Logical argument, however, did little to dull her disappointment that Patrick would be absent from the merry circle gathered around the campfire.

As she changed into jeans and a long-sleeved T-shirt later that afternoon, Rachel tried a sterner line of persuasion with herself. After all, what *did* she want with Patrick? In keeping with her pact with Richard, she was supposed to be seeing other men. Did that automatically place Patrick in the same category as Corbett Williams, the genial date with no cumbersome emotional baggage? Hardly. Yet only a few days earlier, she had done her best to convince herself that any serious relationship between them was limited by the divergent contours of their lives.

Rachel had not come any closer to answering the question by the time she and Gran pulled into one of the campground's graveled parking slots. She was grateful for the coterie of campers who immediately descended on them, leading the way to the picnic area. Surrounded by a throng of exuberant young people, she would find it impossible to spend the evening brooding.

That the campers regarded them as honored guests was clear from the very start. Under the guise of outfitting her with a roasting fork and a ringside seat by the campfire,

Milton smoothly took Gran in hand. As Rachel helped Jody skewer hot dogs onto straightened coat hangers, she kept a discreet eye on the white-haired couple.

"They're kinda cute together, aren't they?"

Rachel glanced up in surprise from the buns she was wrapping in foil.

Jody gave her a matter-of-fact grin. "Your grandmother and Mr. Weber," she added, just in case her adult companion was a bit slow on the uptake.

Rachel tried to look demure. "Well, yes, they are. I mean, I'm glad they enjoy each other's company."

"He'd better get with it and ask her out on a real date pretty soon." Jody studied the two senior citizens seated by the fire as if they were two classmates in the throes of puppy love. Her wide mouth pulled to one side thoughtfully. "I wonder if he knows she likes to dance."

"Gran likes to dance?" Rachel almost gasped. In the twenty-nine years she had known her, Gran had never once expressed the slightest inclination to move her feet in anything more frivolous than a brisk walk. "How do you know?"

"She told me," Jody assured her. "She even showed me some steps your granddad and she used to do. The waltz. The foxtrot. The cha-cha." Her purple high-top basketball shoes did a syncopated two-step beneath the picnic table. "Someone needs to give Milton the scoop."

Looking at the unabashedly freckled face, Rachel had few doubts who that "someone" might be. *And why not?* she thought as she followed Jody to the campfire. Squeezing in between Tanya and Mutt, she realized what a blessing it would be for both Gran and Milton if some seeds of affection had taken root in their many years of friendship. They had both been widowed for a long time. More importantly, they shared a host of common interests, were firmly anchored in Scarborough and committed to the tiny burg's concerns. *Unlike Patrick and me.* The thought rose in her mind, vying with the crackling fire for her attention.

"Your hot dog's gonna be all black."

Rachel looked down to find Mutt tugging gently at her sleeve. "I like 'em well done," she quipped, holding the charred sausage up for the little girl's inspection. Sliding the hot dog onto a bun, she waited while Mutt carefully concealed the damage beneath a thick layer of mustard and ketchup.

On the far side of the dancing fire, a few desultory guitar chords twanged over the night air. Squinting through the flames, she saw Trip tuning up. As the bags of marshmallows began to travel around the campfire circle, someone broke into the first measures of "Blowin' in the Wind." Soon the young voices rose in a spirited chorus, joining in a medley of folk songs. More than a decade had passed since Rachel had heard the sweetly off-key melodies drifting through the dark trees, but she was pleased that this latest brood of Onoconohee campers was familiar with many of her old favorites. When Milton rose to bring the evening's festivities to an end, she felt as reluctant to douse the fire as the youngsters seated around her.

"Go on back to camp, Milton. I'll take it from here and see that the fire's banked properly," a familiar low-pitched voice announced from somewhere behind Rachel.

Spinning around on her split-log seat, Rachel was startled to find Patrick standing on the edge of the clearing.

Without thinking, she scrambled to her feet. "When did you get back?"

"Just a few minutes ago." The guttering firelight illuminated his face, revealing the deep circles carved beneath his eyes. "Did everyone have a good time tonight?"

"Yes, but we all missed you." *I, especially.* Hands clasped behind her back, Rachel hung back slightly, waiting for him to step out of the shadows. When he did, she was startled by the bone-weary lines of his craggy face. "You look as if you've taken on the entire Department of Human Resources single-handedly."

Patrick plied the back of his neck with one hand. "Actually, I had some police business to take care of." He hesitated. "Just some stuff to iron out with my supervisor. Say, are there any hot dogs left? I'm starving," he quickly went on.

"I think we can probably rustle up a couple." Rachel folded her arms, quelling the impulse to loop one through his. She had never seen him look so tired or psychologically drained. A tiny bit of guilt nibbled at her conscience as she recalled her self-centered pique at his absence.

On their way to the littered picnic table, Rachel saw Milton squiring Gran along the path behind the last of the campers. "We're just going to have a look at the finished costumes, dear. I promise not to be too long," Gran cupped her hands to call over her shoulder.

"Take your time," Rachel told her. When she turned back to Patrick, she was grateful for the darkness that concealed her delighted smile.

"I was hoping you wouldn't mind hanging around while I eat," he said quietly.

"I don't, not at all." Rachel's melodic voice seemed to harmonize with the rhythmic night sounds of the forest.

"C'mon." He nudged her arm gently, drawing her back to the campfire.

The once-lively bonfire had subsided to a bed of glowing coals. Entrusting the roasting fork to Rachel, Patrick squatted by the fire and fanned the embers. Soon bright flames curled around the simmering logs. Patrick held his hands over the little blaze for a moment and then settled against the rough split log with Rachel.

All during the long, dull drive back from Hartford, he had thought about her, conjured up her lovely image to exorcise the demons laying siege to his mind. Now, looking at her smooth, patrician profile set off against the wavering firelight, he marveled that such a beautiful being could coexist in the same world with the miscreants he had concerned himself with that afternoon. Closed inside Arnie Nordstrum's cluttered office, surrounded by police reports and mug shots and disposable cups filled with equal parts of cold coffee and cigarette butts, Patrick had felt as if he had stepped into another dimension, totally alien to Scarborough.

Arnie and he had spent the whole day and part of the evening going over the evidence, preparing Patrick's testimony for the upcoming hearing. The ordeal had set off a freshet of rage at the vicious criminals who had gunned down Alvaro. It had also left Patrick profoundly depressed. As he had scrutinized the pictures of the defendants' hard, contemptuous faces, reviewed the volumes of sordid evidence, relived every excruciating moment of the back-alley ambush, Patrick felt as if he had plunged into a sewer and were drowning. Now he was too exhausted for even his anger to buoy him, wanting only to blank the agonizing memories from his mind.

"You're as bad as I am at cooking these things." Rachel's laugh was soft as she gently took the roasting fork from him and pointed it away from the fire.

Patrick had been so numbed by his thoughts he had forgotten about the damned hot dogs, had been only dimly aware of the smells and sounds of the night forest around them. As he turned to look at Rachel, however, a great wave of emotion washed through him, sweeping through all the fatigue and pain.

Did she realize, could she possibly know how much she meant to him right at that moment, how the simple act of joining him in this pathetic, belated meal kept him from tipping over into the abyss? Could she understand how her sweet smile soothed him, eased his mangled spirit with its gentle caress? And was she even vaguely aware of how much he wanted to reach out to her just then, unburden his mind of its oppressive load, seek her comfort?

As Rachel handed him the burned hot dogs on a paper plate, she rested her hand lightly on his wrist. "I'm sorry you've had such a grueling day."

"All that matters is that I'm here right now. With you." Driven by sheer impulse, Patrick covered her hand with his. He felt the small fingers quiver, but she didn't pull away. For some time now—Patrick couldn't place the exact point since he had met her—he had longed to touch her, had craved even the chaste pressure of his hand against hers.

Rachel must have sensed the import of that deceptively casual gesture for she gently eased her hand from his grasp and busied herself with one of the abandoned coat hangers. Her fingers seemed to tremble slightly—or was it just the shimmering firelight?—as she threaded marshmallows onto the wire.

"So I guess I'm going to have the full campfire works, after all." Patrick managed his first heartfelt smile since he had left Scarborough that morning.

Rachel turned the coat hanger carefully over the blaze. "You certainly are. We can even sing a few songs if you like."

"How about 'Moonlight Bay,' or is that too corny?"

He watched her gingerly test one of the marshmallows with her finger. "Tonight has convinced me that there's no such thing as too corny. 'We were sailing along...'"

"'On Moonlight Bay,'" Patrick chimed in. As they began to sway in time with the old song, he sidled closer to her and slid his arm around her shoulders. Something in the familiar lyrics and the half-forgotten memories of a simpler time that they evoked lifted his spirits, helped put his troubled mind at rest.

While Rachel held the last note of the tune, Patrick sang in exaggerated harmony, "'On...Moon...light...Ba-a-y!'"

Both of them chuckled, low, throaty laughter that sounded intimate against the night's background. As Rachel reached to retrieve the toasted marshmallows, Patrick relished the feel of her slender shoulders inside the protective curve of his arm. When she pulled one of the sticky confections off the bent wire, he leaned forward and let her pop it into his mouth. His tongue flicked the tips of her fingers and for a moment, she touched his lips. It was the lightest of caresses, softer than the brush of a butterfly's wing. Yet for that brief, precious second, everything—the fire, the stars, the whisperings of the night—hung suspended around them, frozen in time.

He was so close to her, he could see the quickened pulse beneath her throat's translucent skin. His hand stirred, unable to resist the longing to reach up and trace the soft curve of her cheek. As his palm cupped her face, he felt a tremor pulsate through her.

"Oh, Patrick..." When her lips parted, they had never looked more inviting.

Suddenly, Rachel stiffened. Patrick's hand froze against her cheek as the sound of leaves crunching underfoot intruded on their solitude. He hastily withdrew his hand just as Jody Marshall emerged from the shadows.

"All done?" She halted on the footpath, so abruptly, Patrick was certain, she had assessed the situation with one glance. Jody took an awkward step backward. "Mrs. Chase is waiting in the car, but she said not to hurry."

Rachel had already leapt to her feet and was dusting pine straw off her jeans. "That's fine. I'm on my way." As she looked down at Patrick, he tried to gauge the feelings brewing behind the level gray eyes, but she was too quick for him. "Good night, Patrick." Turning, she hurried up the path behind Jody.

Patrick took his time collecting stray paper plates and marshmallow-coated coat hangers and smothering the fire. He had been unprepared for the turbulent surge of emotion that the last few short minutes with Rachel had unleashed, and he needed the cool night air to clear his head. He was thirty-four years old, and she was not the first woman he had ever been attracted to. He was hardly an uninitiated kid, inflamed by the mere suggestion of a kiss. Privately, he had even prided himself on his ability to shut off distracting emotions, focus solely on his mission when the job demanded it. Why, then, was this heady, gnawing feeling still roiling inside him?

Patrick had no ready answer. But as he knelt to sift ash over the charred white logs, he realized that the fire Rachel had ignited within him would be much harder to extinguish.

Chapter Seven

"There's absolutely no point in taking up valuable parking space!" Gran thrust out her chin in front of the hall mirror, firmly knotting the polka-dot scarf around her neck. "With half the county descending on the camp for the fair today, they'll have quite enough cars to manage without our adding another one to the mess."

Rachel was searching for her sunglasses amid the jumbled contents of her straw shoulder bag, but she gave Gran a dubious look in the mirror. "Let's hope that many people will turn out. At any rate, I don't want you to tire yourself unnecessarily."

Gran gestured toward her own sprightly reflection. "Come now, Rachel. Does that woman look like a feeble old lady?"

Rachel frowned as she pulled the sunglasses out of the bag, hauling a crumpled grocery tape and a leaky ballpoint pen to the surface with them. "No, of course not."

"Good, then we'll walk." Gran spun on her heel and marched to the front door, with the defeated Rachel bringing up the rear.

If the truth be known, she would gladly have carried Gran on her back to the camp if it would have guaranteed a heavy turnout for Camp Onoconohee's Colonial Fair. Heaven knew, the campers had worked hard enough in the past month; they certainly deserved for their endeavor to be a success. And poor Patrick and Milton! As she and Gran walked across the meadow, Rachel felt a knot growing in her stomach at the thought of the blow both men would be dealt if the fair drew only a trickle of visitors. She had tried to do everything in her power, had spent most of the past two weekends driving around the county with Jody, sticking posters in shop windows and restaurants. *Let's just hope someone saw half of those signs.*

As Gran and Rachel picked their way through the wooded acreage separating Heathervale from Camp Onoconohee, the sound of a fife-and-drum corps carried through the trees to welcome them. What the musicians lacked in polished skills they compensated for in enthusiasm, and Rachel unconsciously quickened her step in time with the drummers' spirited beat. At the edge of the picnic area, Gran snatched at Rachel's sleeve and pulled her to a halt.

"Isn't this exciting?" she gasped under her breath, and Rachel could only nod her agreement.

Sometime during the past forty-eight hours, a beneficent fairy had swept over the camp and magically transformed it into an eighteenth-century village. That was the only explanation Rachel could imagine for the colorful pageant unfolding before her eyes. Rustic wooden signs had rechristened the footpaths with names like Candlestick Alley and Dollmakers' Row. The stable had been reincarnated as a blacksmith's shop, courtesy of Owen's collection of ancient tools and a rusty anvil borrowed from Heathervale's barn. Crates, tables and bales of straws had been fashioned into attractive displays for an astonishing multitude of crafts. The soft, natural shades of the campers' costumes contributed to the authentic flavor of the bazaar; Rachel smiled as she recognized the various dyes they had used, mustard-yellow goldenrod, woodsy alder green, the rosy pink of the coreopsis blossom.

Best of all, that fairy must have waved her wand over the entire county on her way back to her castle in the clouds. What else could have summoned the large numbers of people now milling past the booths laden with homemade candles, dried flowers, soap and other handicrafts? Surely not the modest signs she and Jody had posted.

Magic or not, Rachel was heartily grateful to find most of the crafts booths too crowded to permit more than a quick peek as she and Gran jostled through the throng.

"Hear ye! Hear ye!" The doleful ring of a large hand bell cut through the crowd's murmur.

Catching Gran's hand, Rachel shouldered her way to the edge of the path. She broke into a big grin when she recognized the town crier, dressed in knee breeches, ruffled shirt and vest for the occasion. Swinging the bell in time with his measured steps, Patrick was making his way toward a makeshift pillory that had been set up in the middle of the camp. A downcast Trip, similarly clad, followed at a respectful distance; the sign around his neck proclaimed for all to see that he was A Laggard, Given To Much Sleep And Little Labor. Amid the onlookers' uproarious laughter, Patrick locked Trip in the pillory and then proceeded to expound on his shortcomings. Despite the good-natured spirit of the crowd, Trip looked more than a little relieved when the tableau ended, and Patrick freed him from prison.

"My, don't you two gentlemen look marvelous!" Gran exclaimed as they joined the town crier and his lazy charge in the square.

Patrick looked slightly discomfited as he glanced down at his hosiery-encased calves. "You're too kind, Eleanor."

"Nonsense, my boy! You've a well-turned leg, and so has young Trip," she declared. The cackle that followed was positively devilish.

Fortunately, the hapless men were spared any further teasing by Milton's sudden appearance. As he tipped his tricorn hat to the two women, Rachel was struck by how appropriate the antique clothes looked on the courtly white-haired gentleman. In contrast to Trip and Patrick, who wore their costumes with as much ease as they would have donned hula skirts or togas, Milton looked as if he had just stepped out of a Gilbert Stuart painting.

"This is simply grand, Milton!" Gran's eyes were dancing with excitement and, Rachel noted, not above a swift appraisal of Milton's "well-turned leg."

Beneath the shadow of the tricorn's brim, two bright spots were barely discernible on Milton's normally pale cheeks. "The young people deserve most of the credit," he insisted modestly. "Any remaining praise belongs to you. I still cannot believe that you single-handedly managed to turn this diverse group of youngsters into such fine crafts-people."

"Willing hands are easy to teach, Milton," Gran advised him with a philosophical wink. "But I am eager to see how their things look on display. Where is the candle shop? Please show me." Without waiting for Milton to take the cue, Gran slipped her hand through his arm.

Patrick and Rachel exchanged glances as Gran headed for a promising-looking row of booths with Milton firmly in tow. "Is there anything *you're* dying to see?" Patrick took Rachel's arm in a sly imitation of Gran's no-nonsense approach.

"Anything but the candles. Gran's already got dibs on them." Rachel giggled as she tightened her clasp on his arm.

Trip eyed his two companions and then shrugged. "Well, it looks like I'm just the third wheel," he complained good-naturedly.

Patrick fixed him with a mock-severe look. "Careful, my lad, or it's back to the pillory with you!"

Throwing up his arms to ward off an imaginary attack, Trip grinned as he jogged off to join a group of morris dancers performing in the square.

"I'm so glad all these people showed up," Rachel whispered as she and Patrick began to weave their way through the crowd. "And it looks as if they're actually buying things." She tugged Patrick's arm, gesturing toward a couple with two young children carrying a basket filled with herbal wreaths.

Patrick nodded. "This is better than anything we could have hoped for. The gate fee alone should do the trick for us. But believe me, I worried right up until the last minute. I kept waking up last night, trying to figure out what we would do if we had a hurricane or an earthquake or something awful like that!"

Rachel nudged his shoulder lightly with her head. "You should have seen Jody and me last weekend. We were so desperate to get the word out to everyone, we even considered driving to New York and plastering a few signs around Penn Station."

"Jody's been a real trouper with this project." He glanced over the heads of the crowd to an open-air display of corn-husk dolls. Seated on an upturned keg, her spiky hair concealed under a starched white mob cap, Jody was presiding over her wares with the air of a true colonial dame. "I never thought I'd see her come out of herself this much."

Rachel smiled. "I'm sure Gran would have a pithy comment to make on the subject, something about little seeds needing fertile soil in which to grow. Jody and she have struck up quite a friendship, you know.''

''Your grandmother is a gem.'' Patrick pulled her to a stop and a smile broadened his face. ''Speaking of priceless relations, I've spotted someone I want you to meet. Hey, Peter!'' Throwing up his free hand, he waved to a group of people clustered around a table of herb-flavored vinegars and oils.

Rachel watched a man, who was holding one of the bottled decoctions up to the light, wheel suddenly. One glimpse of his ruddy, laughing face and she had no doubt that Morrissey blood flowed in his veins.

''Patrick!'' The man's hearty voice boomed over the noisy chattering. He took the hand of a pretty chestnut-haired woman carrying a baby in a shoulder pack and then plowed through the crowd. ''I owe you an apology, Paddy. I thought you were stretching the truth, raving on about such a wonderful fair just to lure us out here today. This is great, isn't it, Maureen?''

The woman smiled and nodded as she gently jostled the infant sleeping against her chest. ''Your kids have certainly done an admirable job.''

Patrick noticeably beamed at the phrase ''your kids,'' but he was quick to move on to introductions. ''Rachel, this is my sister-in-law, Maureen, and, of course, my brother, Peter. Since we're twins, I suppose you could call him my better half.'' The joke was obviously a well-worn one, for Peter snorted and rolled his eyes as if on cue. ''And this little fellow is Edward James Morrissey.'' Patrick bent over the baby, both hands clasped behind his back as if he were both tempted and afraid to touch the chubby pink face.

Although Rachel had never spent much time around babies, she had no such reservations. Wiggling her finger inside the tiny, damp hand, she dandled it playfully. "Pleased to meet you, Edward. I'm Rachel Chase."

Maureen and Peter both laughed as only proud parents can. "He's our first," Maureen put in confidentially.

"Our future contribution to the Morrissey clan touch-football team," Peter added, regarding his brother with a pronounced glint in his eye. "When Dad finally retires from the game, we'll need a quarterback to take his place, and so far, Patrick hasn't given us much help along those lines."

Patrick came as close to blushing as his naturally high color would permit. "Lay off, Pete! Just because you've become a father yourself is no reason for you to start sounding like our Dad." Glancing at Rachel, he grinned. "My family! Take 'em or leave 'em!"

Rachel smiled back, but she sensed that Patrick's jocular bantering concealed a sore spot in his life. "Has either of you eaten?" she asked, turning to that perennial peacemaker, food, to change the subject. When the Morrisseys shook their heads, she strained for a glimpse of the camp's cafeteria through the throng. "I'm not sure how extensive the menu is going to be, but I know for certain that Kohler's Bakery has donated a big supply of gingerbread muffins and molasses cookies to the fair."

That simple incentive was enough to get everyone moving toward the cafeteria. Although the airy dining room was filled with patrons, Tanya immediately singled out the newcomers as guests of honor. Ushering them to a small table between two wooden benches, she skirted the line and soon returned with a plate of saucer-sized cookies and four cups of apple cider.

As she nibbled the chewy molasses cookie, Rachel chatted with the Morrisseys about their life in Hartford. For once, she decided, she had met two people who were as healthy and well-adjusted as they appeared. Peter talked about the rose garden he was planting in the backyard of their new home, and Maureen recounted her plans to return to teaching as soon as Edward was in nursery school. Both of them mentioned old friends from high school whom Patrick knew as well, the kind of enduring friends who rejoiced together at christenings and weddings and appeared at the door with soup and good wishes whenever someone was ill. Listening to the Morrisseys' conversation, Rachel was struck by how different their life was from her own—and by how happy they seemed to be.

That their warm, open life-style extended to new acquaintances was apparent, too. Peter had just related an anecdote about an argumentative cousin when he winked at his brother. "Of course, you'll be bringing Rachel to the family reunion next weekend, so she'll get a firsthand look at Terence herself. Or firsthand earful, I should say."

Rachel looked down at the crumbs littering her corner of the table and began to scrape them onto a napkin. If Patrick hadn't intended to invite her to the get-together, she had no desire to see him put on the spot. Fortunately for everyone involved, tiny Edward chose that moment to test his developing vocal cords. Hastily scooping up the fretful baby, Maureen hurried out of the cafeteria with Peter close behind her.

"Poor little thing, he's getting tired. It's time we got him home, Pete." Swaying the temporarily subdued infant, Maureen gave Rachel an apologetic smile. "We'll look forward to seeing you next Saturday," she added in parting.

"Thanks."

Patrick waved to his departing relatives, but Rachel could tell he was watching her out of the corner of his eye. When they had disappeared into the crowd, he shoved his hands into the pockets of his knee breeches, striking the classic pose of indecision.

"Look, Rachel," he began. "About this family thing... uh, I don't know how to put this, but I'm not sure you really want to attend this reunion. You see, I'm not even sure *I* do." He shook his head irritably. "Oh, for God's sake, I didn't mean that the way it sounded, but..."

Rachel placed a hand on Patrick's arm, forcing him to look her in the eye. "What this *does* sound like is that you need to talk. Why don't we find a place where we can sit down away from the crowd?"

Patrick looked grateful for the suggestion. He let her lead the way through the bustling camp ground until they reached the well-worn footpath snaking into the forest. When they reached the pond's cool, mossy bank, Rachel dropped onto the damp grass and pulled her knees up. Resting her chin on her knee, she watched Patrick select a flat stone and hurl it over the pond. The stone skittered across the iridescent surface, cutting chinks in the green glaze, and then abruptly sank.

"What do you think of my brother?" Patrick asked, his eyes following the next missile as it arced and then plummeted.

Ordinarily, she would have dismissed such a loaded question, but she sensed that Patrick was sincerely fishing for some kind of honest answer. "He's very nice, even if he does like to rib you. In fact, I liked him and your sister-in-law a lot. It's refreshing to meet people who are so normal."

"Normal as apple pie and Monday night football." Patrick chuckled under his breath. "Pete's just like Dad, always has been. God knows, I love 'em both." Dropping the stone he held, he sank back onto his heels. "But sometimes when I'm around them, I get this funny feeling." He broke off, prompting Rachel to nod encouragingly. "It's hard to describe, but it's sort of like they're expecting me to be more like them. To be someone I'm not."

"You did follow in your father's footsteps and become a policeman," Rachel reminded him gently.

"Yeah, but even that's turned out different." Patrick stared across the pond. "You know, when Pete and I first joined the force, we knew we had separate goals. Pete had wanted to be a neighborhood cop almost from the time he was Eddie's size and Dad had swung him up onto the saddle in front of him. But I had different ideas. I was determined to make detective, get in on the heavy stuff. So I threw myself into the thick of it, learned to live on greasy hamburgers and four hours sleep, worked my rear off until I got that badge."

He looked down at the sliver of slate cradled in his hand, turning it over to examine it. "Dad was the first person to congratulate me when I got promoted. In a lot of ways, I guess I did it to impress him, make him proud of his other son. But now, sometimes, I wonder what all that nasty work has really gotten me. A lousy piece of tin with Lieutenant Morrissey engraved on it? Sometimes I wish I could be like Dad and Peter, join a bowling league, sing in the church choir, have my normal little house in a normal little neighborhood. With a normal little family of my own." He shook his head and tossed the shard of slate aside.

Rachel stretched her legs out in front of her, propping herself on her elbows. "Maybe your dreams aren't that different from your father's or Peter's. Maybe you're pursuing them from a different direction. You know, I believe when you get right down to it, everyone wants the same things out of life."

Patrick leaned to one side and gazed down at her. "What do you want, Rachel?"

The shadows cast by the over-hanging trees had deepened the blue of his eyes to the color of a dusky summer sky. Looking up into those eyes, Rachel felt as if they could see beyond the flesh and bone of her substance, deep inside to the place where she hoarded her innermost thoughts.

"The same things everyone wants," she repeated, this time in a whisper so faint he moved closer to catch her words.

At the first light caress of his lips against hers, Rachel closed her eyes, savoring the wondrous shape and texture of his mouth. He kissed her gently, first her upper lip, then the lower, teasing her responses. Then the pressure grew more ardent.

Lying back on the grass, Rachel reached up to capture his face in her hands. She could feel his ragged breathing, the quivering anticipation that matched her own. How easy it would be to lose herself in this fevered heat of passion! How easy to forget, for the moment, everything but the warm, vital man who held her locked in his gaze. His kiss, his touch, his very presence seemed to transport her out of time, free from the fetters of yesterday and tomorrow, living only in the intensity of the moment.

What do you want, Rachel? Patrick's question echoed in her head, calling her back to reality. Easing up on her elbows, Rachel let her hand linger on his face. Yes, she wanted him, more than she had ever desired any man in her life. But that yearning was larger, more powerful than even the rapturous excitement of his kiss. With Patrick, Rachel knew she wanted to share tomorrow as well as today.

As if he could read her thoughts, Patrick slowly rose and then offered her his hand. Gently pulling her to her feet, he encircled her waist with both his arms. His lips grazed her ear, but this time they imparted a treasure more precious even than a kiss. "Rachel," he whispered. "My sweet Rachel."

Chapter Eight

If Rachel didn't exactly look forward to the mundane task of changing beds, she never failed to relish a trip to Gran's linen closet. Sorting through the shelves piled with neatly folded sheets and pillowcases was always a treat for the senses. The silky-smooth texture of pure cotton tantalized her touch; dainty lace trims and embroidery enchanted her eye, while the dusty fragrance of lavender delighted her nose. Tonight, she had narrowed her choices to a pale blue set of sheets with matching ribbon laced through crocheted edging and a white set appliquéd with soft pink tea roses. She was preparing to reshelve the blue sheets when a muffled thud sent her swiftly retreating into the hall.

The noise had come from Gran's room; she was sure of it. Dropping the sheets, Rachel dashed down the hall. The frightening thought that Gran may have fallen overrode normal courtesy and she flung open the door without knocking. She frowned as her eyes swept the normally tidy bedroom that was now as disorderly as a rummage sale.

Both the bed and the armchair were piled with skirts and blouses. Dresses hung from the wardrobe door, their hangers sticking out at odd angles, while a couple of items—what looked like a floor-length black gown and a bottle-green velvet bolero—had been summarily dumped on the floor.

Gran was hunched over the open cedar chest, digging through its contents like a pirate in search of buried treasure. Her face was flushed as she glanced over her shoulder at Rachel.

"Are you all right? I thought I heard something fall," Rachel said, still unsure what to make of the chaotic scene.

"Well, it wasn't me, just the lid of this chest. And I'll be quite all right as soon as I find a suitable outfit. Something dressy but not overdone. And festive. How does a nice lively print strike you...?" Gran's voice drifted off, her attention now centered on the cedar-scented clothing.

"Maybe if I knew what the occasion was, I could help you decide," Rachel suggested, cautiously stepping over the crumpled velvet jacket.

"Milton has asked me to go out dancing with him Saturday evening." Gran made the announcement briskly, shaking out the petit-print silk dress she had just unearthed with a smart snap. Whirling around, she watched the bias-cut skirt unfurl. "Goodness, I wonder when was the last time I wore this dress?"

"Dancing?" Rachel tried to sound properly surprised but approving. Bless her spiky little head, Jody certainly hadn't wasted any time planting a bug in Milton's ear!

"Yes, ballroom dancing to be precise. There's a lovely hotel in Hartford that features big-band music on the weekend. And, Rachel, I don't want to hear one word from you about minding my hip." Gran's pleased smile softened her tart tone. "When you think about it, dancing is really no more than walking back and forth and around in little circles. Besides, it will give me something to do while you're off at Patrick's family reunion."

"You won't hear any objections from me," Rachel promised her. "And I think that dress is perfect."

"So do I." Gran's eyes sparkled, and she couldn't resist humming a few bars as she gave the full skirt one last swing.

Rachel's applause was cut short by the jingling telephone. Leaving Gran to fuss over her wardrobe, Rachel jogged downstairs. Since the intimate moments they had shared at the Colonial Fair, Patrick had called her every day and Rachel's expectations rose as she grabbed the receiver.

"Hello?"

"Rachel? Damn this miserable connection!"

Rachel swallowed, gulping down the shock that threatened to twist her vocal cords into a sailor's knot. "Mother, is that you?" she finally choked out.

"Yes, of course, it's me!" her mother insisted, the characteristically impatient tone confirming her point. "Are you okay? You sound a little shaky."

"Oh, I'm fine. I just wasn't expecting you when I picked up the phone." *Especially since I haven't heard a word from you in over five months.* "What have you been up to?" Rachel asked, hating the childlike tenor creeping into her voice.

"Just the usual. Spent the last two weeks on assignment in Pakistan, shooting border refugee camps, guerrillas in exile, that sort of thing. I'm in Brussels now for a few days, covering one of those boring economic summits, but at least the water's safe to drink." Rachel's mother rattled off her itinerary as if it were a calendar of PTA meetings and hairdresser's appointments. "Next week I've got to be in Vancouver. No politics this time, thank God—I'm sick of politics—just a color spread for *Earthworks* magazine. What about you?"

Rachel did a rapid scan of her mental files, vainly searching for something that would be of even marginal interest to a woman who has just circled the globe. What in Heathervale's quiet, slow-paced life-style *would* interest her mother? Spring planting? The bicycle trip with Patrick and the campers? The Colonial Fair? Shuffling through her own life's recent milestones, Rachel felt like a bag lady trying to outdress a socialite. She finally settled on one catch-all sentence. "I'm keeping busy helping Gran here at the farm."

Her mother's response was equally noncommittal. "That's good. How is Gran doing, anyway?"

"She looks and acts as fit as ever. In fact, the last time she went to the doctor he told her—" Rachel broke off as her mother cut in.

"Rachel, excuse me, please."

Pressing her lips together, Rachel toyed with the phone cord and waited while her mother exchanged a few muffled lines with someone.

"Sorry, dear, but Malcolm tells me we've got to run for it or we'll miss the big politicos sleepwalking out of their meeting. What are you doing Saturday?"

The question was so unexpected, for a moment Rachel drew a blank. "I've been invited to a family reunion. A friend's family, that is."

"Think you might have time to drive up to Boston around nine o'clock on Saturday morning? I'll be flying out to Vancouver, but I have a two-hour layover at Logan."

"Well, the reunion is in Hartford and they're expecting me around one," Rachel hedged.

"If it's too much of a hassle, don't worry about it," her mother cut in. "I just thought it would be a chance for us to see each other."

"It would be," Rachel insisted, suddenly engulfed by a great, suffocating cloud of guilt. "Where shall we meet in the airport?"

"Let's shoot for the TWA ticket counter. Gotta run now. See you on Saturday." Her mother's quick, abbreviated sentences collided like runaway freight cars, abruptly terminating in the phone's click.

Let's shoot. Gotta run. See you. Her mother's conversation had always been peppered with those kinds of clipped, telegraphic phrases, lean, stripped down words that conveyed meaning without a lot of frills. Janet Chase had never been one to waste time on frills.

To be fair, Rachel reminded herself, her mother's nonstop schedule left little time to spare for leisurely pursuits. Like a restless bee, she was perpetually on the wing, never really stopping in any one spot, only hovering long enough to dispatch with necessary business and then move on. How fitting that an airport should be the site of their latest hit-and-run meeting. Of course, by now she should be accustomed to the hectic pace of her mother's life, accept it in the same way she took for granted her height or the color of her eyes. Still, Rachel could not help wishing that her mother were not always going *somewhere else*.

She had subdued, if not entirely conquered, that wistful thought by the time she climbed into her station wagon early Saturday morning and pointed it toward Boston. Certainly, Patrick had done his best to put her in a lighthearted frame of mind.

"Two family affairs in one day?" he had exclaimed into the phone when Rachel had told him about her mother's call. "You're going to be up to your chin in nostalgia by Saturday evening. But seriously, take your time and enjoy visiting with your mother. If she's anything like my mom, I know you'll have a hard time catching up in just a couple of hours. And anyway, the Morrissey reunion will be in full swing all day. If you're a bit late, you're not going to miss more than a touch-football scrimmage or the home movies of our 1964 vacation at Disneyland. Come to think of it, maybe you should skip those movies! I don't know if I'm ready for you to see me as a knock-kneed preteen dork.''

Rachel had laughed at Patrick's self-deprecating joke, but privately the prospect of watching jerky amateur movies of a happy family sharing time together did not strike her as all that unappealing. Now, as she cut and wove her way through the steady traffic channeling into Boston's Logan International Airport, she was already mentally calculating the drive time back to Hartford.

Rachel parked her car in the short-term lot nearest the terminal and hurried into the ticketing hall. When she reached the TWA counter, she checked her watch. It was only ten to nine. She had made better time on the road than she had expected and could relax now. Rachel scanned the hall, in case she had overlooked her mother among the milling travelers. Finally satisfied that her mother had not yet arrived she selected a seat within view of the TWA counter and sat down to wait.

Fifteen minutes had passed the next time she allowed her eyes to drift back to her watch. Rachel crossed her legs and then recrossed them. She picked up a tattered copy of *People* magazine someone had discarded on the adjacent seat and began to flip through the glossy pages, trying to distract herself from the burning sensation gnawing at her stomach. She had been foolish to skip breakfast. Rushing to an airport made her nervous. Especially when she was rushing to meet her mother.

Irritably tossing the magazine aside, Rachel glanced at her watch and then up at the posted arriving flights. If only she'd had the presence of mind to ask her mother for her flight number! It was already 9:20, no, make that 9:22. What if there were some kind of delay? What if her mother had somehow wandered past the counter unseen while Rachel was reading the magazine? She *had* said TWA, hadn't she? Worse yet, what if her mother had been called to cover a breaking news story, an uprising or a military coup and something had happened...

"Rachel Chase, please come to the TWA ticket area. Rachel Chase, please come to the TWA ticket area."

The summons warbling over the PA catapulted Rachel out of her seat. Hurrying to one of the closed ticket stations, she leaned across the counter. "I'm Rachel Chase. Did someone just page me?"

The ticket agent smacked his stapler smartly, securing a bundle of receipts, before looking up. "I'll check for you, miss."

As he turned to question one of his co-workers, Rachel's fingers anxiously clamped the edge of the counter. The two men whispered between themselves and then looked back at her. A faint ringing filled her ears as she watched the ticket agent, discreet white slip of paper in hand, walk in slow motion to the place where she stood.

"I'm sorry, Miss Chase, but I'm afraid we have some bad news."

Rachel watched the man's lips move, her eyes following the contour of the words. *Bad news? Oh, God, no! Please no! Don't tell me something has happened to my mother! Anything but that!*

"...But I'm afraid Mrs. Chase had an unexpected change in her travel plans." A perplexed expression spread over the ticket agent's face and he hesitated. "Miss Chase? Is something wrong?"

"No, no. I... It's just awfully warm in here." Rachel folded her hands to conceal their trembling and tried to collect herself. "What was the message again, please?"

The ticket agent gave her another dubious look and then reread the note. "Mrs. Chase is very sorry, but she has been delayed for two additional days in Brussels and will then be flying directly to her next assignment. She says she tried to phone you this morning, but you had already left home."

The note rustled in the man's hand as Rachel let out a sigh. "Thank you. Thank you very much," she repeated. She forced a feeble smile, then turned and fled.

She needed to find a quiet corner, someplace where she could sit down and get herself together. That coffee shop didn't look terribly busy and at least the lights were low. Stumbling over a pile of luggage someone had parked by the cash register, Rachel entered the coffee shop and made a beeline for an empty booth. When the waitress approached her, she ordered orange juice and scrambled eggs without even looking at the menu.

You almost lost it back there, didn't you? You thought this was it, the disaster you've been dreading since you lost Daddy. So much for being all grown up, big, smart Rachel Chase with her M.B.A. to prove it! Who do you think you're fooling? You may know all the moves, put on a business suit and talk a good line, but back at that ticket counter, you were right back in your navy-blue school uniform, you're little hand sweaty inside the headmistress's, eyes fastened on Gran's ashen face, waiting for her to tell you what your child's intuition already knew.

Rachel took a sip of the juice, both hands encircling the clammy glass. She forced herself to pick up the fork, take a bite of the eggs, chew, swallow. The food had no taste in her mouth, but going through the familiar motions helped to calm her. By the time the waitress delivered the check, the heart-fluttering anxiety had subsided, supplanted by a dull numbness.

It was eleven-thirty when Rachel finally roused herself from the green vinyl booth. If she left now, she could arrive at the family reunion almost as she and Patrick had planned. The first wave of steaks and hamburgers had probably hit the grill; everyone would be warming up with the football and the badminton rackets, clowning around for the benefit of the omnipresent cameras.

Pulling out her compact, Rachel pretended to check her makeup. She looked normal enough, like someone who has just spent an hour or so with her mother, catching up on the past few months over a cup of coffee. Snapping the compact shut, she thanked heaven that appearances could be so deceiving.

For as Rachel walked to the parking slot where she had left the Volvo, she realized that she would not, *could* not tell the Morrisseys what had actually transpired that morning—not even Patrick. He cared about her, of that she was certain, but what would he think if she told him she had gone into a blind panic at the TWA counter and assumed her mother had met with tragedy? That she was neurotic? Or worse? Rachel had gotten only a glimpse of Patrick's family, but it had been enough to convince her that his childhood had left him mercifully free of such recurring nightmares. No, what Patrick didn't know about her couldn't hurt either of them.

As she accelerated onto the turnpike, jockeying the station wagon into the left lane, another disturbing thought loomed in Rachel's mind. What *would* she tell them about that morning? She could pass off her mother's change of plans, but how in the world could she account for the two-hour stupor she had spent in the coffee shop? Rachel still had not formulated a satisfactory explanation by the time she turned into the quiet, middle-class Hartford neighborhood where Patrick had grown up.

She recognized the house without even reading the number. Clusters of people—some older than Gran, others tiny enough to curl in their parents' arms, still others in-between—filled the front porch and spilled onto the front lawn of the modest green-shingled house, clearly identifying it as the site of a big family gathering. Before Rachel had switched off the ignition, a welcoming committee descended on her.

"Glory be! And this must be Rachel!" A middle-aged man, his curling brown hair laced with streaks of iron, thrust his ruddy face into the open car window. "Kevin Morrissey, Patrick's old dad," he announced. Giving her hand a hearty shake, he helped her out of the car while a contingent of Morrissey relatives looked on approvingly.

"I'm pleased to meet you, Mr. Morrissey."

The jovial face contorted in mock horror. "Now, now, none of this mister business. It's Kevin to you, my dear. Next thing you know, you'll be calling me Officer Morrissey." He shook his head, winning a ripple of laughter from the onlookers. "But come along now and meet the clan. This is my brother Edmund. My cousin, Colleen. Jimmy O'Rourke here." He winked at Rachel. "Jimmy, now he's special. You see, I've been married to his sister for over thirty-six years."

Large hand anchored firmly on Rachel's elbow, Patrick's father guided her up the walk, past what had become a substantial receiving line. At the foot of the porch steps, he relinquished his hold to shout into the house.

"Patrick, my boy, where are your manners? This lovely young lady is here and you're nowhere to be found!"

Patrick was grinning when he appeared in the front door. Clearing the steps two at a time, he hurried to take Rachel in hand.

"I'm glad you're here." In the wake of his father's boisterous hospitality, Patrick's voice sounded low, almost hushed. "You and your mom must have had a nice, long visit."

Rachel licked her lips, but before she could say anything, an attractive auburn-haired woman hailed them from the doorway.

"Patrick, do bring your guest around back. We're just about ready to eat, and I'm sure she'd like something to drink."

As Patrick obediently escorted Rachel to the foot of the steps, the woman's full, pretty face broke into a big smile. "I'm Kate Morrissey, Rachel. We're so delighted to have you join us today."

"Thank you for including me."

Patrick's mother fell in step with her son and his guest as they walked around the house to the backyard. "Oh, don't mention it! Why, we've enough steaks and baked potatoes for an army. When Patrick told me you were meeting your mother today, I said, 'Invite her, too! We'd love to have her!' Maybe the next time she visits you. Where was she off to, anyway? Florida?"

"Vancouver," Rachel told her.

"Rachel's mother is a photojournalist, Mom," Patrick put in, giving Rachel's shoulders a squeeze on the sly.

"I bet that's an exciting job!" Patrick's mother was beaming as she lifted the lid of an insulated cooler and surveyed the selection of beer and soft drinks. "You two must have had a lot to talk about today."

"Oh, yes." The words had slipped off her tongue and leapt out into the shady, hickory-smoked-filled air of the Morrisseys' backyard before Rachel had even thought about it.

"Now what would you like to drink? We have all kinds of beer...." Mrs. Morrissey's hands plunged fearlessly through the melting ice chips, excavating an array of tinted bottles and brightly colored cans.

"I'll have a ginger ale, please." Maybe if she put something in her mouth, Rachel thought, it would prevent any more lies from slipping out.

Kate Morrissey popped the soft-drink can open. She waited for the overflowing fizz to subside before presenting it to Rachel. "What's your mom going to be doing out in Vancouver?"

Rachel took a quick sip of the tangy beverage. "She's photographing a spread for *Earthworks* magazine."

"I love that magazine! They always have such gorgeous pictures. Fred!" Kate reached out to grab the arm of a passing man dressed in green Bermuda shorts. "Guess what? This young lady's mother is a photographer for *Earthworks,* and she's going to be taking pictures up in Vancouver. Fred's the fisherman of the family," she informed Rachel in an aside. "He and Dolly spent two weeks salmon fishing in British Columbia last year."

"Your mother works for *Earthworks?*" There was an element of awe in Fred's voice.

"No, actually she free-lances. She's just doing this one assignment for *Earthworks.*"

"Rachel's mom travels all over the place, Fred," Patrick added in what Rachel could tell was an attempt to be helpful. "For instance, she was working in Brussels this past week, and before that she was in Pakistan, shooting pictures of Afghan refugees."

"Wowee!" Fred whistled under his breath. "I know you must get tired of dumb questions like this, but what did she have to say about those refugees? You see such awful stories on the news."

"Well..." Rachel began. She lifted the soda can, wishing it were large enough for her to crawl into it. "The camps are very crowded. The relief organizations are doing their best, but you can imagine the problems—so many sick children, wounded guerrillas and the like."

"Did she actually see any of the real fighting?" Fred asked in a voice loud enough to attract another half dozen eager listeners.

"No, she pretty much stayed on the Pakistani side of the border." A lie was like an insidious weed, Rachel thought. Once it took root, it kept growing, no matter how badly you wanted to stomp it out.

With a mounting sense of helplessness, Rachel watched her audience grow—and with it the myth she was spinning. With each question, she found herself stretching the truth a little further. No, her mother had not brought her any silk from Pakistan, but she had wanted to shop for lace in Brussels. Too bad her schedule had been so packed. Oh, well, maybe next time. Yes, she had been a bit tired, but only from jet lag. By now, Mother was a seasoned traveler.

Rachel risked a glance at Patrick, wondering if he somehow sensed that her narrative was ninety-nine percent embellishment, but his relaxed smile told her that he, too, took what she was saying at face value. Apparently, unless her nose started to grow like Pinocchio's, no one would ever suspect she was making it all up. The thought that her deception was a complete success only compounded her misery.

When Kevin Morrissey at last ordered everyone to grab a paper plate and line up by the grill, Rachel was overwhelmed with relief. She hung back, giving Fred and his cohorts a chance to get well ahead of her in the line.

"Sorry if you feel you got put on center stage," Patrick whispered into her ear as they moved along the picnic table.

Rachel gripped an ear of steamed corn with a pair of tongs. "That's okay," she murmured as she deposited the corn on her plate.

"Your mom does have an interesting job," he remarked, reaching for the potato salad.

"Oh, yeah. You can't argue with that."

Rachel skipped the potato salad and moved on to the coleslaw. As soon as Kevin had served her a perfectly cooked steak, she headed for a small table near the back porch. Most of its occupants were children and young teens, guests who would be the least likely to demand yet more details of her bogus visit with her mother.

When Patrick slid in beside her, he was still smiling, but a hint of concern had crept into his blue eyes. "Are you feeling okay?"

"I'm fine." She gave him a smile that felt as phony as the stories she had spun for Fred. "Just a trifle tired, that's all."

But not too tired to fabricate more lies, Rachel reflected after dinner when Peter and Maureen challenged them to a game of horseshoes. With Patrick's mother and Fred acting as an advance team, Rachel had no hope of steering her conversation with the gregarious Maureen away from the morning's activities. By the time Patrick had made their last toss and then conceded defeat, Rachel had repeated her fiction yet again.

"We may have lost, but at least we lost with honor." Patrick dropped his arm around her shoulders as they made their way to the cooler for some after-game refreshments.

At the word *honor*, Rachel almost cringed inside his solid, straightforward embrace. One little slip of the tongue, and she had managed to spoil the whole afternoon for herself. Worse still, she knew her discomfort was beginning to show, at least to Patrick.

"Something on your mind, Rachel?" Patrick touched her shoulders gently. "You've been awfully quiet."

"No." That had to be one of the hardest words to fake convincingly—even for someone who had as much recent practice in deception as Rachel. "I guess all the driving today has tired me," she told him, falling back on her earlier excuse. If she was going to lie, at least keep it consistent.

Patrick looked unconvinced as he fished a soda out of the cooler. When he handed it to Rachel, she shook her head. "Uh, Patrick, I've had a wonderful time, but I think getting up so early this morning is starting to catch up with me. Do you think anyone would mind terribly if I went home now?"

Patrick juggled the can of soda for a moment and then replaced it in the cooler. "No, of course not."

Her mouth ached, rebelling at being forced to mimic yet another smile. "I want to thank your parents again." Her eyes nervously swept the crowded backyard in search of Kevin and Kate Morrissey. She found them seated side by side on the hammock, feet dangling as they swung their grandson and kibitzed a volleyball match. At least she could sincerely tell them she had appreciated their hospitality.

Patrick accompanied her around the house to the street. As the lively sounds of the reunion began to recede, the unnatural silence between them became painfully noticeable. When they reached her car, Rachel fumbled for her keys, trying to think of something to say that would break the awkward moment.

Patrick, I didn't see my mother today, but I lied about it because I didn't want you to know what a basket case I am. No, if that was what it took, then she would just have to endure the discomfort. As she reached for the door, Patrick caught her hand.

"Rachel, are you sure something isn't bugging you? Have I said or done anything that's put you off?" Patrick's earnest eyes were probing.

"No!" Rachel pulled her hand free and dove behind the steering wheel. "You keep asking me if I'm okay. Honestly, I'm fine." *Honestly, indeed!*

Patrick stepped back from the car and folded his arms across his chest. "You just haven't seemed yourself this afternoon."

"Oh, please!" In her frustration, Rachel ground the ignition. "Look, I'll talk with you later this week, okay?"

Patrick only nodded.

"Thank every one again for me." With that one last stab at decency, Rachel put up the window and wheeled away from the curb.

On the way back to Scarborough, she tried to put things into perspective. None of Patrick's relatives would ever realize that she had lied to them. Even Patrick would never have to know. She should put the unfortunate sequence of events behind her and vow never to repeat the mistake. But a nagging sense of dishonesty continued to dog her even as she turned onto Heathervale's winding drive. Without intending to, she had betrayed the trust and affection deepening between Patrick and her. She had been afraid to let him see an aspect of herself that she didn't like very much. In trying to conceal that one little part, she had managed to build a wall between them.

The house was dark, save for a single table lamp in the front room and the meager threads of dusky light still visible through the lace curtains. Rachel found a note propped next to the lamp, along with a plastic-wrapped plate of oatmeal cookies.

Dearest,

I hope you had a pleasant visit with your mother and

a thoroughly marvelous time at Patrick's family reunion. The band plays until 1:00 a.m., so I may be
rather late. Please don't feel obliged to wait up for me.
Enjoy the cookies! I warned Noodles to keep his paws
off them. Love,

Gran

Rachel sank down into the chair and fumbled with the
plastic wrap. Breaking off a chunk of cookie, she patted her
knee with her free hand, beckoning Noodles onto her lap.
His furry bulk felt good, vibrating with a deep, husky purr,
and she was grateful for the warmth. Despite the summer
day's heat, an odd coolness seemed to pervade the room, the
chill of a dark, empty house.

She started when a car door slammed somewhere on the
drive. Easing Noodles gently onto the floor, Rachel walked
to the window and parted the curtain. She drew back when
she saw Patrick walking purposefully up the flagstone path.

He hammered the brass knocker against the door and
then stepped back to gaze up at the dark second-story windows. "Rachel?" His voice sounded as determined as his
gait had looked.

Rachel opened the door a crack. "Patrick, what are you
doing here?"

"May I come in?" His unyielding stance added an element of command to his request.

He had taken her by surprise, and she was in no condition to deal with surprises tonight. Still, she hadn't much
choice but to let him in. "Sure." Rachel stepped back, reluctantly admitting Patrick into the house.

He walked straight to the front room, halted in front of
the fireplace, and then swung around to face her. "Rachel,
something is bothering you and we need to talk about it."

His announcement was so direct, it sounded as if he had rehearsed it in advance.

Rachel opened her mouth to deny his accusation, but then she caught herself. *No more lying.* "Patrick, believe me, it's a personal thing. It has nothing to do with you." She shook her head, wishing she could do something to banish the strained look on his face. Since there didn't seem to be, she turned to stare out the curtain-shrouded window.

"Like hell it doesn't!" The vehemence of his protest spun her around. When she faced him, his voice softened. "All afternoon, I've felt as if we were talking at each other, saying meaningless things to fill the void. I've never seen you like this before. I don't know...you seem so distant, as if something were preying on your mind and you were afraid to tell me. And the more you try to cover it up, the more obvious it becomes."

Rachel took a deep breath. "Please, Patrick. This is something you don't want to know...." She broke off, pressing her lips together.

In an instant, he was by her side, his hands on her arms. "There isn't anything about you I don't want to know, Rachel. Please trust me." His fingers tightened, adding import to his words.

Rachel stared down at the broad, tanned hands. They looked so strong and capable, as if they could protect and heal and make what was wrong, right. Those hands were reaching out to her, but her secrecy had placed a barrier in their way. And nothing could remove that barrier but honesty.

Suddenly, Rachel drew herself up, pulling her arms free. "All right, I'll tell you." She thrust out her chin, almost managing to look him level in the eye. "I lied to you and everyone at the reunion today. I acted as if I had met Mother at the airport today, but I hadn't. She had to change her plans at the last minute.''

Patrick frowned and shook his head. "I don't understand. I mean, that doesn't sound all that awful."

Rachel held up her hand, cutting him off. "Wait, you haven't heard it all. You see, when I got to the airport, I didn't know she wasn't coming. So I waited for her. When she didn't show up, I started getting nervous. I began to imagine all kinds of dreadful things, plane crashes, taxi accidents, disasters." She licked her lips and willed herself to stay calm. "And then they paged me. I—I don't know what came over me, but all I could hear was the man saying, 'I'm sorry.' And—and I just knew something horrible had happened to her." A tremor tore through her voice and she looked down.

She felt Patrick's muscular arms close around her, holding her close to him, swaying her gently. "There. It's okay. Nothing awful has happened to your mother. She's all right," he murmured into her hair.

"I know it sounds crazy, but when I talk with her, I'm almost afraid to ask where she's been or where she's going, always scared that she'll tell me about some dangerous assignment." She clasped his neck, holding on with all her strength.

"That doesn't sound crazy to me. After losing your father, you're terrified of the same thing happening to your mother, and who wouldn't be?" His calm, understanding voice was as soothing as his touch.

She felt so snug and secure in Patrick's arms that, for a moment, Rachel wished she could remain there forever. "You know, I think I would have let myself get a lot closer to Mother if I hadn't carried this fear around with me for so long. Most of the time, I suspect I'm actually grateful I *don't* know what she's up to." Her cheek rubbed against the smooth fabric of his chambray shirt when she looked up at him. "You must think I'm a first-class neurotic."

She stood stock still, not daring to move, scarcely able to breathe as Patrick lifted his hand to stroke her face. She savored the deliciously rough texture of his finger as it followed the contour of her cheek down to her lips. "I think you're the most beautiful, kind, strong, generous woman I've ever known in my life."

Rachel's breath shortened when his finger slid across her lips, gently testing the damp curve. Watching his full, sensual lips part, she felt a well spring of yearning swell within her. When his mouth met hers, she closed her eyes, letting her emotions ride free on the heady wave of the moment. He tasted her lips, then her cheek, his warm mouth caressing her forehead down to the tip of her nose.

"Oh, Rachel!" she heard him breathe into the cleft of her neck as she clasped his head, digging her fingers into the thick, curling hair.

For so long, their contact had been circumscribed by the gentle rhythms of country life. Working together to prepare for the fair, bicycling, wandering through the woods— the simple activities they had shared had given them precious hours together, time to get to know each other, a chance for their friendship to ripen into something deeper. For some time, Rachel had been aware of a powerful undercurrent building under the surface, like a fiery river of magma coursing beneath the earth's crust. It had threatened to break loose before, but they had held it in check, subduing it in the name of prudence and caution. Tonight, the volcano was ready to erupt, and Rachel had no desire to hold it back.

She plowed her fingers through the crisp, dark curls and then let them trip down his neck. When they reached his collar, they glided beneath the starched fabric, stretching to explore the sculpted muscles of his back. She felt a shiver ripple through the warm skin, responding to her touch. When her fingers grazed a hard ridge slashing across the shoulder, they hesitated. Reaching up to catch her hand, Patrick drew it to his mouth and kissed it. "It's just an old scar. Don't worry about it," he whispered into her palm.

Now his hands were following the example set by hers, exploring the outline of her shoulders and back. Cool air licked her sensitized flesh as he pulled her blouse above the waist of her skirt. His palms slid up her rib cage, building her anticipation with an almost painful slowness. Then they turned to cup her breasts. As his thumbs lightly flicked her nipples through the sheer lace, Rachel moaned.

Both hands resting on his shoulders to steady the swaying of the room around her, Rachel arched her back as he lifted her blouse over her head. Still holding on to him, she closed her eyes, letting her tactile sense trace the kisses his lips trailed from her waist to her chin.

When his mouth reached her ear, she heard him whisper, "Let me take your hair down."

She answered him with a sigh laden with desire. As he reached to unbind the French braid, his chest pressed against her taut breasts and a yearning ache flooded her entire body. While he deftly loosened the thick plaits, Rachel's own hands were busy undoing the row of shirt buttons. As his fingers sifted through her hair, she pulled open his shirt to caress the silky mat of hair covering his firm chest.

Patrick scooped a handful of her hair and then let it tumble over her bare shoulders. "I never knew a woman could be so beautiful," he murmured.

His fingers curled beneath the straps of her bra, gently sliding them down her arms. Following the heartshaped curve of the bra, they circled her breasts. As he began to ease the bra down the slope of her breasts, Rachel sucked in her breath. Holding the lace lingerie poised on the edge of her nipples, Patrick knelt to tease the flushed aureoles with his tongue. When the bra at last fell away, Rachel grasped his head, drawing his face into the heated cleft of her bosom.

Radiant was the only word Rachel could have found to describe his face as he looked up at her. In the soft lamp-light, his gemlike blue eyes seemed to glow, fired by the passion simmering within him.

"I want to make love to you, Rachel." He whispered the longing that his look, his touch, his whole being had already so eloquently spoken.

Rachel followed his beckoning gaze as he rose and took her hand, leading her up the staircase. When they reached the landing, it was her turn to guide them. Inside her dark bedroom, she turned to face him. Pulling his shirt off his shoulders, she completed the task she had begun down-stairs. As her hands wandered to his belt, she watched the muscles of his midriff tighten, signaling the shock wave of excitement she had set off. With a leisurely pace calculated to fan his desire, Rachel loosened first his belt buckle and then the brass rivet of his jeans. She slowly edged the zip-per open to reveal the burgeoning evidence of his arousal outlined in the shadowy light.

With a quickness that both startled and excited her, Pat-rick slipped out of his remaining clothing. The moonlight filtering through the curtains bathed his naked body with a soft-focus sheen as he scooped Rachel into his arms and carried her to the bed. His touch was hungry, direct as he removed her skirt and tossed it onto the floor. His hands sculpted the curves of her hips, freeing them from the transparent wisp of lace panties.

At the first pressure of his body, stretched full length against hers, an uncontrollable trembling raced through her. Opening her legs, she laced them around his back, molding him to her. At first slowly, then gradually building to a fever pitch, the rhythm of their desire meshed. Rachel gasped as an uncontrollable tide engulfed her, sweeping her along on undulating waves until she floated in the sweet, euphoric sea of release. She felt a shudder of ecstasy pass through Patrick's body. Then he rested against her, his chest rising and falling in unison with her own breathing.

The antique bed murmured beneath them as Patrick shifted his weight from her. Lying on his side, he looked at her with an expression of such exquisite tenderness, her eyes began to fill. As one tiny tear overflowed the rim, he leaned to staunch its trickle with a kiss.

Her lips trembled into a smile. Closing her eyes, she curled into the inviting pocket of his shoulder. "It feels so good being with you. Stay with me awhile. Let's make this last just a little longer."

Through the curtain of her hair, she heard him whisper. "Let's make it last forever."

Chapter Nine

Hand poised on the bedroom door's white porcelain knob, Rachel pressed her ear to the wood and listened for any stirring in the hall. She slowly twisted the knob, easing the door open so as not to rankle its testy hinges, and peeked into the hall. All clear. Rising on her bare toes, she made a swift dash for the bathroom.

Inside the cool yellow-tiled room, she inspected her face in the oval mirror. Her cheeks were a bit rosier than usual, but that was probably due to the sun she had gotten in the Morrisseys' backyard. Hands braced on the edge of the sink, Rachel eyed herself critically. No, regardless of what some old wives' tales would lead you to believe, a woman who has been loved—and loved well—doesn't look all that different the morning after. At least she hoped not, she thought as she doffed her robe and climbed into the bathtub.

Of course, she wasn't a little girl anymore, she reminded herself beneath the shower's brisk spray. Gran and she were both grown women, mature adults, each entitled to a private life of her own. Still, she wasn't sure she was ready to burst into the dining room that morning and announce how she had whiled away the time during Gran's absence the previous night. If the subject came up, she would simply say Patrick had stopped by and let it go at that.

As Rachel descended the stairs, the aroma of sizzling bacon and freshly brewed coffee beckoned her to the kitchen. Swinging open the door, she found Gran bustling around the shiny new restaurant stove, humming to herself as she scooped poached eggs out of a saucepan.

"Good morning!" Gran's greeting rode on a little melody of its own. "I hope I didn't wake you when I sneaked in last night."

Rachel selected a knife from the silver tray and began to pry warm bran muffins from their tin. "I was sleeping like a log. What time did you get in anyway?"

Gran shrugged. "Oh, I don't know. Around three. Maybe a little later."

Rachel looked up in surprise. "You must have had a really good time."

"Just marvelous! Milton is a heavenly dancer. Who would have guessed that he had such . . ." She paused, a peculiarly mysterious smile enlivening her face. "Such *verve* in him!" Picking up the platter of bacon and eggs, Gran swayed in a few steps of a solo rhumba. Still moving to the music in her head, she backed into the swinging door and held it open for Rachel. "But what about you, dear? I want to hear all about your mother and the reunion."

Rachel deposited the basket of muffins on the dining table and reached for the pitcher of orange juice. "As it turned out, Mother's plans changed at the last minute and she was detained in Brussels. I got her message at the TWA counter." Perhaps it was just the effect of the fresh morning air and her cheery surroundings, but somehow that all sounded very ordinary and inconsequential right now. Or perhaps, Rachel suspected, honestly talking about her fears with Patrick had helped cast things in a more realistic light.

"That's too bad." Gran shook her head as Rachel handed her a glass of juice. "I wish Janet would slow down some-day, take time to smell the roses, as they say."

"So do I," Rachel agreed. "But let's not hold our breath."

"No, that might be dangerous." Gran chuckled as she jiggled the salt shaker over her eggs. "So, tell me about the reunion."

Rachel took a bite of a muffin. "Well, the Morrisseys were just the kind of family you would expect Patrick to have—warm, open, bighearted. Everything was very nice and homey, with hammocks and horseshoes and corn-on-the-cob."

A wistful look drifted across Gran's face. "It's a real pleasure to open one's home to good people and entertain them. You know, that's one reason I'm anxious to begin serving lunches here. I've been rattling around alone in this big old house for so many years. The rafters need more than one old lady's laughter to clear out the cobwebs."

"Don't tell me you're discounting my giggle fits?" Rachel feigned an insulted frown.

"You know what I mean, Rachel," Gran insisted. "And anyway, you'll be leaving someday, all too soon."

Rachel laid a loving hand on her grandmother's wrist. "Not that soon, Gran."

"Soon enough." Gran sniffed in resignation.

Rachel gave the fine-boned wrist an emphatic squeeze. "Look, I've already thought of asking Marquette for a lit-tle extra time," she began, but Gran was already shaking her head.

"I can't possibly allow you to jeopardize a fine career for my sake."

"Should I interpret that as a threat to throw me out?" Rachel teased. "Seriously, Gran, I've put so much of my-

self into the farm in the past months, I'd hate to leave before..." She hesitated, suddenly at a loss to identify the
exact point at which she *would* be willing to abandon her life
at Heathervale.

Gran smiled. "You know you're welcome for as long as
you like. In fact, I wouldn't mind one bit if you decided to
stay for good. I've grown rather accustomed to having a
partner in the past few months." She eyed Rachel carefully, obviously gauging her reaction. Then she sighed. "Of
course, I know that's asking too much. Heathervale can't
begin to compete with Marquette Brothers."

"Oh, Gran, don't say that!" Rachel protested with unexpected vigor.

Gran shook her head, indicating that she was disappointed but not offended. "You do agree that I'm going to
need lots of help getting the lunch service rolling. It's so
hard to know if we should hire a waitress from town or try
to manage things ourselves to start with. I'd hate to promise a girl work and then not have enough business to make
it worth her while."

"Don't forget my one college-vacation summer of hash-
slinging on Cape Cod," Rachel reminded her. "I may be
rusty, but I'm willing."

"But you're so busy already!" Gran protested. "You
know, last night I was talking with Milton—" She broke off
as a horn tooted from the yard.

Gran and Rachel both rose and walked to the front door.
As they opened the door, they found Patrick wrestling the
ponderous anvil, borrowed from Heathervale for the fair,
out of the back of Milton's station wagon. Jody and Milton were looking on, offering free advice.

"Pretend you're a weight lifter. This is the Olympics, and
you're the United States' last shot at the gold medal," Jody

suggested, propping her purple-high-top foot on the bumper.

"Ugh!" Patrick heaved the anvil out of the tailgate and anchored it on the ground.

"For heaven's sake, don't hurt yourself!" Gran rushed to intervene, with Rachel right behind her.

Patrick pressed his hand into the small of his back and straightened himself stiffly. "The anvil isn't all that heavy. I'm just a little tired. Must have worn myself out yesterday." The mischievous look he shot Rachel brought a surge of warmth to her cheeks.

"I'll get the wheelbarrow and you can roll it into the barn," she volunteered.

"Excellent idea, Rachel! It's a good thing you men have three women to do some clear thinking for you," Gran teased. "In the meantime, do I have any takers for coffee or juice?"

"You certainly do!" Milton hastened toward the house, a big smile crinkling the lines of his normally sober face.

With the men firmly in Gran's tow, Rachel jogged to the barn to retrieve the wheelbarrow. As she was trundling it up the garden path, she was surprised to find Jody sitting on the fence, staring out across the meadow. The sad expression on her young face looked out of place, like a black dress worn by a small child.

"I'll bet you could talk Gran into throwing in a couple of bran muffins with that juice." Rachel propped the wheelbarrow against the fence post and rested her folded arms on the rail next to Jody.

The slumped shoulders rose and fell in a lackluster shrug. "Thanks, but I'm not hungry."

Rachel had met Jody early enough in her camp experience to recognize the girl's capacity for sullen behavior.

Right now, though, something in her downcast expression told Rachel that this was no routine teenage sulk.

"I'm gonna miss this place," Jody said without looking at Rachel.

So that was it! Rachel had known, of course, that this was the final week of the first camp session. She and Gran had even planned a special batch of Heavenly Heathervale Mint Brownies to take to the farewell campfire party scheduled for Friday. She had expected fond goodbyes and some reluctant parting between new-found friends. That the impending departure would weigh so heavily on Jody, however, had not occurred to her.

"We're going to miss you, too, both Gran and I. But I bet your mother will be glad to have you and Mutt back."

Jody shot her a skeptical glance, but said nothing.

Rachel settled her hand on the girl's knee and gave it a sisterly pat. "I'm sorry for trying to cheer you up with stupid remarks. I always hated it when people used to try that kind of stuff with me. And you may not believe it, but I think I know exactly how you feel right now."

Jody shifted on the fence, regarding her with guarded interest.

Rachel shook her head, her eyes following a sparrow hawk wheeling over the herb field. "I used to get so down at the end of the summer. I was never ready to leave Gran and go back to school. I remember one time, I even thought about running away, planned it all in my head, how I would slip out of the school dorm and hitchhike back to Scarborough."

"Did you?"

Rachel laughed softly. "No. And don't you get any ideas! But I'll make you a promise. If you ever want to come back to Heathervale to visit, all you need to do is pick up the phone and call me. Okay?"

"You really mean that?"

"Of course, I do!"

Jody looked uncharacteristically shy as she nodded. "Okay, Rachel. I'd like that. A lot."

"So would Gran and I." Rachel elbowed her knee. "Now, let's try to get some of the goodies before everyone starts straining and sweating over that anvil again."

Jody slid off the fence and the two of them walked back to the house. No sooner had Rachel parked the wheelbarrow by the station wagon than Patrick ambled onto the stoop.

"Did you save any muffins for us?" Rachel grinned.

"Of course, we did!" Patrick managed to look offended. "Although we were beginning to wonder where you were. Your grandmother is getting a little impatient. You're both wanted in the dining room, double-quick time."

Rachel and Jody exchanged puzzled looks, but they dutifully trooped into the house. They followed Patrick as he walked briskly to the dining room.

Hands folded in front of her, Gran was standing at the head of the table, looking for all the world as if she were about to convene a board meeting. "Please sit down." She gestured toward the two vacant chairs. As soon as the stragglers had done as they were told, she cleared her throat. "Before I begin, I know there may be some objections to what I am about to propose. However, I ask that you both hear me out before raising them." She looked first at Rachel, then at Jody.

"As you know, Jody, Heathervale will begin serving lunch next week. While I am confident I can manage most of the cooking, serving the dining room leaves me in a bit of a quandary. Rachel will be acting as hostess, but I need someone industrious and reliable to handle the dining room." She gave Rachel a gently deprecating look. "Now, dear, I know you insist that you can also wait tables, but frankly speaking, you've never had much knack for balancing things, and I don't want my customers doused with hot soup and ice water.''

Rachel glared at Patrick, who was making a manful effort to keep a straight face.

"That's where you come in, Jody," Gran went on. "To get right to the point, I need a waitress. I think you would be perfect for the job, and Milton and Patrick agree with me.''

Jody's mouth flew open, but Gran stilled her with an upheld hand.

"I can't pay you much—just tips, plus room and board and a little pocket money on the side.''

"Oh, Mrs. Chase, that would be totally terrif—'' Jody leaned forward, resting one knee on the edge of her chair.

"Do sit down, child and let me finish! This would only be until school starts, of course, but by then I trust our business will warrant a full-time waitress. I am afraid I will want you to start next week—if you accept and your mother is agreeable with the idea.''

"Count me in!'' Jody whooped, finally having her say in spite of Gran.

Rachel could tell that Gran was struggling to control her smile. "I'm glad you're interested, but you still must discuss our arrangement with your mother.''

"She'll agree,'' Jody assured them with a determined glint in her eye.

"I hope she does,'' Gran said, at last allowing her smile full play. "Very well, then. If everything works out, I'll expect you back here next Monday evening. Patrick tells me he has business in Hartford that day and will be happy to deliver you back to us. So, do we have a deal?'' She proffered her hand.

Jody seized the small hand and gave it a solid yank. "It's a deal!"

By MIDAFTERNOON the following Monday, Patrick felt sure there was one person who would be even happier than Jody Marshall to get back to Scarborough: himself. In fact, he would have been relieved to go about anywhere, as long as it put considerable distance between him and the day's grueling pretrial hearing.

Although Patrick had been going over his testimony in his mind for months now, priming his memory for the hearing, nothing could have prepared him for spending six hours in a courtroom with one of the men who had tried to kill him and his partner. In the course of his career, he had been called on many times to testify against suspects whom he had helped apprehend. He had won the admiration of his colleagues for keeping a cool head under tough cross-examination. Today, however, he had felt his anger creep several degrees closer to the boiling point with each hostile question the defense attorney hurled at him. By the time the session was adjourned, his shirt was limp with perspiration and his head was throbbing.

"Good job, Pat." Arnie Nordstrom clapped a large hand on Patrick's damp shoulder as they made their way to the courtroom door.

Patrick overlooked the compliment. "Think it'll do any good? Can the prosecution make anything stick?"

The second they were in the corridor, Arnie loosened his tie, freeing his fleshy red neck from its unwelcome constraint. "They've got a strong case. Why shouldn't they nail him?"

"C'mon, Arnie. You know what I'm really asking. Will this guy ever do time?"

Arnie fished in his pocket and pulled out a foil-wrapped strip of gum. "Stuff's loaded with nicotine. It's supposed to help you quit smoking."

Patrick wheeled, blocking his stocky companion's path. "Knock it off, okay?"

Arnie balled the foil into a tiny wad and aimed it at a bullet-shaped trash can. The missile pinged against the can's chrome lid and then skittered across the marble floor. "Okay, Pat, you and me, we both know how these things work. We got a scummy guy here who, we're more than half sure, is working for an even scummier guy. Now let's just say—just for the sake of argument, mind you—that our less-scummy guy decides his hide is more important than this vermin whose dirty work he's been doing. So he agrees to talk. With conditions of course. Bingo." He snapped his thick, tobacco-stained fingers. "Mr. Bigtime Scum is nailed to the wall."

"And Mr. Little Time goes scot-free?" Patrick let out a short, disgusted breath.

Arnie's hulking shoulders rose in a shrug as he shoved the stick of gum into his mouth. "Look, Pat, you know I don't like this kind of stuff any better than you do, but you gotta think positive."

"You're telling me I'm supposed to turn handsprings because the criminal who took Al's future away from him is going to walk out of here a free man?" Anger had congested Patrick's voice.

"Sometimes that's the way the system works, pal." Arnie chewed the gum slowly, giving his words a chance to soak in. "It stinks, but that's the way it is."

"Yeah, well, I'm not real sure I want to be a part of that system anymore." Patrick turned on his heel and marched toward the stairs.

"Hey, we're counting on you, buddy! And you're still a cop. Don't you forget that!" Arnie's choleric voice rebounded off the marble walls, pursuing Patrick down the stairwell.

Once inside his car, Patrick hunched over the steering wheel, trying to calm the fury that had escalated his headache to full-throttle torture. *You're still a cop. Don't forget that!* As if he could ever put that ineluctable fact out of his mind for long. Not that he hadn't tried, pretending that the camp and its gentle concerns were what mattered, that the love blossoming between Rachel and him could continue to grow, unfettered by the strictures of the outside world.

At the thought of Rachel, a vivid pang gripped him. All day, he had carried her memory with him like a talisman, a reminder that a power stronger than violence and cynicism still reigned, at least in her small corner of the universe. Now, however, even that conviction offered him faint comfort, buffeted as it was by the sobering realities of their lives. Another six weeks, and his tenure at Camp Onoconohee would come to an end. He would return to Hartford, reclaim his small, haphazardly furnished apartment from its sublease tenant and resume his place on Arnie Nordstrom's Special Investigation Vice Squad.

As Patrick edged the car through Hartford's lurch-and-stop rush-hour traffic, he wondered if the clock were ticking as ominously for Rachel. Her leave of absence would be up at the end of the year. Barring any setbacks with Gran Chase's health—and Patrick would never stoop low enough to wish for *that*—Rachel would drive back to Boston and pick up where she had left off there. Their lives would diverge, separated by more than mere miles, until the brief, bittersweet summer they had shared was only a fading memory. Unless . . .

Patrick's eyes narrowed against the fierce dying sun as he considered the courses of action that lay open to him. The least complicated and certainly the most direct way of persuading Rachel to stay involved with him was simply to ask her. In fact, she would very likely appreciate his bringing the matter up. After all, hadn't she been relieved when he had refused to ignore her depression at the reunion and had insisted they discuss things honestly?

But how honestly was he willing to talk with Rachel about their future? He cared about her, more than any woman he had ever known in his life, and he was unafraid to admit it. But did he have the guts to tell her that he was an undercover vice cop who placed his life on the line almost daily? Could he summon the nerve to tell her how he came by that scar on his shoulder, a grisly souvenir of his latest assignment? And would he ever find the courage to tell her about Al?

If he had not actually lied to her, Patrick knew he had done his best to keep Rachel in the dark about his work and its attendant dangers. He had never consciously intended to deceive her, of course; he had only wanted to shield her from worry. Her life had already been shattered by tragedy once, leaving her haunted by anxiety, and he had seen no point in adding to her concerns. Now, however, he realized that his motives had been tainted by an element of self-interest and, yes, cowardice. For as he turned into a one-way street and began to scan the drab row houses, Patrick had to confront a long-suppressed fear: if Rachel knew who he really was, she would run scared and he would lose her forever.

Jody and Mutt must have been on the lookout for him, for Patrick had no sooner wedged the Honda Accord into a parking space than their grinning faces appeared in the passenger-side window. Jody rapped her knuckle against the glass, demanding entry, while Mutt yanked at the unyielding door handle. Patrick forced himself to put aside his own concerns enough to smile as he leaned to unlock the door.

"All right!" Jody greeted him as she slung her duffel bag into the back seat. She clambered into the car and then cranked down the window. "Okay, Mutt. You know what Mom said. Keep the door locked until she gets home from work."

Mutt jockeyed to one side of the open window and wrinkled her nose for Patrick's benefit. "I want to go back to camp, too."

"I've told you a trillion-zillion times!" Jody glared at her sister in exasperation. "This is *not* camp. It's work! Besides, Mom practically has to sit on you to get you to set the table for dinner. Some waitress you'd make!"

Mutt ignored the snub. "This would be different."

"Sure!" Jody snorted derisively. "Okay, Mutt. We've gotta go."

Mutt took a hesitant step back onto the curb. Then she abruptly lunged toward the car, thrusting her head through the open window to give Jody a quick hug. "You'll send me a postcard, won't you?"

Jody pretended to adjust one of the three earrings gracing her left ear, doing her best not to look awkward. "Yeah. If it'll make you happy. I mean, *really!* You'd think this was a trip around the world or something," she grumbled, rolling up the window to ward off any more surprises Mutt might have in store. "Back into the house!" She mouthed the command through the glass, shooing her sister toward the steps with a wave of her hand. As Patrick pulled the car away from the curb, she watched until the little girl had disappeared into the house. "Kids!"

Patrick smiled to himself. When he braked at the intersection, he glanced over at Jody. "Anxious to get back to Scarborough?"

Jody slapped the dashboard emphatically. "Am I ever!" She leaned back in the seat and folded her arms across the front of her Bruce Springsteen T-shirt. "I'll bet you are, too."

Patrick would have given her another, more penetrating glance if a sudden break in the traffic had not forced him to maneuver the Accord onto the thoroughfare. "Uh-huh. I like staying out there in the country for a change."

"So do I," Jody agreed. "Scarborough's a nice little town, but it's the people I really miss. I mean like Gran Chase. I think she's a totally awesome lady! And Rachel, too."

Patrick risked a quick inspection and found Jody watching the stream of cars as intently as he was—or should have been. The squeal of brakes somewhere in the throng instantly refocused both of his eyes on the road.

"You know what Rachel told me?" Jody went on.

Patrick swallowed and wondered if he really wanted to know. "No. What?"

"She said if I ever wanted to come back to visit her and Gran, all I had to do was call her and she'd come get me."

Patrick laughed, in part to cover his embarrassment. His ego must be getting the best of him if he suspected Rachel of discussing him with one of Onoconohee's former campers! "That's very thoughtful of her."

"Yeah, she's like that. I think she could tell I was feeling kind of out of it, down because camp was going to be over. She sort of made me talk about it, without being pushy. But you know, it's funny. As much as I wanted to come back to see her and Gran, I don't think I'd ever have had the nerve to ask." Jody crossed one gangly leg over her knee and tightened the laces of her black boxer's boots.

"Why not? You must realize that Rachel and Gran Chase like you."

Jody sighed as she reached for the other foot. "I know, but I'm always too afraid people will say no. Know what I mean?"

The steering wheel wavered in Patrick's hands for a split second and he tightened his grip. "Well, yes, I think I do. I suppose everyone fears rejection, deep down inside." He cleared his throat with pseudoadult authority.

"Lucky for me, Gran Chase can read minds. If she couldn't, I'd probably be flipping burgers three afternoons a week and just hangin' out until school starts." The elfin face reflected in the windshield grew pensive. "And if I hadn't talked with Rachel, I might never have seen Heathervale again. When you get right down to it, there's not much difference in a near hit and a near miss, is there?"

"No, there isn't," Patrick commented weakly, his eyes darting across the acceleration lane narrowing into the expressway. Although years of police work had honed his driving skills to the cutting edge, this passenger-philosopher was definitely interfering with his concentration.

Jody stretched her legs as far as the compact front seat would allow. "You know, I've really learned something from this. If you want something, you need to speak up. Right?"

"Yes. I guess so." Patrick frowned at the black Porsche that had just cut in front of him, and he irritably eased off the gas.

Normally, he could put his reflexes on automatic and readily handle a car with the police radio and his partner's conversation vying for his attention. He was struggling right now, however, to hold his speed down and keep track of the exit signs. Perhaps it was Jody's high-pitched voice that was getting to him, needling him like a tiny splinter he couldn't ignore.

Worse still, Jody showed no signs of letting up. "Way I look at it, you might just get what you want. And if you don't say anything, well, you stand to lose big."

"Uhm." Patrick shifted to one side, digging into his pocket, as he wheeled the Accord into one of the tollbooth lanes. His fingers identified extra keys, a laundry tag and several bits of lint as they futilely plundered the pocket for change.

"Right?"

Patrick slapped his shirt pocket and was rewarded with an empty, jingleless thump. He geared down with a lurch and edged yet another car-length closer to the booth.

"Right?" Jody repeated.

Doing his best to ignore the needle voice probing into his distracted consciousness, Patrick squirmed to explore his remaining pants pocket. Surely, he hadn't driven out of Scarborough that morning with nothing but a gasoline credit card and the few dollars he had squandered on an unappetizing lunch with Arnie. In desperation, he pulled out the pocket's contents and examined the seven pennies cupped in his palm.

"You need something, Patrick?" Jody's voice was infuriatingly calm.

When he looked up from the pitiful collection of pennies, she reached into her pocket and then presented him with the requisite change. Leaning back against the car door, Jody was gracious enough not to look smug. "Like I said, if you want something, you need to ask. Right?"

Patrick tossed the coins into the tollbooth hopper. Glancing at Jody, he conceded with a grin. "Right."

Chapter Ten

"How are we doing?" Rachel smiled as she peeked around the edge of the swinging door.

"*We're* doing just fine, thank you!" Bustling around the big restaurant stove, Gran sounded just the slightest bit harried. She lifted the lid from a stainless-steel stock pot, releasing a cloud of thyme-scented vapor into the already steamy kitchen, and gave the soup an energetic stir. "How many tables are filled now? I've quite lost track."

"Five. All the reservations showed up."

"Whew!" Gran clapped the lid onto the pot with the vigor of a symphony percussionist. "Four more guests and we'll be filled to capacity."

"That's right," Rachel agreed cheerfully. "If the food starts to run low, let me know and I'll tell any latecomers to come back some other time," she teased.

"Oh, Rachel, do be serious!" Gran scooped up a handful of fresh tarragon and scattered it over a dish of poached chicken breasts. Smoothing her apron with her hands, she surveyed the row of arugula-and-leaf-lettuce salads lining the kitchen island. She poked at the crisp leaves, making the sort of adjustments to the carefully garnished salads that only a proud proprietor would notice.

"Stand clear!" Tray poised on her shoulder, Jody swooped through the kitchen door so rapidly, Rachel had to dance a hasty two-step to avoid a collision. "Got another hungry-looking couple at the door, Rachel. I told 'em to wait in the front room and you'd be right with them." Jody settled the tray onto the counter with a clatter and began to load the salads onto it.

Gran eyed Jody and the salads appreciatively. "Thank goodness, I don't have *two* lollygaggers loitering about the kitchen, giving me grief, while honest customers wait around untended."

Rachel pretended to scurry toward the door. "I'll have them seated in a jiffy, Gran," she promised before ducking back into the dining room.

On her way to greet the latest arrivals, Rachel smiled and nodded to the diners seated at the pink-linen-skirted tables. Of course, they had only been serving lunch for two weeks now, far too briefly to proclaim the venture an unequivocal success. If the steady increase in patronage were any indicator, however, Gran's dream of establishing a showcase for herbal cookery was off to an excellent start.

Rachel paused in the hall to collect two of Gran's calligraphy-lettered menus that listed each day's special entrées along with interesting lore about the herbs used in the dishes. Then she headed for the front room. She broke into a big smile as she recognized the young couple admiring the antique decoys arranged on the mantel.

"Maureen! Peter! What a pleasant surprise!" Rachel extended her hand in welcome to both Morrisseys.

"I hope we didn't make a mistake by not phoning ahead for reservations," Maureen apologized. "But we weren't sure Grandma Morrissey could baby-sit until the last minute."

"It's no problem at all," Rachel assured her as she led the way to the dining room. "And anyway, you do have reservations of a sort because Patrick's been telling us you were planning to come out the first free Saturday you had. See, we've even saved you a table." She pointed toward the window table for two that, fortunately, was still vacant.

"Patrick is turning into a walking advertisement for Heathervale's kitchen," Peter joked, taking the menu Rachel offered. "When he goes back to Hartford, I imagine he'll talk this place up so much, you'll have half the police force out here for lunch."

Rachel smiled as she pocketed a couple of rose petals that had fallen from the table's bouquet. "Patrick has been awfully busy with the last group of campers, but he's still managed to give us some help taste-testing recipes. And eating up the leftovers!"

"I'll bet! I've never known him to be too busy to eat. If he's not careful, he's going to be doing overtime in the police gym, working off those extra pounds." Peter chuckled at the prospect of his lithely-built brother fighting an unfamiliar battle of the bulge.

Rachel joined in the laughter. Privately, however, Patrick's imminent return to Hartford was not a subject she wanted to dwell on just then and she was grateful to reroute the conversation to the menus. After helping the Morrisseys settle on cream of sorrel soup and lamb chops broiled with rosemary, she hurried back to the kitchen.

"Be extra nice to the couple sitting by the window on the right," Rachel whispered to Jody as they pushed through the swinging door together.

Jody paused to peer over her tray at the guests in question.

"They're Patrick's brother and sister-in-law," Rachel explained, drawing Jody gently by her elbow into the kitchen.

"O-h-h!" Jody's amber eyes widened and she nodded slowly. A knowing smile spread across her freckled face as she selected two water tumblers and carefully checked them for fingerprints.

Something in Jody's *Mona Lisa* expression prompted Rachel to lend a hand with the water service. "I mean, they've driven all the way down from Hartford. We wouldn't want them to be disappointed." She filled one of the tumblers and placed it on the tray.

"Uh-huh!" Jody twisted a slice of lemon and perched it on the edge of the glass.

Rachel frowned at her young companion and tried to figure what sort of mischief might be computing beneath the spiky pate. If this teenaged yenta had managed to get Milton Weber and her grandmother out on the dance floor until three in the morning, who knew what she had in mind for her and Patrick? Of course, she might be overreacting, jumping to conclusions, Rachel reminded herself. After all, she and Patrick had both been discreet enough to conceal their growing attraction from the campers. Or had they? While Rachel nestled warm cheese breadsticks inside a napkin-lined basket, she scoured her memory for any lapses that might have caught Jody's attention.

The wink Jody gave her as she hoisted the tray onto her shoulder did little to ease Rachel's misgivings. "Don't worry about a thing!"

Indeed! thought Rachel, but she only swung the door open for Jody. Under the ruse of chatting with guests, Rachel wandered through the dining room, all the while keeping a sharp eye on Jody. As soon as the young waitress had taken the Morrisseys' order, she returned to the kitchen, with Rachel right on her heels.

Jody clipped the order onto the rack next to Gran's work station. "Now I remember them. They were at the fair. He looks a lot like Patrick," she went on, taking a surreptitious sample of a breadstick crumb. "Only not as cute."

For want of anything better to do, Rachel grabbed a napkin from the stack of fresh linen and began to roll it around a silver setting. She was *not,* under absolutely no circumstances, going to engage in giggly girl talk with this adolescent matchmaker.

Jody, however, apparently had other ideas. "I think Patrick's cute. Don't you?"

"Well, I guess. I mean, of course, he is." Rachel irritably shook out the napkin she had rolled around two spoons and a fork and rearranged the mismatched cutlery.

Jody reached across the counter and gingerly lifted one of the hot soup plates Gran had just filled. "He likes you," she remarked as casually as if she were commenting on the soup or the weather.

The rapid hammering of Gran's kitchen knife against the chopping block at the far end of the counter was the only sound in the big kitchen.

Jody eased another bowl of soup onto the tray without spilling a drop. "I can always tell when a guy, you know, like, really *likes* someone. It's all in the way he looks at you," she added sagely.

The stack of clean napkins was now exhausted, leaving Rachel frantically scanning the counter for another task to cover her consternation. Fortunately, circumstances intervened to get her off the hook, at least for the moment.

"There we are." Hurrying down the counter, Gran christened the creamy soups with a final sprinkling of minced herbs. "Now run along, dear, before the soup gets cold."

Jody obediently shouldered the tray, but the worldly-wise look she gave Rachel signaled that their conversation had been only temporarily interrupted.

Forewarned is forearmed, thought Rachel. As soon as Jody was out of the kitchen, she took steps to circumvent any further opportunities for cozy chitchat. After making sure that Gran had the last dessert preparations well under control, she headed for the dining room. Except for the Morrisseys, the remaining diners were eagerly awaiting coffee and the day's special blueberry tart. Ignoring the loaded glances that Jody gave her in passing, Rachel lent a hand with the dessert service. Soon the guests had dwindled to only Maureen and Peter lingering over their tart à la mode, with Jody hovering like a guardian angel by the coffee warmers.

"Why don't you help Gran tidy up in the kitchen?" Rachel suggested as she lifted the freshest pot of coffee from its hot plate. "I'll take care of the last details out here."

"Gotcha!" Jody smiled as she unfolded her arms and sauntered toward the kitchen. Luckily, the Morrisseys were too preoccupied with their desserts to notice the thumbs-up she flashed Rachel from the door.

As Rachel approached the table, Maureen was folding her napkin. "That was the best blueberry pie I've ever eaten in my life!" Covering her cup with her hand, she shook her head. "No, thanks."

"How about you, Peter? Care for a refill?" Rachel held the carafe invitingly near his cup.

Patrick's twin checked his watch and then looked at his wife. "What do you think, sweetheart? How close do you think we can cut it and still make it back to Hartford before Mom and Dad's bridge game gets underway this evening?"

Maureen cast a rueful glance out the window. "Well, I had wanted a chance to see just a little of the gardens."

Without waiting for further instructions, Rachel filled Peter's cup with aromatic coffee. "If you don't mind sipping this along the way, I'll be glad to give you a streamlined tour."

Both Morrisseys were delighted with her offer and contrary to the ulterior motives Jody was sure to infer, Rachel took genuine pleasure in escorting her new friends along the flagstone paths crisscrossing Heathervale's herb beds. She did her best to give them a condensed introduction to the farm's more unusual crops, concluding with a tour of the drying shed. Maureen was fascinated by the fragrant bundles suspended from the shed's rafters; armed with a complimentary copy of Gran's booklet *Putting Herbs By*, she was soon absorbed in examining the farm's latest harvest. When Peter wandered outside to one of the benches, Rachel decided to join him.

"This place is incredible. Just listen to those birds." Peter cocked one ear to the canopy of leafy branches and smiled. "It's hard to believe there are still places where the only arguments you hear are between the sparrows. Believe me, I could get used to living out here real fast." Cradling the empty coffee cup in his hands, he contentedly stretched his legs out in front of him. "No wonder Pat has managed to get a handle on himself," he added as Rachel sank down onto the bench beside him.

"I remember Patrick's talking about how burned out he felt at the beginning of the summer," Rachel commented quietly. Those days seemed so remote now, blurred by the profound emotional experiences they had since shared. In a brief two months, Patrick had come to occupy a larger part of her life than she would ever have imagined possible. Talking with Peter now, she realized that she had unconsciously begun to reckon time by two sharp divisions: Before Patrick and Now. "I'm glad the medicine has worked."

Peter glanced over at her, an incongruously shy look playing on his ruddy, open face. "You know, you're a big part of that medicine. I don't think he'd be the same man today if he hadn't met you."

Rachel smiled down at her hands. "These things work both ways, Peter. I'm really grateful that circumstances brought us together—especially since those circumstances weren't all that fortunate to begin with. After all, if Gran hadn't broken her hip, I would never have come back to Heathervale to live. And I suppose Patrick's situation was much the same—if he hadn't needed a break from police work, he wouldn't have ended up working with Milton at the camp."

Peter shook his head, rolling the porcelain cup around in his big hands. "I was really worried about him after that drug bust blew up in his face. At first, of course, we were just praying that he'd be able to use his arm all right again. But after a while, we could see that the scars went a lot deeper than those bullet wounds."

Rachel stared at Peter, waiting for him to poke her arm or laugh or do anything to show that he had only been joking. But he only continued to gaze out across the peaceful meadow, his rugged face solemn as a pallbearer's. *Drug bust. Scars. Bullet wounds.* She formed the words silently in her mind, as if they were obscenities too foul to utter.

"I think it's Al that bothered him most. Still bothers him. Those guys were like brothers." He held up one hand and pressed two of his fingers together tightly. "In fact, sometimes I think Pat was a lot closer to Al than he is to me. I can understand it, though, their being partners so long, going through so much together. And now to have Al suspended in a coma..." His voice caught. "I guess we're just lucky Patrick didn't end up like that, too."

No, no! I don't want to hear this. Please don't tell me!
The urge to clamp her hands over her ears, to spring up
from the shady bench, bolt across the green-gold fields and
cower in the woods like a small, hunted animal seized her.
But a chilling numbness had begun to creep through her
limbs, holding her powerless to escape Peter's low, serious
voice.

"Of course, undercover work is risky, especially when it
involves dope." Peter sighed heavily. "God knows, I'm a
cop and I realize someone has to do it. It's just that sometimes I wish that someone weren't my brother." He looked
slightly embarrassed. "Sorry to dump my own worries on
you like this. I guess I figured you'd understand, after all the
soul-searching you've probably gone through with Patrick."

Rachel was too stunned, too psychologically paralyzed by
his revelations to speak. She could only nod, the stupid,
will-less bob of a rag doll.

Patrick was an undercover cop, investigating illegal drug
dealing. He had been shot, his partner nearly killed. The
harsh facts bombarded her consciousness, battering her
cherished image of him like vandals sacking a cathedral. As
the shocking realization settled into her mind, another, even
more devastating thought rose to taunt her: he had deliberately deceived her, tried to avoid conjuring the fears her
own father's death had left in her, would have let her go on
thinking he was a genial cop-on-the-beat until... Until
what? The next drug dealer's bullet found its mark? An
uncontrollable shudder passed through her, causing her to
grip the edge of the bench to steady herself, hold onto reality.

"Uh-oh! I'm afraid I lost track of time," Maureen apologized as she jogged up the path toward them. She smiled

at Rachel. "This has been such a treat, I wish we could stay longer."

"I wish you could, too." Rachel was startled by how even her voice sounded, calm as death.

"We'll be back, have no fear on that count," Peter promised, placing an arm around his wife's shoulders as they sidled toward the drive. At the gate, he turned to give Rachel's hand a grateful shake. "Thanks for taking such good care of us. And of Patrick."

Rachel's lips twitched into what she supposed passed for a smile. "Goodbye." Her hand felt limp as she waved to the young couple climbing into their Dodge Astro. No sooner had the minivan disappeared onto the main road than she spun around and fled into the house. She pressed her lips together, fighting the ache that was spreading over her face, as she made a dash for the stairs.

"Boy, did Gran ever plan this one right!" Jody called from the end of the hall. "We have exactly five pieces of blueberry tart left—one for her, one for Milton, one for me, one for you, and one for...Patrick...." Rachel heard the girl's voice drop, cut off as the bedroom door slammed behind her.

FOR SOMEONE WITH such a quantity of Irish blood flowing in his veins, Patrick had rarely put much stock in luck. He had always preferred to rely on more logical explanations, to base his decisions on calculable facts rather than trust in the fickle fortune of shamrocks and leprechauns. His experiences that summer, however, had done much to erode those long-held notions. After all, how else could he account for the series of random events that had brought him and Rachel Chase together?

No, luck must have played at least a small role in placing their lives on converging courses. Now, if it would just give him a hand in keeping things that way, he thought as he scaled the mortarless stone fence bordering Heathervale's ripening fields.

Of course, he could always rely on Jody to give luck a little push in the right direction. In the first place, it had been her oblique pep talk during their drive back to Scarborough that had prompted him to make plans to discuss the future with Rachel. He had considered it a good omen that afternoon when Jody had phoned the camp to tell him that Maureen and Peter had spared them five pieces of blueberry tart, one of which had his name on it. Patrick felt so buoyed by good, honest Gaelic luck, he had to restrain himself to keep from running up the path to the house.

He bridled his boisterous smile, trying to strike a reasonably sober appearance as he rapped the brass knocker soundly against the front door. He felt his face fall, but only a little, when Jody answered instead of Rachel.

"So I hear you gave Pete and Maureen the royal treatment." In spite of himself, Patrick glanced into the front room and up the stairs, hoping to find Rachel.

"Yeah. I think they had a good time." Jody took a step backward and gestured clumsily toward the rear of the house. "Uh, why don't you have a seat in the dining room with Gran? I'll see if Rachel . . . I'll go call her. Upstairs."

Patrick eyed Jody suspiciously. "Is Rachel all right? She's not sick or anything, is she?"

"Oh, no," Jody assured him, almost too quickly. "She was probably real tired after lunch today. I think she's been taking a nap."

"Don't wake her on my account," Patrick felt obliged to say, although he secretly hoped his vigorous knocking would have already had the same effect.

Jody seemed eager to dispatch him to the dining room. "Tell Gran we'll be right there," she said, waving him away as if he were a pesky winged insect.

Inside the dining room, Patrick found Gran Chase arranging a silver coffee service on the sideboard. "Good evening, Patrick!" she greeted him warmly, but he noticed the slightest dimming of the mirth in her lively gray eyes. "Milton decided not to come along?"

"He really wanted to, but he was already committed to officiate at this evening's tennis match. He asked me to extend his regrets. And ask for a rain check."

"Well, certainly! There will always be other times and other desserts." Gran covered her disappointment with a smile as she held up a bone-china cup. "By now I should remember how you take your coffee. Just black?"

"Yes, thank you." Patrick surveyed the table set with five dessert forks and napkins and then glanced back at the door. When Jody appeared, he was surprised to find her alone.

"Please sit down." Gran beckoned with the pie server.

As she slid into her seat, Jody avoided looking at Patrick—or so it seemed to him. He took the dessert plates Gran handed him, passing them around until four place settings were filled.

"There!" Gran placed the tart tin on the sideboard and then brushed her hands together. As she sat down at the head of the table, Patrick and Jody looked at her and then at each other. Then they all three looked at Rachel's conspicuously empty chair. Gran frowned. "Jody, is Rachel not feeling well?"

Jody squirmed in her seat, but before she could answer, Rachel appeared in the dining room door.

"I was beginning to worry about you, dear. Do you have a headache?" Gran asked.

"No. I'm fine," Rachel told her in a flat voice that sounded anything but fine.

She paused, giving the two vacant chairs a hard look. One was positioned directly across from Patrick, the other next to him, and she appeared to be weighing the consequences of sitting down in either of them. After what seemed an inordinately long time, she settled on the chair opposite him.

"Jody tells me you rolled out the red carpet for Maureen and Peter," Patrick began, in hopes of easing the awkwardness hanging in the air between them, but her unsmiling glance promptly silenced him.

What on earth was wrong with Rachel? Between bites of tart, Patrick fished for possible explanations for her unapproachable mood. Usually animated and sociable, she said fewer than a half-dozen words while they ate their desserts, and then only to request cream and sugar. Maybe it had something to do with her mother, he guessed, falling back on the only other occasion when Rachel had seemed withdrawn. But if Janet Chase were in some sort of dangerous situation, wouldn't Gran be a little flustered? Right now, the elderly lady's only concern appeared to be her granddaughter's flagging appetite.

"You're not hungry, dear?" Gran eyed Rachel's untouched slice of tart uncertainly.

"Not right now. I'll put it away and have it later, if that's all right." Springing up from the table, Rachel grabbed the dessert plate and pivoted toward the kitchen.

Gran rose more slowly. "Perhaps a bit of fresh air would do you good. Why don't you take a little stroll?" She gave Patrick a look that clearly included him in her suggestion.

Patrick could see a protest building behind Rachel's tightly clamped lips, but before she could object, Jody swiftly relieved her of the dessert plate. "Take your time. More than two cleaning up in the kitchen and you just get in the way." The swinging door whooshed behind her as she followed Gran into the kitchen.

For a moment, Rachel only stared at the deserted table. Then she turned and headed for the hall door. As she passed Patrick, his hand moved at his side, stirred by the impulse to take her arm. The withering look she gave him instantly squelched the urge.

Not waiting for him to catch up with her, Rachel marched out of the house and down the flagstone path. Patrick broke into a jog, finally drawing alongside her at the sundial.

"For God's sake, Rachel, what's on your mind?"

Rachel spun around, fixing him with eyes as hard as chips of gray flint. "You really want to know?" She posed it as more a challenge than a question.

Patrick stood his ground, forcing himself to meet her discomfiting glare. "Yes, I would. You look as if the world has just caved in on you. The last time you were upset, we talked things through—"

"We have such an honest relationship, you and I," she cut in.

The brittle edge on her voice put him on guard, but he had no choice but to go on. "Yes, I think we do. I've told you, if something is bothering you, I'm always here to talk it over."

"Like you talked over getting shot up?"

The words struck him with the force of a well-directed bullet, slamming into him with searing pain. "How do you know about that?" In his agitation, he was on the verge of stammering.

"Peter mentioned the incident today. Apparently, he has no idea that you've been carrying on this charade with me for the past two months."

Patrick took a step toward her, but she shrank back. Struggling to collect himself, he lifted both hands in a powerless gesture and then let them drop. "Rachel, believe me, I intended to tell you about all that someday," he began, but she was in no mood to listen.

"When? The next time some criminal gets you in his sights?" Her breath was ragged now, punctuating her words with short, angry spurts. "That's a gamble, isn't it, Patrick? You might not be able to talk about anything at all after the next time."

"Rachel, please!" In his frustration, he was almost shouting. "I honestly..."

"Don't use that word with me! I won't stand for any more manipulation with talk about openness and communication. 'If something's bothering you, I want to know.'" Her voice quavered slightly as she threw his own words back into his face. "Never mind that you kept the truth about your own life hidden behind fluff about an ordinary cop just doing his ordinary job." Anger had drained her face of its normal color, blanching it to an unwholesome, chalky pallor.

"I swear, Rachel! I'll never lie to you again!" Patrick instinctively reached out to touch her trembling shoulder, but she pulled away from him as if he were carrying the plague.

"No, you never will, Patrick. Because I'll never give you the chance again, as long as I live!"

Turning on her heel, Rachel raced up the garden path. The wooden gate shuddered on its hinges as she slammed it behind her. Watching her disappear into the house, Patrick could feel the early-evening darkness enveloping him like a shroud.

Chapter Eleven

Sprawled against the pillows, Rachel listlessly thumbed the pages of the fashion magazine. The glossy images fluttered before her eyes, blurring into an indistinguishable smear of meaningless shape and color. Pulling her knees up to her chin, she tossed the magazine onto the floor beside the bed and tried to focus her attention on the TV miniseries that had been droning away in the corner for the past half hour. A brusque knock at the bedroom door interrupted her wavering concentration.

"Yes?"

The door opened a crack and Jody's scrubbed, freckled face appeared. As had so often been the case in the three weeks since the rift with Patrick, she wasn't smiling. "Telephone. It's a man," she added in the same tone she would have used to identify a cockroach.

"Thanks." Rachel climbed out of bed and pulled on her bathrobe. As she padded down the hall, she watched the tail of Jody's acid-green sleep shirt disappear into the guest room. The door closed—none too quietly, to Rachel's way of thinking.

Damn it! It wasn't her fault that things had gone sour between Patrick and her! In any case, she certainly didn't owe Jody an explanation. Not that the teenager had demanded one. She simply never passed up a chance to demonstrate her disapproval of the situation.

But then, Gran wasn't much better, either, Rachel reflected as she entered the downstairs sitting room that doubled as the farm's office. Gran was working on a piece of cross-stitch, but when she saw her granddaughter, she pointedly gathered up her work and headed for the door.

"Don't leave on my account," Rachel told her.

"It's time I got to bed anyway," Gran assured her. "Milton has invited me to the campfire breakfast tomorrow morning, and that means getting up with the chickens. Of course, I wouldn't miss it for the world," she added with a tight little smile.

Rachel sighed and tried to overlook the reminder that she was now excluded from such activities—or more accurately, had chosen to exclude herself. As Gran's footsteps petered out on the stairs, Rachel picked up the receiver. "Hello?"

"Rachel? For a moment there, I thought they were having a hard time finding you in that big old farmhouse." Richard's chuckle rumbled on the other end of the line. "How are things?"

"Fine. Just fine." Rachel thought she would choke on the words, but she managed to get them out. "How are you? And *where* are you?"

"A., I'm doing just great, and B., I'm in Boston. Just got back from Rio about an hour and a half ago, but that's a long story and it's been a long night already. I'll tell you when I see you, which is why I called in the first place. When can we get together?"

"Oh, I don't know," Rachel hedged. She was so surprised by his phone call, she had no idea what she should—much less wanted—to say. "I mean, how can we work this?"

"My place or yours, to coin a phrase," Richard shot back, his sense of humor obviously unimpaired by the lengthy flight. "Seriously, I could drive down to your corner of the wilderness some weekend. Or you could come up to Boston, whichever you like. I have to admit, though, that a lot of people are hoping you'll opt for choice number two. You know, I'm not the only person who'd like to see you. Just the most eager," he added. When he laughed, Rachel envied him the carefree music that seemed to flow so effortlessly from his chest.

She briefly considered the risk of inviting Richard into a household where her decisions about men were already severely questioned, and then picked the latter option. "I'll come to Boston. Shall we set a date?"

"How does next Saturday sound?"

Rachel hesitated. For a moment, she almost said, *But that's Camp Onoconohee's last day.* Just as quickly, she reminded herself that the camp's closing ceremonies now had no effect on her schedule. "That sounds great," she told him, hoping the long-distance connection would obscure the uncertainty in her voice.

"See you on Saturday. I can't wait, but I guess I'll have to." Richard's parting remark was full of confident anticipation.

"Goodbye." Rachel hung up the phone, holding the receiver down with both hands as if she feared it might spring back up to her ear and permit Richard yet another onslaught.

As she had expected, Gran and Jody greeted the news of her trip to Boston with cool-but-polite disinterest. They were far too absorbed in the farewell festivities Milton and Patrick were planning for the last group of campers to give Rachel's announcement more than a passing nod—or at least they pretended to be. Whatever the case, the follow-

ing Friday night, Rachel set her alarm clock early enough to
get herself up and on the road before either of her house-
mates stirred. The next morning, after sipping a quick cup
of instant coffee with only Noodles for company, she slipped
out of the house and into her car with the stealth of a bur-
glar.

Although Richard was an early riser, conditioned by his
meteoric career to survive on four hours of sleep, Rachel
realized that her daybreak departure would put her in Boston much sooner than they had planned. She, at least,
wasn't prepared to start their first meeting in over six
months with one of them dressed in pajamas. Far better to
kill a little time on the way. She needed to tank up the car
anyway, and a bit of breakfast might even nix the queer
gnawing in her stomach. With those thoughts in mind,
Rachel turned onto the parking apron of Scarborough's
lone twenty-four-hour convenience store.

She was too busy latching the recalcitrant nozzle onto the
Volvo's gas tank to notice the Honda Accord nosing up to
the lead-free pumps. When she finally looked up, she caught
her breath, sucking in a nauseating gulp of petroleum-laden
air.

Patrick was still bent over his car, unscrewing the gas-tank
cap and for a split second, Rachel tried to calculate the speed
with which she could cut off the pump, run into the store,
throw a few bills on the counter, sprint back to her car and
tear out onto the highway. Probably not fast enough. Certainly not before Patrick saw her, something he was already
in the process of doing.

Patrick's eyes traveled from the steadily escalating numbers on the pump's meter to Rachel, regarding both with
equally neutral interest.

Following his lead, Rachel focused on the gallons and
dollars and cents flipping past the little glass windows.

Never in a thousand years would she have expected fate to propel Patrick Morrissey to the Mini-Magic-Mart at exactly 6:36 a.m. on this particular Saturday. It was almost as if he had planned to intercept her there just to needle her.

Rachel's eyes strayed from the pump long enough to give him a suspicious glance. No, that was a ludicrous assumption. Besides, for all she knew, Patrick hadn't the faintest idea she was going to Boston today, much less at this unholy hour. Their meeting was simply one of those crazy coincidences.

The two pumps shut off almost simultaneously. Rachel forced herself to take her time as she disengaged the nozzle and replaced the gas-tank cap. Patrick, too, went about his business slowly and methodically, refusing to rush. With the precision of a Marine drill team, they both turned and walked to the store, keeping an even distance between them.

The door was going to be a problem, Rachel realized. She hesitated, holding back enough to give Patrick a few paces' lead. A little bell jingled as he opened the door, then stepped aside and held it for her. He nodded curtly, signaling her to enter. Rachel headed for the candy rack, determined to give him ample time to pay and be on his way. To her consternation, Patrick sauntered to the cooler and began to look over the selection of bottled fruit juices.

"Good morning, Rachel! Patrick!" Terry Matthews, the friendly high school student minding the store, pushed aside the newspaper he had spread open on the counter and walked to the cash register. "What brings you two out so early this morning?"

"I'm going to Boston..." Rachel began.

"I was up anyway, so..." Patrick chimed with her.

Terry's myopic eyes narrowed behind the thick lenses. "Going out of town today?"

"Yes." Rachel deposited two Mars bars and a bag of M&Ms on the counter and fished in her shoulder bag for her wallet.

Terry fingered the bag of M&Ms as if he were reluctant to ring it up on the register. "But I thought the camp was having its gala this afternoon."

"It is," Patrick informed him, scooting two eight-ounce bottles of grapefruit juice into line behind Rachel's candy.

"Then I guess it's good you're getting an early start this morning." Terry gave each of them a hopeful look.

Rachel nodded, and Patrick shrugged.

The youthful clerk's smile faltered slightly as he surveyed the assortment of products they had placed on the counter. "Uh, is this all together?"

"No!" Patrick and Rachel chorused.

Chastened, Terry quickly totaled Rachel's candy-and-gasoline purchase. She could hear the register buzzing through Patrick's purchases as she pushed open the door. She was securely ensconced behind the wheel of the Volvo by the time he emerged from the store. Her hand was on the ignition key, her attention focused on a clean getaway, but she started when he walked up to the car.

Patrick gave the driver's-side window the brief, authoritative tap of a seasoned police officer. Trapped, Rachel reluctantly lowered the window a few inches.

"You know this is pretty ridiculous." Patrick didn't smile; he didn't scowl. He simply stated a fact.

Rachel drew a deep breath, but she knew any argument would be futile. And it *was* ridiculous, two grown people refusing to exchange normal pleasantries. "I'm sorry I didn't speak. Good morning, Patrick."

"Good morning, Rachel." Patrick gave an abbreviated half laugh. "Now that that's out of the way, when are we really going to talk?"

"There's nothing to talk about." Rachel reached for the ignition once more, but Patrick sidestepped, as if he intended to block the car with his body.

"That's nonsense and you know it. For God's sake, Rachel, look at all we had. You can't seriously mean it's over, up in smoke just like that." He snapped his fingers.

"I have to get to Boston." Rachel shifted gears and eased off the clutch slightly.

Patrick was walking alongside the car. As she picked up speed, he threw up his hands and then stepped back. "Go on then and run away. But you can't keep running forever."

Rachel grappled with the window crank, struggling to block out his parting jibe. As the convenience store's big sign receded in the rearview mirror, she let up on the gas pedal. She wasn't running away, she told herself fiercely. And if not wanting to fall in love with a man who might be gunned down at any minute *was* running, then heaven give her speed.

Falling in love. Locked inside the insulated solitude of her car, Rachel could admit that was exactly what had been happening to her all summer. She had been slow to recognize it at first, she realized, because the symptoms were unfamiliar to her. Before Patrick, no man had ever made her feel so vibrant, so joyful—and so terribly vulnerable. It was a double-edged sword, this quirky, unpredictable thing called love, and she was mature enough to acknowledge the risks involved in caring a great deal about someone. In Patrick's case, however, those risks carried deadly consequences.

She should consider herself lucky that the truth had come out before she had become more deeply entangled with him. As it was, she needed to concentrate on the aspects of her life she could control, stay busy and give time a chance to dull the nagging ache that filled her whenever she thought about him. Rachel refused to calculate just how much time that transition would require as she switched on the radio to fill the void.

By the time she reached the popular upscale neighborhood where Richard's renovated brownstone was located, Rachel had heard enough pop singers bemoan fickle emotions and foundered love affairs to last her a lifetime. After she had parked the car in Richard's tiny driveway, she took a few minutes to check her lipstick and adjust her expression in her compact mirror.

Today would be a good chance to put her recovery plan into action. She would be seeing old friends, visiting familiar turf, reconnecting with a life that, up until a few months ago, had suited her to a T. That her encounter with the first old friend was not going to be entirely carefree, however, became apparent the second Richard responded to the buzzer.

"You look terrific!" With a maneuver that would have done Valentino proud, Richard swept her into his embrace, planting a jolting kiss on her lips as he drew her into the foyer. Rachel tried to gather her wits as he held her out at arm's length and looked her over with avid eyes. "God, it's good to see you!"

"It's good to see you, too, Richard." Rachel gently disengaged herself from his hold and straightened the clip anchoring her hair at her nape. "I'm sorry if I caught you a bit early."

Richard glanced down at his health-club T-shirt and gray sweat pants. "Yesterday wouldn't have been too early."

As he moved toward her, Rachel neatly sidled around the coat rack. Richard had to push the sleeve of a brown leather bomber jacket out of his face, but he was still smiling.

"Have you had breakfast yet?" she asked, staying a few steps ahead of him in the hall.

"No. I was waiting for you. Want me to whip up one of my famous cheddar-and-hot-sauce omelettes?" He cast a hopeful eye toward the door opening onto a gleaming granite-and-stainless-steel kitchen.

"Actually, I was hoping we could go out to Jamison's. If we get there before noon, we're certain to run into some friends," she quickly went on, hoping to banish the shadow that had just fallen across his good-looking face. "Wouldn't it be nice to have a couple of Bloody Marys with Chris and Sam?" She almost added *just like we used to do,* but for some reason thought better of it.

Richard agreed with her point, albeit with some reluctance. "Sure. Just give me a chance to change." He turned toward the stairs and then looked back at her. "Come on up, if you like."

Rachel smiled—not too awkwardly, considering the circumstances—as she ducked into the living room. "Let's see what you've been reading these days," she said, loudly enough for him to hear her on the landing overhead. Perching on the edge of the Italian leather sofa, she sorted through the books stacked on the coffee table. Mixed in among popular titles on investing and negotiating were a few bestsellers and an illustrated guide to toning the abdominal muscles. Rachel was paging through the ghost-written autobiography of a famous real-estate tycoon when Richard appeared in the doorway.

To judge from the supple torso outlined beneath his navy-blue polo shirt, the fitness book, at least, had been worth its jacket price. For someone who kept up a twenty-five-hour-a-day schedule, Richard always managed to look as if he had just returned from a restful sojourn at a tropical resort. Looking up at him, glowing with good health and anticipation, Rachel was struck by his extraordinary good looks, the face and physique of the classic golden boy. As his hand clasped her shoulder, however, the feelings it elicited in her were oddly lacking in passion. The palpable yearning in his touch only underscored their contrasting emotions.

As they walked to Jamison's Bar and Restaurant, Rachel congratulated herself on having skillfully maneuvered them out into a public place. The intimate confines of Richard's town house afforded far too many opportunities for unwanted romantic overtures and clumsy evasions to suit her just then. During the short stroll, she was pleased to turn the conversation to his recent adventures in Brazil, and Richard willingly obliged with a witty narrative.

Just as Rachel had predicted, they found several friends and business associates sprinkled among Jamison's midmorning brunch crowd. For once, she made no attempt to shun the spotlight, eager as she was to deflect Richard's attention. Over Eggs Benedict and coffee, Rachel listened to several months' worth of news about new jobs, new homes and new significant others. She, in turn, provided an entertaining description of life at Heathervale, liberally laced with anecdotes about Gran and the tourists and Camp Onoconohee. She had to catch herself several times to avoid mentioning Patrick.

"Sounds like a far cry from the Marquette pressure cooker," Maddie Cusack commented, briskly stirring artificial sweetener into her coffee. "Think you'll have trouble swinging back into the saddle after a whole year's vacation?"

"I haven't been on vacation." Rachel was quick to protest. "Granted, Heathervale is an idyllic setting, but running the farm is a full-time business, and that means lots of hard work. Although you couldn't have told me so this time last year, I've discovered that managing Heathervale is as challenging and rewarding as anything I was doing at Marquette Brothers. It could never be reduced to routine drudgery because the farm is so special to my grandmother. And to me," she felt compelled to add. "I've even thought about staying on at Heathervale, for a while at least."

The curious look that Maddie gave her told Rachel that this last admission could lead the conversation into unplumbed waters. As often as Gran had joked and cajoled her with offers to stay at the farm, Rachel had never seriously voiced the possibility until now. Her own thoughts on the subject were still too scattered, too unripe to explore with a table full of acquaintances she hadn't seen in almost a year. Fortunately, Maddie's quicksilver attention had now been redirected to the Arts and Leisure section of the morning's newspaper.

"I've always loved Georgia O'Keefe, and I've been dying to see that collection," Maddie gushed over the listing of gallery and museum offerings. "Those massive flowers are so *sensual*. Have you seen the exhibit yet, Jack?"

Jack shook his head, setting off a chain reaction around the table. By the time the waiter had returned the credit card receipts, an expedition of six had formed to visit the Boston Museum.

As they filed out of Jamison's, Richard plucked at Rachel's sleeve, pulling her to one side of the restaurant's mahogany-paneled foyer. "You never said anything about staying at the farm." His hoarse whisper sounded more than a little miffed.

Rachel shook her head, trying to assuage his pique. "That's because I haven't thought it through yet," she told him honestly. "Besides, we haven't had much time yet to talk about anything important, have we?"

The moment she recognized the eager look flaring in his eyes, she realized she had chosen the wrong words. "That's why I've made reservations for dinner at La Grotta tonight. Just for two, okay?"

Rachel nodded. "Okay." It was sheer foolishness, in any case, to hope that she could rely on a buffer of acquaintances to shield her from a one-on-one encounter with Richard. With several months of their trial separation behind them, he quite naturally would want to talk about the relationship, assess their feelings, discuss the future. If only she didn't feel so woefully unprepared for the task.

How did she feel about him anyway? Rachel scoured her mind—and her heart—for an answer to that question over the elegant Northern Italian dinner they shared that evening. Looking at Richard's all-American features delineated in the soft candlelight, she knew she found him attractive—but only with the detached, impersonal appreciation she would have for a handsome movie star or athlete. She liked Richard—in much the same comradely way she liked Chris Bradley or Maddie Cusack. Most importantly, she didn't love him. That single, unassailable truth overshadowed all other considerations—not least of all because she knew she would have to reveal it to Richard before the day was over.

"The harbor is beautiful this time of the evening. Why don't we go for a walk?" Richard suggested after they had finished their cappuccino.

The walkway along the harbor was dotted with Bostonians bent on taking advantage of the dwindling summer sun. Panting joggers and dogs walking their people hurried past Richard and Rachel as they paused at the rail to gaze out across the black-green water dotted with vessels.

"You know, I don't think I realized how much I've missed you until today," Richard began, not looking up from the brackish froth lapping at the pier.

"I've missed you, too." Rachel spoke slowly, giving herself a chance to frame her thoughts. "We had some good times, didn't we?"

Richard folded his hands on the rail. "We could have them again, only better. I know there were times in the past when I was pretty self-centered, but I've grown a lot. I guess being thrown back on my own, without you to depend on, has forced me to take a hard look at myself. I'm willing to give it another try, if you are." When he looked at her, it was not with the calculating gaze of the wily negotiator, but with the guileless eyes of a man pleading for a second chance.

"I'll always care a great deal about you, Richard." She heard him sigh, watched his expectant expression slowly fade. "And because I care for you so much, I have to be honest. Please try to understand."

"I was afraid of this." Richard's effort to keep the bitterness out of his voice was not entirely successful.

"I can't pretend to be in love, Richard," she said gently. "No more than you can."

"Who's talking about pretending?" Richard shot back, and then caught himself. "I'm sorry, Rachel. But look how much we have in common—friends, goals, interests. We could be a winning team, you and I."

"But does that mean we're in love?" Rachel took a deep breath. "I don't think so. Believe me, I know how easy it is to confuse affection, strong attraction for love. But real love...it feels different."

Richard smiled sadly. "You sound as if you've experienced the real thing."

Rachel gripped the rail tightly, focusing on a lighted buoy winking on the distant horizon. "I thought I did. Once."

"But it didn't work out?" The question was free of rancor.

Rachel bit her lip, struggling with the emotion swelling inside her throat. "No."

She felt Richard's hand settle on the back of her neck, the comforting touch of a true friend. His voice was as soothing as the warm night air. "I don't know who he was, but I'm sure of one thing—he was a very, very lucky man."

Chapter Twelve

"Snag any fish?" Charlene Jefferson hailed Patrick from the end of the hall.

Patrick turned, shaking his head, and waited for the petite woman to catch up with him. Dressed in powder-blue jogging shorts and matching singlet, she looked more like a carefree coed headed for her afternoon run than the competent undercover policewoman she actually was.

"We didn't even get a nibble." Patrick kneaded his stiff neck muscles. "I don't know what I hate the most—sitting cooped up in the surveillance van, waiting for something to happen, or hanging around the street, afraid it will. What about you?"

Charlene wrinkled her short, turned-up nose. "Apparently our campus mugger has decided to cool it during this heat wave. Give the guy credit for something. It was all I could do to pretend to walk out there today, much less jog." She eyed Patrick critically. "You know, you look as if the heat might be getting to you, too. I'm going to tell Arnie he needs to put air-conditioning in the back of that van."

Patrick plucked at the seedy T-shirt that perspiration held plastered to his chest. "If he listens to you, you'll be the first person who's ever gotten through to him."

Charlene's wide brown eyes traveled over Patrick's shoulder. "Speak of the devil..."

Patrick turned to find the portly police lieutenant bearing down on them. "Scott tells me you guys didn't have any luck today, eh, Jefferson?" he bellowed, fanning himself with a sheaf of police reports. Before Charlene could reply, he charged past them. "We'll have to keep trying then, won't we?"

Charlene rolled her eyes and mouthed the word *we* behind Arnie's back. She abruptly sobered when he glanced over his shoulder.

"You got a call, Morrissey. Whoever it is wanted to hold."

"Catch you later," Patrick told Charlene before hurrying to his office. If the caller was willing to wait, it could mean he was an informant. As he slammed the door behind him, Patrick surveyed the cluttered desk. His mind was beginning to resemble that desk, jumbled with unrelated facts and random information. Since his return to the force two weeks ago, he had struggled to whet the skills that had once served him automatically. It wasn't that he had lost his fire. He had merely gotten rusty over the summer, he assured himself as he tugged a notepad from the standing file and picked up the receiver.

"Officer Morrissey here. Can I help you?" he snapped into the phone.

"Goodness, Patrick, you sound so official!" Gran Chase exclaimed with a laugh.

"Eleanor! I wasn't expecting you!" Patrick sank down into his seat, as grateful for the familiar, sprightly voice as he was for the comfortable old chair.

"No, I suppose not," Gran agreed with just a touch of irony. "I won't keep you long, busy as I know you must be.

I only wanted to ask if you would like to come to dinner this Sunday evening."

If the drug kingpin his undercover team had been tracking for the past two weeks had just phoned to invite him to tea, Patrick would not have been more at a loss for words. A dozen qualifying questions jammed in his throat, all of them concerning Rachel, none of them coherent enough to be shared with Gran Chase.

With the aplomb of someone who has lived eighty years and learned much from experience, Gran smoothed the way for him. "My granddaughter can be very stubborn, Patrick. But I can't very well fault her for it because she gets it from me. I know you and she haven't had much to say to each other lately, but I think she'd secretly welcome the chance to do something about that. She's just too proud to admit it." Her chuckle reminded Patrick of the happier days they had all shared. "Pride, that's another virtue she inherited from me. So what do you say? Can we expect you?"

Gran Chase had a way of posing questions that didn't give you much chance to think and even less to say no. "What time?"

"Around seven o'clock will be fine." Gran sounded immensely pleased with herself as she bade him goodbye. "I know we're all going to look forward to the occasion!"

THE CATNIP MOUSE SCUTTERED across the floor, followed by a racing ball of gray fluff. Rachel hurried to retrieve the toy from Noodles's frantic grasp. She laughed as she held it just out of range of the cat's flailing paws. When she tossed it again, the agile animal pounced, this time clamping the gingham rodent firmly with his claws.

"Okay, Noodles, you win." Rachel bent to give the cat's ears a playful scratch before joining her grandmother in the office.

Gran Chase was just hanging up the phone. When she looked up, her face wore the telltale expression of someone who has been shaking gifts under the Christmas tree.

"Who was that?" Rachel asked on her way to her desk.

"Patrick." With her hands folded behind her back, Gran looked just a little defiant.

Rachel pretended to examine a stock sheet listing Heathervale's Christmas specialty items. "I didn't hear the phone ring," she remarked coolly.

"That's because I called him."

Rachel frowned over the descriptions of bay-leaf wreaths and hot-cider spice packets, trying to think of a suitable response. Whatever had prompted Gran to phone Patrick, it couldn't bode well.

"I invited him to dinner this coming Sunday," Gran went on, in the same cheeky tone.

Rachel slowly replaced the stapled papers on the desk.

"Patrick is a friend of mine, Rachel, and as such, he is always welcome in this house. I will expect you to treat him with the same civility you would accord any of my other friends."

Rachel tried to look offended. It was the best she could do at this point, with Gran clearly on the offensive. "I have no intention of insulting him, Gran. As far as I'm concerned, this will be a cordial dinner party, to be enjoyed by everyone involved." When her eyes drifted to the phone, she was struck by a sudden inspiration. "In fact, I'd like to invite another guest, if you don't object."

Gran eyed her warily, but said nothing.

"I'm going to call Milton and see if he has anything planned for Sunday evening," Rachel announced gleefully. The retired principal's presence would put a damper on any designs for mischief Gran might have brewing in her mind; with Milton, she was always on her best behavior.

That Gran surely had a plan up her sleeve was evidenced by the uneasy glance she gave the phone. "You can ask him, I suppose," she conceded with noticeable reluctance.

Rachel smiled as she picked up the receiver and dialed Milton Weber's home. When the elderly man answered, she looked directly at Gran. "Hello, Mr. Weber. This is Rachel Chase. How are you today?"

"I'm doing well, thank you, Miss Chase. And you?"

"Just fine. I was calling to see if you could join us for dinner on Sunday." She wove the phone cord through her fingers, relishing the discomfiture growing on Gran's face.

Milton hesitated. "Well, that's very kind of you, Rachel, but I'm afraid I won't be in town that evening. I don't suppose your grandmother has mentioned it, but the Golden Years Globetrotters group is leaving Sunday for a week in Bermuda. I figured I had earned a vacation after overseeing everyone else's this summer," he added with a spry chuckle.

"That's wonderful, Mr. Weber!" Rachel congratulated him, doing her best to conceal her disappointment. "We'll have to invite you over to show us your vacation pictures when you get back. Have a good trip." After she had hung up, she grudgingly shared the news with Gran. "He's going to Bermuda on Sunday."

A look of unmitigated relief washed over Gran's pale pink face, but she had the good grace not to crow. "I've been telling Milton it was high time he did something for himself" was her only comment.

The battle lines might be drawn, but Gran had proven she was willing to conduct herself as a gentlewoman. With this thought in mind Rachel spent the remainder of the week mapping her strategy for dealing with Patrick's impending visit. Of course, Milton Weber could have made things a whole lot easier if he had delayed his vacation by just one more week. A threesome would be a much trickier situation to handle, riddled with unseen pitfalls. For a time, Rachel toyed with the idea of going out for dinner and a movie that evening, but she realized that Gran would hold such a maneuver against her. Far better to stay put and get it over with.

By Saturday evening, she had decided the best approach would be to maintain a polite but distant demeanor with Patrick and let Gran do most of the talking. After all, Gran had insisted that he was her guest; let her entertain him. As proof of her good intentions, Rachel lent a hand with the advance dinner preparations on Saturday morning. While she was arranging a lattice crust on the cherry pie, Gran startled her by putting an arm around her.

"I know you might not understand some of the things I do, dear, but you know I mean well, don't you?" Gran jostled Rachel's shoulders lovingly.

Suddenly gripped with guilt, Rachel dropped the strip of pie dough to give her grandmother a hug. "Of course I do, Gran. And I promise to behave myself tomorrow."

Gran patted her back. "That's all I wanted to hear!"

Poor Gran! Rachel reflected after she had gone to bed that night. She must have been as anxious about the Sunday dinner as Rachel, worrying that an angry spat would erupt over her roast chicken and corn pudding. When Rachel awoke the next morning, she vowed to bottle her feelings and treat Patrick as cordially as she could without raising false hopes in him.

For some reason, Noodles was pacing the upstairs hall, his thick tail fluffed out like a plume. When he saw Rachel emerge sleepily from her room, he dashed in front of her and tore down the stairs. He sprang onto the front room's window seat and stared intently out at the yard.

"Are the squirrels giving you a hard time, old boy?" Rachel asked, parting the curtain to inspect the dewy lawn.

The cat arched his back, doing his best to reply.

"Come on. Let's get some breakfast. Take care that we don't wake Gran," she warned him as she tiptoed to the kitchen.

Apparently, Gran had taken care not to wake her, for Noodles's food dish had already been filled with Cat Chow and the aroma of fresh coffee hung in the air. Wiping her still-groggy eyes, Rachel selected a mug from the cupboard and then shuffled to the coffee maker. Only when she reached for the pot did she notice the handwritten note taped to the side of the machine.

Dear Rachel,

I'm really sorry I didn't wake you to say goodbye, but I hope you will understand why. The Golden Years Globetrotters flight to Bermuda left at six this morning. By the time you read this note, I should be well on my way to a dream vacation. Trust me, Rachel, I did want to tell you, but I feared you would discourage me from taking the trip. You always do worry so about my health. So I just decided to do it and talk about it later. That way, it will be more fun for both of us. I must admit I was afraid Milton would let the cat out of the bag when you phoned him this week, but, bless him, he can keep a secret! I've engaged Mrs. Clark to cook the lunches next week, so you only need bother with dinner this evening. Don't forget to baste the chicken frequently. Please give Patrick my regards. I'll see you next week.

Love,
Gran

For a long moment, Rachel was too stunned to do more than stare at the neatly written note. As the impact of its shocking message began to seep into her consciousness, she reread it, then turned it over in the vain hope of finding some reassuring disclaimer on the other side. There was none.

"Bermuda." Rachel sank onto the kitchen stool, oblivious to the persistent pressure of Noodles's head at her shoulder. *Gran has slipped off to Bermuda for a week.* She rolled the alien idea around in her head, trying to get accustomed to it in much the same way one adjusts to false teeth or an ill-fitting toupee. Only when the full consequences of Gran's surreptitious departure hit her did she suddenly sit bolt upright. Patrick was coming to dinner tonight and she would have to face him all by herself.

Rachel jumped off the stool as if someone had just driven a tack through the seat and began to pace the kitchen. What on earth was she going to do? Call him up and cancel? The impulse sent her dashing to the office, but the moment her hand touched the phone, she froze. No, that wouldn't do. There was no way to disinvite someone without being miserably rude. In any case, Gran would never, ever forgive such a transgression.

Rachel stalked back to the kitchen. When Noodles looked up from his breakfast to meow at her, she realized that her support had dwindled to one affectionate cat with a pathetically limited vocabulary.

Maybe Patrick would cancel on her, she thought as she roamed the kitchen, slopping cereal into a bowl and stuffing bread slices into the toaster. With each passing hour, however, that possibility grew fainter. By midafternoon, Rachel had abandoned any hope of Patrick not showing up and reconciled herself to putting the chicken into the oven.

With the bird browning nicely and the side dishes ready to rewarm in the microwave, nothing remained but to set the table. Even with Noodles's help, however, that task proved to be a problematic one. At first she placed the settings at opposite ends of the big table, but the question of how they would go about passing food to each other, much less carry on the pretext of conversation without two-way radios quickly changed her mind. Next she tried spacing the plates with two seats between them. The asymmetrical arrangement looked awkward and contrived, however, and Rachel was certain the evening was going to be awkward and contrived enough without any help from her. She finally settled on seating herself at the head of the table with Patrick a decorous space-and-a-half to her right.

Despite the lingering unseasonable heat wave, Rachel selected a black cotton knit dress with a severe high collar. She completed the forbidding image by foregoing perfume and pulling her hair into a tight knot at the base of her neck. Satisfied that she had set the correct tone for the evening to come, she went downstairs to await her fate.

Since childhood, she had always loved Gran's old-fashioned grandfather clock. Now, however, its doleful ticking drummed on her already frayed nerves. When she heard tires crunch on the gravel drive, her stomach contracted palpably. Not giving herself time to do something crazy like run out the back door or hide upstairs, Rachel marched to the front door. As soon as Patrick rapped the knocker, she opened the door.

He seemed surprised by her swift response. "Uh, good evening, Rachel." He looked as if he wanted to smile but unsure if he should.

"Hello, Patrick. Gran has gone to Bermuda, so it's just us tonight," she announced tersely, acting on the urge to get the news out without mincing words.

The uncertain smile flickering on Patrick's lips shifted into a startled gape. "Bermuda?"

Rachel nodded. "Yes, Bermuda. With Milton." Pulling the door open wider, she beckoned with a grim gesture. "Please come in."

"I can't believe this." Patrick was shaking his head as he walked into the hall. "Your grandmother and Milton Weber took off for a fling on a sun-drenched island?"

"I don't know if I would put it exactly that way," Rachel told him primly. She started for the dining room, bent on getting the business of eating and drinking underway as expeditiously as possible.

Patrick broke into a hearty laugh, but quickly sobered when Rachel shot him a disapproving look over her shoulder.

"Please sit down." Rachel indicated his seat on her way to the kitchen. "I'll serve the salad."

"Let me help," Patrick suggested hopefully.

He reached for the candlesticks standing on the sideboard. While he plundered the drawer in search of matches, Rachel switched on the overhead light, turning the dimmer switch to its brightest level. When she returned from the kitchen with two plates of marinated cucumber salad, she discovered that he had lighted the candles anyway. Rachel placed a salad in front of him and then seated herself.

"This looks delicious." Patrick studied the translucent disks of cucumber speckled with dill. He took a bite. "Tastes great, too."

"Gran will be glad to know you like it. It's one of her specialties," Rachel informed him.

"She's a great cook, your grandmother."

"I've always thought so."

Patrick chewed steadily, lifting one forkful after another to his mouth like a child charged with cleaning his plate. "By the way, how's the luncheon business doing?"

"Very well."

Rachel had been gauging his progress with the salad. No sooner had he swallowed the last bite than she rose and collected the plates. Inside the kitchen, she surveyed the counter and tried to figure the most efficient way to get all the food to the table. Too many trips, and Patrick was sure to offer his help. The last thing she wanted was any chummy bumping together around the work island. Perhaps if she delivered the chicken first, she could occupy him with carving it while she brought out the side dishes. She was arranging the carving knife and fork on the platter when Patrick poked his head around the door. When he spotted the implements in her hands, she imagined he drew back a bit.

"Need help?"

Rachel laid down her weapons and handed him the platter. Gathering up the corn pudding and steamed green beans, she followed him back to the dining room. Patrick needed no prompting from her to take charge of the carving. After the bird had been disjointed and the vegetables passed between them, they turned their attention to eating.

"Uhm. Delicious," Patrick commented between bites.

"Gran has always made wonderful corn pudding," Rachel remarked, and then broke off. Better to eat in silence than to repeat the stilted conversation that had accompanied the salads.

Patrick, however, was of a more tenacious bent. "So tell me what you've been up to."

Rachel stared at him for a moment, as if she were uncertain he was addressing his remark to her. "We're gearing up for Christmas now. The mail orders should really start to increase next month, and Gran wants to be prepared. Other than that . . ." She broke down enough to smile briefly and then shrugged. "I guess I've just been doing the usual, helping Gran keep the farm running smoothly."

"You're going to be doing more than helping this week. Can't you imagine your grandmother lolling on some glistening beach while you're running yourself ragged back here with lunches and mail orders?" When Patrick chuckled, Rachel found it impossible not to join in.

"Maybe I should pull the same trick on her someday," she remarked.

"That wouldn't be a bad idea."

"No, it probably wouldn't. And I've never been to Bermuda." When Rachel met his gaze, she was startled to recognize that humorous yet tender expression that she had assumed she would never see again. She hastily looked back at her plate. Already she had said far more than she intended, and she felt her voice, her expression, her whole posture relaxing. A few more minutes and she might do something she would live to regret.

"Care for another helping of chicken?" Patrick reached to spear a sliver of white meat.

"No, thank you." Rachel concentrated on the food remaining on her plate, doggedly intent on concluding the meal without further delay.

The carving knife clicked against the stoneware platter, followed by the serving fork. She heard Patrick clear his throat. When she inadvertently looked up, he gave her a smile that could have been conciliatory or sarcastic or both.

"You know, you could ask me what I've been doing. That's the way these things usually work. I ask you, then you ask me. Tit for tat." He leaned back in his chair, draping one arm over the ladder back. "So aren't you going to ask?"

Rachel poised her fork carefully on the edge of her plate. "I'm not sure I want to know, Patrick." It was the first straightforward statement she had made all evening, and she could tell it had hit the mark.

"Damn it, Rachel! You never miss a chance to get back to *that*, do you?" Patrick shoved himself away from the table and threw his napkin onto the empty plate.

"You asked me and I told you." Rachel sprang up from her chair, the better to defend herself.

"There's only one thing you've told me clearly, Rachel—that you're afraid. You're like a kid who refuses to go into a dark room—not because of what's really there, but of what she's afraid she might find."

"Those bullets weren't imaginary, Patrick." A metallic taste flooded her mouth, the acrid flavor of pent-up frustration and anger. "No one fantasized those drug dealers who attacked you and your partner."

"It was a freak slipup that should never have happened." Anguish tore through his voice, draining it of its earlier fire.

"But it did." The moment she uttered the words, she felt horribly cold and heartless. Watching the spectrum of agonizing emotions wash over Patrick's face, she longed to reach out to him, wrap him in her arms, tell him that she was sorry and nothing else mattered. Most of all, she longed to tell him that she loved him and would stand by him, come what may. But as Rachel watched Patrick turn and walk out of the house, she realized that saying those few simple words was what she feared most of all.

Chapter Thirteen

The crisp breeze whistled through the trees, dislodging a fresh downpour of gold and russet leaves. Patrick rested his hands on the rake and waited for the shower to abate.

"It's the world's most pointless task, son," Kevin Morrissey remarked sagely as he cut the motor of the leaf blower he was wielding along the edge of the walk. "No sooner do you sweep up a few of them than another hundred or so take their place."

Patrick took a swipe at the latest additions with the rake. "Perverse as it may sound, I've never minded raking leaves. It reminds me of the fun we had as kids, running and jumping into the leaf piles. Pete and I thought we were big shots, helping you with the yard work, but I guess we were more of a nuisance than anything."

Patrick's father chuckled. "That you were at times, but you've more than made up for it as grown-ups. Here, lend me a hand with this bag, will you?"

Patrick obligingly shook open the green plastic bag and then began to scoop leaves into it. Despite his father's good-natured grumbling about the futility of leaf raking, he was genuinely grateful for the slow-paced, monotonous work that afternoon. At this point in his life, he welcomed almost any activity that took his mind off police work for a few hours. If the accompanying fatigue dulled his persistent thoughts of Rachel, all the better.

"About ready for a beer?" Kevin Morrissey clapped a big hand on his son's shoulder after they had consigned the last bulging bag to the curb.

Patrick nodded as he propped the rake against the side of the house. Dusting the knees of his faded jeans, he followed his father up the porch steps. The enticing aroma of cinnamon-laced baked goods wafted from the kitchen to lure them through the door. From the far end of the hall, Patrick could hear a television chef—no doubt the source of the irresistible spicy goodies—leading his audience through a complicated culinary technique.

"Your mother's always trying out something new in the kitchen. Of course, I'm glad she took up cooking as a hobby and left the gardening to me. That way I get to eat like a king and still manage to work off the calories. Or at least some of them." Patrick's father gave his comfortably solid waist a rueful pat. As they entered the cheerful blue-and-white kitchen, he sniffed the air appreciatively. "Something smells good enough to eat!"

"Shhh!" Not taking her eyes off the tiny television perched next to the range, Patrick's mother impatiently waved them toward the refrigerator.

Kevin grinned over his shoulder as he pulled two bottles of beer from inside the refrigerator door. After dumping the bottle caps into the waste can, he led the way out of the kitchen. In the living room, he handed Patrick one of the beers and then settled into his favorite recliner.

Patrick sipped the beer and stared out the window at nothing in particular, letting his thoughts drift. When he turned, he was surprised to find his father watching him closely.

"You know, when you were little, you never could fool me if you had something on your mind. And now that you're big, you don't do any better job of it. What's eating at you, son? You've been brooding all afternoon."

Patrick's first instinct was to deny his father's suspicion, contend that his life had never been better, crack a dumb joke or two to illustrate how lighthearted he felt. But even that well-intentioned subterfuge required more energy than he could muster just then.

"Somehow I can't seem to latch on to anything anymore, Dad. The only thing I've ever been good at is detective work, but these days, I'm not even sure about that."

"Because of Al?" his father asked gently.

Patrick frowned. "No, this is different. I remember how I felt back in the spring, right after the incident. Every hour of every day, I used to tell myself to stay on my toes, concentrate, think of the other guy's move before he did. But in the back of my mind, there was always this nagging suspicion that something would slip, that I'd blink for just one wrong split second and another innocent person would have to pay. It's strange, but I don't feel that way now. When I'm out with a team, I'm as steady and confident as I've ever been...." His voice tapered to a murmur and he looked back at the empty street.

"But that's not the problem?"

Patrick covered the neck of the bottle with his palm and leaned back in the armchair. "I guess what really bothers me is that I just don't get much out of it all, you know the stuff that keeps a detective sharp, the hunt and chase, the setup, the spring. I try to imagine what would make the way I spend my days worthwhile. Nailing the guys who shot Al?" He shrugged. "They're already in the hands of the judicial system, and even if they get a dozen consecutive life sentences each, it wouldn't do Al a damn bit of good. I don't know. Sometimes I wish I could just be more like Peter."

The recliner's springs creaked as his father tilted the backrest. "Why don't you try to be more like Patrick?" he suggested matter-of-factly.

Patrick gave him a puzzled look. "What do you mean?"

"Follow your heart, son." Kevin Morrissey placed the bottle on the end table and rubbed his large, rough hands together. "What you've just told me, if I understand correctly, is that your heart isn't in your work the way it once was."

"But I've always been a cop! My brother's a cop. You were a cop. Your father was a cop."

"This is beginning to sound pretty boring, wouldn't you say?" His father chuckled softly, the warm, deep-chested laugh Patrick remembered from his boyhood. "And anyway, you already broke tradition when you made detective."

Patrick looked directly into the blue eyes that so closely mirrored his own. "I wanted you to be proud of me."

Kevin clapped the worn arms of the recliner with both hands. "Lord, son! I'll be proud of my boys if they just lead decent lives, put some good back into the world and find a little happiness for themselves." His eyes traveled to the frayed toes of his gardening sneakers. "Of course, I'll admit I was pleased when both of you joined the force. I dare say most fathers secretly wish for a chip off the old block, just to pump up their own egos. If I gave you the impression I expected you to pattern your lives on mine, well, I guess that was my insecurity getting in the way. But for heaven's sake, don't cling to that pattern if it doesn't work for you. If you can find something that gives your life meaning, go after it."

For a moment, the ghost of Rachel's lovely face floated through Patrick's mind, conjured by his father's admonition. He shook his head, trying to dislodge the uninvited specter. "Maybe that's the real problem. I don't know what I want."

His father lifted the empty bottle and pursed his lips, pretending to study the label. "Seems to me you were certain enough about one thing this summer. You still find time to see that young woman?"

"Rachel and I are finished," Patrick told him bluntly. The words sounded crude, clumsy, but then that was the way their relationship had ended, wasn't it? With blunders and bungling and insurmountable misunderstandings.

"It isn't over, son, until you quit thinking about her." The elder Morrissey tapped his forehead with one finger. "And I can tell you're still doing a lot of that."

"I'll get over it in time," Patrick insisted. *Just give me another hundred years or so.*

"I'm sure you will," his father remarked dryly. "But wouldn't it be a lot more pleasant to talk with her and work things out?"

In this one matter, Patrick had trained himself to be adamant. "I've tried that, but her mind is set and she'll never change it."

Kevin Morrissey drummed his fingers against the recliner's arms, tapping an impatient beat on the black vinyl. "You're too old, my boy, to be using the word *never*. If you love that woman, then show it. Pursue her. Woo her. Don't let up until she comes to her senses. Chances are she loves you, too. She just needs a little help recognizing it."

"You don't know Rachel, Dad. Nothing short of a miracle is going to turn her around."

His father narrowed his eyes, leaning back in the recliner with a contented sigh. "Ah, Paddy, but miracles *do* happen!"

IF THEIR CONVERSATION had not actually solved anything on a practical level, Patrick's talk with his father had gone a long way toward clearing the air between them. He had always revered his father, looked up to him. For the first time, however, they had managed to talk as two adults, each with his own strengths and insecurities. As a child, Patrick had taken comfort in the belief that Daddy was as invincible as Superman; as a grown man, he found it oddly reassuring to know that his father was human, just like himself.

He tried to hang on to that warm, solid feeling the following Friday evening when he stopped by the hospital to see Al. How strange it seemed, after all the radical upheavals in his own life this past summer, that Al should remain unchanged, immutable, frozen in time. Every time he visited the shadowy hospital room, Patrick searched for a sign of the faintest alteration, a slight shift of the head position, a scarcely imperceptible curve in the left wrist, a tiny variation in the contour of the upper lip. Every time he searched in vain.

The nurses were busy organizing charts when he arrived on the floor, and he passed the station unnoticed. The door to Al's room stood slightly ajar, wide enough for Patrick to slip through. As he was about to enter the room, however, he hesitated.

The young woman standing next to the bed had her back to him, but Patrick recognized Kitty Ruiz's slight figure and abundant dark hair. Surrounded by the sturdy hospital furnishings, she looked frail, weighed down with the burden of her pregnancy's final month. He could hear her talking softly to the man lying inert in the bed, telling him the heartbreakingly mundane details of the life they could no longer share.

Patrick had not been expecting to find Kitty there that evening, and he felt as awkward and out of place as if he had blundered into a sacred rite. He was about to withdraw into the hall when she turned.

"Patrick! I didn't hear you come in." When she stepped into the light produced by the red call buttons, Patrick could see the moisture gleaming on her cheeks.

"I didn't mean to disturb you." He hung back, still unwilling to violate the privacy of Kitty's vigil.

That she could still manage such a genuine smile was testimony to the resilience of the human spirit. "You're not disturbing me. And I know Al would be glad you're here. Wouldn't you, sweetheart?" Her voice dropped to a shaky whisper as she looked back at her husband. She reached to smooth a few small wrinkles from the sleeve of the hospital gown and then rested her hand on Al's. "It's still so hard to believe, isn't it? He looks just the way he would if he were sleeping. You know, for a long time I tried to convince myself that he *was* simply asleep, that someday I'd walk in here, pat his shoulder and call his name and he'd wake up. And it would all be over, like a bad nightmare. I guess a part of me is always going to believe that." She broke off, biting her lip to quell its trembling.

Patrick placed his hand on her shoulder in a clumsy gesture of comfort. He wanted to say something that would make Kitty feel better, but his reserve of consoling phrases and encouraging homilies had been stripped bare by his own despair. What was left to say anyway? Where there's life, there's hope? There's always the chance he'll come out of it someday? Let's try to be strong, like Al would want us to be? He recoiled at the thought of offering this brave woman such meaningless platitudes. Humbled by his own sense of inadequacy, Patrick stepped back, letting his hand drop from her shoulder.

As he withdrew to the door, Kitty seemed not to notice. She was bent over Al now, her free hand smoothing his forehead. "I love you, Al," he heard her murmur. "No matter what, I always will. I just want you to know that. You do, don't you?"

An unseen, viselike hand suddenly grabbed at Patrick's throat, threatening to wrench a sob from him. Gulping a quick, ragged breath, he bolted into the corridor. He braced his hand against the cool green wall, trying to get his bearings. How long had it been since he had felt this throbbing ache building inside him, threatening to burst forth in an anguished wail? How many years had passed since he had cried?

A shriek from the hospital room hit him like a splash of cold water in the face. Spinning around, Patrick dashed back into the room. He found Kitty standing by the bed with both hands pressed to her face.

"Kitty?" His heart was pounding as he rushed to her side, but he forced himself to ask the dreaded question. "What is it?"

But Kitty could only shake her head and point to her husband lying in the bed.

"I'm here. It's going to be all right." Acting on pure instinct, Patrick enfolded her in his arms, but she immediately shook herself free.

"He moved!" she finally managed to gasp.

Patrick felt the blood draining away from his face, the room closing in on him. When Kitty clasped his arm and shook him, he blinked and the tears rolled freely down his cheeks.

Her face was ecstatic as she looked up at him. "His fingers, Patrick! I felt them in my hand! He moved his fingers!"

HIS FATHER HAD BEEN RIGHT; miracles did happen. Having witnessed one himself that night in Al's room, Patrick wasn't too proud to abandon the skepticism he had spent thirty-four years cultivating in favor of his father's more optimistic viewpoint. In fact, in the week that had passed since Al had shown that first glimmer of returning consciousness, Patrick had decided his whole attitude could stand a little readjustment—starting with his notions about Rachel Chase.

By Saturday, he had convinced himself to take action. The only question that remained was exactly what he should do. The first, and most obvious, move that occurred to Patrick was simply to pick up the phone and call her. After brief consideration, however, he rejected the idea. It was too easy to evade an unwanted caller, and even if he did succeed in getting her on the line, he would lack the added impact of eye contact and facial expression. With something as important as the rest of their lives hanging in the balance, Patrick wanted a full arsenal of auxiliary supports to drive his point home.

The solution that finally occurred to him was startlingly simple and direct. He would drive to Scarborough, arrive at Heathervale without advance warning and insist she hear him out. The bold plan would require little preparation, save a brief bit of reconnaissance. With this last thought in mind, Patrick phoned Milton Weber, just to make sure that Rachel would be home on Sunday.

Milton had seemed delighted to hear from him and readily provided the necessary information. "They're all as busy as Santa's elves, making Christmas things for the mail-order business. I believe Miss Marshall is spending the weekend at Heathervale, just to lend them a hand.''

"That's great!'' Patrick had exclaimed. With both Jody and Gran on hand, he could count on a solid fifth column of support within the Heathervale household. After promising to stop by and visit Milton while he was in town, Patrick confirmed his plan to drive to Scarborough the following day.

The first inkling that the operation might not progress as smoothly as he had hoped came to Patrick before he had even pulled out of his apartment complex's parking lot. An early snow had arrived in the night, frosting his car with a tenacious coating of ice. Patrick grumbled to himself as he gave the windows a slapdash scraping. Why couldn't the decent weather have held out just one more day? He had envisioned walking through Heathervale's dormant gardens with Rachel, relying on the pleasant, familiar atmosphere to soften her up. At the rate the snow was coming down, however, any outdoor strolls would have to include boots and parkas—not the most romantic attire he could imagine.

On the turnpike, the wet flakes were coming down so thickly, he had trouble seeing more than a few cars' lengths in front of him. The hazardous conditions demanded that he pay strict attention to his driving and not let his mind wander to the upcoming assault on Heathervale.

The moderately nasty snowstorm that had followed him from Hartford had escalated to a near-blizzard by the time he reached Scarborough. Still, there was something to be said for the appeal of a snow-blanketed eighteenth-century farm. Surrounded by plump, unsullied snowdrifts, with a feather of smoke curling from its chimney, the old house looked as if it had been lifted from a nostalgic Christmas card.

Patrick tried not to feel like an intruder as he plowed through the pristine banks covering the drive. Unable to see where the drive ended and the yard began, he parked the car a judicious distance from the frost-laden rose bushes and climbed out, ready to lay siege to Rachel's heart. Narrowing his eyes against the pelting flakes, he slogged toward the house.

As he rapped the brass knocker, he could hear the faint melody of a Christmas carol from somewhere inside the house. He could imagine Gran, Jody and Rachel sitting beside the crackling fire, busy with their Yuletide handcrafts. Noodles would be curled up on the braided rug or perhaps in someone's lap. Gran would serve mugs of hot chocolate, each with a cinnamon stick and a couple of marshmallows. Everyone would join in on the favorite songs, just as they had around the campfire last summer.

The door opened suddenly, catching Patrick in the middle of his reverie.

"Hey, Patrick!" Jody's face lighted up in surprise. "We weren't expecting you!"

That was exactly the point, Patrick thought. "I decided to drive out to Scarborough this morning and thought I'd drop by while I was in town." The moment he offered his rehearsed explanation he realized he should have updated the script to suit the weather. After all, only a lunatic would choose near-blizzard conditions for an impromptu drive in the country.

Jody gave him a dubious look, but she graciously beckoned him into the hall. "You should have worn your boots," she remarked, eyeing his snow-encrusted shoes and soggy pants legs.

Patrick glanced down at the puddle forming around his feet. "Yeah, I guess I should have. Uh, where is everybody anyway?" He couldn't restrain his eyes from a hopeful peek into the front room. Contrary to his cozy projection, only Noodles was taking advantage of the fire simmering in the grate.

"Gran has a bad cold and she's taking a nap," Jody informed him. "But I know she'd like to see you."

"Perhaps later when she wakes up, but please don't disturb her on my account." He hesitated, waiting for Jody to go on. When she didn't, he was forced to prompt her. "What about Rachel? Is she around?"

Jody nodded. "She's upstairs. Want me to tell her you're here?" Her question had a challenging ring to it.

"Yes, please." He tried to look confident and dignified in spite of the gleeful grin spreading across Jody's face.

"Way to go, Patrick!" She thrust her fist triumphantly into the air before pivoting on the heel of her green leather granny boots and charging up the stairs.

He listened to the sound of the boots clomping down the hall overhead. He heard a brisk knock, then the creak of yielding hinges. Patrick strained, without success, to catch the muffled verbal exchange that followed. When the boots once more breached the stairs, they moved at a noticeably slower pace.

"She's taking a bath," Jody announced from the foot of the stairs.

"Oh." Patrick quickly tried to regroup. "I'll pay Milton a visit and come back later."

Jody's mouth pulled to one side and she shrugged skeptically. "She said she planned to soak for a *long* time."

Patrick could feel himself getting angry, something he hadn't reckoned on when he had laid his optimistic master plan back in Hartford. "Well, then I guess I'll have to pay Milton a *long* visit. I'll see you later, Jody." He turned and let himself out the door.

On his way back to his car, Patrick cast a sullen glance back at the house. When he chanced to see a curtain stir in one of the upstairs windows, his temper surged anew. Even through the screen of thick snowfall, the face peeking from behind the chintz panel had been unmistakable.

Patrick waded through the snow to the side of the house, his breath forming little vapor clouds in the chilly air. He halted right below the chintz-curtained window.

"Rachel!" Head thrown back, Patrick shouted up at the window through the falling snow. "Okay. If you want to hide behind the curtain, that's fine. Pack up and run back to Boston. Pretend that nothing deep and strong and real has passed between us. Do what you like. But there's no way you can stop me from saying what I came here to tell you. I love you, Rachel. Do you hear me? I loved you back when we were friends and rode bikes together and walked by the pond. And I loved you when we got closer and I thought we had a future together. A lot has happened since those days. Maybe we're not friends anymore. But, damn it, I still love you. I guess I always will." He paused, taking a deep breath of icy air as he straightened his shoulders. "I've had my say."

And so he had. As he squinted up at the silent window, Patrick felt the last of his buoyant anticipation ebbing away. Scrunching his neck down into his wet jacket collar, he turned and trudged slowly back to his car.

RACHEL WAITED UNTIL she heard the car's engine grind before she dared touch the bathroom window curtain again. Why, oh, why hadn't she just stayed put in her nice, relaxing bubble bath and let him drive off, unseen and unheard? Dropping the thick bath sheet she had wrapped around herself, Rachel climbed back into the tub.

Thank God, she had been quick-witted enough to run for the bathtub the second she recognized his voice carrying up the stairwell. He had certainly taken her by surprise, showing up without warning in the middle of a blizzard. At least she could safely assume he wouldn't be back. After all, he had had his say, as he put it.

A wayward bubble floated up from the stirred water, tickling Rachel's nose with its lilac sweetness. Frowning, she rubbed her nose and then sneezed. Some nerve he had, telling her to run back to Boston, as if he had any jurisdiction over Heathervale and her presence there. The farm belonged to *her* grandmother. Rachel had put in long hours to keep Heathervale thriving and she was welcome to stay there as long she pleased. Forever, if she liked, Gran had said. Wouldn't he be surprised if she decided to take Gran up on her offer of a partnership?

But of course, Patrick would be unlikely to hear anything about her, one way or the other. Something in the determined way in which he had turned his back on the farmhouse told her that Patrick Morrissey had made his final attempt to penetrate the barrier she had erected between them.

I still love you. I guess I always will. Rachel squirmed uneasily, lapping the sudsy water over her shoulders. Obviously he had wanted to make her feel guilty. He might as well have said, "I love you even though you've been stubborn, cowardly, unyielding, implacable, unreasonable and a lot of other things I'm too polite to mention."

Rachel irritably plunged her hand through the froth and pulled the plug. Okay, maybe she should have been more willing to talk things through with him in the first place. That would have been a more civilized, adult way to break off the relationship than just going on the lam—and a lot riskier. As she stepped onto the plush bath mat, Rachel re-

minded herself of how close she had come to capitulating on
the few strained occasions she had encountered Patrick face-
to-face. Heaven only knew what would have happened if he
had managed to intercept her today before she had barri-
caded herself into the bathroom, armed as he was with
professions of love. As it was, she was having a hard enough
time putting his parting outburst out of her mind.

What kind of a man would pull a stunt like that anyway?
He would have to be crazy or... Rachel slowly blotted the
moisture from her legs, resisting the obvious corollary. *He
would have to be crazy or very much in love.*

Whatever his faults might be, Rachel didn't think Patrick was crazy. And whatever her faults might be, she wasn't
too blind or too pigheaded to accept that he still loved her.
Staring into the foggy bathroom mirror, Rachel did a long
minute's soul searching and then headed for her bedroom.

Piling on heavy winter clothes was at best a tedious undertaking. In her haste, Rachel snatched gloves and caps
and sweaters from her closet shelves without any thought to
style or color coordination. Shoving her feet into a pair of
snow boots, she grabbed her keys and then tromped down
the stairs.

Jody was in the office, watching MTV on the midget Sony
television as she sorted packets of holiday potpourri. She
seemed surprised to see Rachel in full polar regalia.

"Where did Patrick go?" Rachel demanded.

Jody switched off the TV, ready to give the question her
full attention. "To Milton's. But why—?"

"I have to talk with him," Rachel told her, trying to circumvent a lengthy discussion.

Jody followed her to the door. "You'd better hurry. The
last time I turned on the radio, they said the state police were
going to close some of the roads. We're going to be snow-
bound pretty soon."

Rachel zipped the ski jacket up to her chin with the resolute gesture of an Admiral Byrd setting out on an expedition. If she had to walk to Milton Weber's house, she was determined to find Patrick before he headed back to Hartford.

That walking might have been a more prudent mode of transportation occurred to Rachel several times as she maneuvered the Volvo slowly over the nearly impassable road. Worse yet, when she reached Milton's house, her heart sank, for Patrick's Accord was nowhere in sight. As she was climbing out of her car, the porch light flicked on and Milton appeared in the door.

Urgency prompted her to dispense with preliminaries. "Have you seen Patrick?" she called from the drive.

Milton nodded. "He left here about thirty minutes ago. I tried to talk him into staying—there have been a lot of accidents out on the road, you know—but he was eager to get back to Hartford."

"Oh, no!" Rachel ducked back behind the wheel and pulled out of Milton's driveway as quickly as a foot of icy snow would permit.

If she hadn't cowered in the bathroom like an idiot instead of talking with him, this would never have happened. As it was, her intransigence had put them both in jeopardy. One thing was certain. She wouldn't rest until she was sure Patrick was safe, even if she had to drive all the way to Hartford.

The windshield wipers skidded across the icy windows, grating on her nerves with every sweep. Rachel leaned forward and squinted into the gale. Her heart almost stopped when she spotted a dark blue Accord angled off on the shoulder. Clouds of fresh snow spewed around the car as Rachel pulled over behind the disabled vehicle.

So much snow had fallen around the Honda, she couldn't tell if it was damaged. Stumbling through the deep drifts banked against the car, Rachel clawed at the driver's window. Her gloved fingers cut through the layer of sleet enough for her to see that the car was unoccupied.

What if he had been injured when the car careened off the road and was trying to walk back to town? Thoroughly alarmed, Rachel floundered back to the Volvo. Inside the car, she took a few deep breaths to calm herself. If he were on foot, he would still follow the road. She should drive slowly and keep an eye peeled for him.

That she would not be driving at any speed became woefully apparent as soon as Rachel attempted to pilot the car back onto the road. After a few minutes of wheel-spinning, she was forced to admit that she was marooned in an ever-deepening snowdrift.

Rachel wrestled the door open and climbed out of the car. If she could only reach a phone, she could call the state police. Hunched against the swirling snow, she set off in the direction of Milton Weber's house. It was slow going, stumbling through the knee-deep snow against a stiff head wind. Her face was beginning to feel numb, sensitive only to the biting sleet pelting it. Her eyes burned, unaccustomed to the stark, unrelieved whiteness. When she saw something move in the distance, she needed a few seconds to focus.

"Hey!" Rachel called to the figure plodding along the shoulder ahead of her. When the man turned, a surge of elation coursed through her chilled limbs. It was Patrick!

Rachel half ran, half staggered to meet him. "Did you have a wreck? Are you hurt? I've been worried sick about you since I found your car on the side of the road."

The wind had burnished two red patches on Patrick's cheeks. "I swerved to avoid a snowplow and got stuck. But I'm no worse for wear."

Now that she was sure he was uninjured, Rachel could afford to vent her annoyance. "That was insane, trying to drive back to Hartford in this mess!"

"Yeah, well, at least I wasn't out for a leisurely Sunday afternoon spin. Which, I suppose, is apparently what you were doing."

"I was not!" Rachel insisted huffily. The frigid air stung her nose as she drew in a deep breath. "I was looking for you."

The apple patches on his cheeks brightened. "You were?" He sounded genuinely surprised.

"Yes. You had your say and I wanted to have mine." She looked up at him, defying the snow peppering her face.

Patrick licked his wind-chapped lips, but said nothing.

"First of all, I don't like being accused of running. Even if I were going back to Boston, it wouldn't be because of you."

"'Even if'? You mean you aren't leaving Heathervale?" The cold, damp air sharpened the edge of surprise in his voice.

"How could I?" Rachel thrust out her chin, not giving herself a chance to check the flow of long-secreted conviction flooding to the surface. "Heathervale is where I belong. Helping the farm thrive and grow has been the most meaningful work I've ever done in my life. Gran has often said she would like for me to be her partner, and I've come to realize I'd be a fool to turn down her offer."

"Well, this is news—" Patrick began, but Rachel silenced him with an upheld gloved hand.

"I haven't had my say yet." She cleared her throat and took a deep breath of biting arctic air. "I love you, Patrick.

I loved you when we gathered wild flowers to make dye and cooked over an open fire and sang 'Moonlight Bay.' And I loved you when I confided in you and you helped me be less afraid. You made it hard for me, Patrick, and for a long time I thought loving an undercover cop was too big a risk. I guess that's what any coward would think.''

"Don't say that, Rachel!" Patrick protested. "You, of all people, are not a coward."

"Then why did I keep telling myself that facing my fear was too big a price to pay for caring about you?" Rachel refused to be sidetracked by his generous heart. "No, Patrick, I was determined to play it safe—even if I made myself miserable in the process. I suppose a person's secret terrors can get to be rather comfortable over the years; after all, they do come in terribly handy when you need something to hide behind."

Her eyes traveled across the monochrome white landscape. "I had to come close to losing my chance at happiness to realize what I was doing. When I was stumbling through the snow just now, looking for you, I imagined all the terrible things that could have happened to you. I was very afraid, but I realized that if I wanted to live fully, I couldn't insulate myself from fear. Somehow, I would have to learn to master it. And I vowed that if I were given another chance, I wouldn't muff it." Rachel bit her cold-numbed lower lip before blurting out, "Damn it, Patrick, I still love you!" She swallowed, waiting for him to react. "So there! Now I've had my say. Are you satisfied?" she prompted.

Patrick shook his head slowly, dislodging some of the white powder glistening on his curly dark hair. "No. I need to hear one more thing from you."

Here it comes, she thought. She had been hardhearted with him, and now that she had humbled herself, he was going to bring her to her knees.

"Will you marry me?"

Rachel blinked into the driving snow. "Marry you? I mean, we're standing out here in the middle of a blizzard and you're proposing to me?" she stammered.

"Just yes or no, Rachel." Patrick took a step closer to her.

"I can't believe this."

He took another step. "Yes or no?"

"Yes!" she cried, just before their lips met in a snowy kiss that sealed their pact.

Chapter Fourteen

"It's simply impossible, Eleanor. One more ornament on this Christmas tree and the floor will give way beneath it." Shaking his head, Milton Weber regarded the delicate crocheted snowflake Gran held out to him as warily as if it were a lead weight.

"Nonsense! Christmas tree decorations are like potato chips. There's always room for one more." To prove her point, Gran anchored the starched snowflake on one of the seven-foot spruce's branches and then stepped back to admire her handiwork.

"Don't worry, Milton. That was the very last ornament." Patrick upturned the empty cardboard box and gave it a shake. "Now, who has the honor of plugging in the lights?"

"Why the happy engaged couple, of course!" Gran informed him gaily. "But first, let me fetch the hot cider and cookies. Then we can all cozy up in front of the fireplace and enjoy our lovely tree before Milton and I have to leave for the caroling concert."

Milton wasted no time volunteering his assistance. "I'll help you, Eleanor." His step was quick, almost boyish, as he followed Gran down the hall.

Rachel looked up from the crumpled tissue paper she was stuffing into the empty ornament boxes and grinned at Patrick. "It looks to me as if we're not the only happy couple around this house."

"But the only one that's happy *and* engaged," Patrick reminded her, giving her shoulders an affectionate squeeze.

"The only one for now." Rachel leaned her head back, inviting him to plant a kiss on her smiling lips.

Patrick promptly obliged. "Maybe we need another blizzard to push them over the brink."

Rachel shrugged beneath the warm hands clasping her shoulders. "I don't know. I used to think Gran was the most stubborn woman in the world, but I don't believe she would ever be as pigheaded with Milton as I was with you."

"Don't be so hard on yourself." Patrick nuzzled the back of her neck, tickling the wispy hair that had escaped her French braid. "Let's not forget that Milton isn't guilty of sugar-coating his profession to make it more palatable to her."

"I guess we both made some dumb mistakes." Rachel evaded his grasp, but only enough to turn to face him. "But all's well that ends well." She slipped her hands around his neck.

"And this is only the beginning." Hands firmly locked around her waist, Patrick back-stepped, guiding Rachel toward the hall. When they reached the doorway, he glanced up at the bunch of mistletoe suspended directly overhead before bending to bestow a lingering kiss on her lips.

Rachel closed her eyes, relishing his closeness and the warm flush it sent coursing beneath her skin. With considerable reluctance, she gently extricated herself from his embrace. "I'd better give Gran and Milton a hand."

These days, Gran never missed a chance to voice her approval of the engagement she had worked so hard to foster.

All the same, Rachel wasn't sure she was ready to have her grandmother—or, heaven forbid, Milton—find Patrick and her locked in a passionate embrace, even with the wedding only six months in the offing. Better to keep things relatively decorous when the older generation was on hand.

In spite of her good intentions, Rachel's mind wandered ahead to the time she and Patrick would have alone later that evening. As she pushed through the kitchen door, she halted, her attention wrenched back to the present by the completely unexpected sight that greeted her. For a moment, she was too startled to do anything but gape at Gran and Milton, wrapped in each other's arms, right in front of the refrigerator.

The elderly gentleman had his back to the door, but Gran spotted Rachel before her granddaughter could recover herself and discreetly withdraw. She stepped back, still keeping one of Milton's hands firmly clasped in her own. Her lively gray eyes sparkled with a pleased defiance as they focused on the stunned interloper. "Why don't you get the cookies, dear?" she suggested, nodding to a plate of golden-brown stars and crescents studded with candied fruit. As Rachel hastened to fulfill her assigned task, Gran smiled up into Milton's pink face. "If you can manage the cider, I'll bring the cups. Take care. The kettle is hot," she admonished him, giving his hand a loving pat as she released it.

Rachel was unsure who looked more sheepish, she or Milton, as they trooped into the living room with their respective burdens. Fortunately, Gran possessed enough cool aplomb to compensate for any deficiency on their part. Blithely humming "Deck the Halls," she dispensed cups of piping hot cider, garnishing each serving with a few cloves and a cinnamon stick.

Patrick's nose hovered appreciatively over his steaming mug. "This smells terrific! But you know, I'm still waiting to try some May wine."

"Well, you'll just have to wait a bit longer," Gran told him with her wise Christmas elf's smile. "Everything in its season. But rest assured that I'll whip up the most marvelous May wine anyone has ever tasted for your wedding."

Patrick seemed placated by Gran's promise. When she shushed the little assembly in preparation for the tree lighting ceremony, he dutifully joined hands with Rachel. Gran and Milton switched off the table lamps and for a moment, the room was dark, save for the split logs glowing in the fireplace and the candles lighting the mantel. Then Patrick and Rachel plugged the extension cord into the socket. A collective gasp rose in the room as the tiny crystal candles winked to life.

Rachel had witnessed many such tree-lightings in the cheerful front room of the farmhouse, all presided over with equal pomp and fanfare by Gran. For some reason, the magic of the evergreen suddenly bursting into a tower of twinkling tapers had never diminished. As a child, she had loved the marvelous spectacle of glass orbs and cranberry garlands glittering with light, a symbol of all the hope and anticipation of the holiday. Now, as a grown woman about to join her life with that of the man she loved, the sparkling tree seemed to offer an even greater promise, one as wondrous and undying as Christmas itself.

"It's time we went a-caroling." Gran's whisper was almost apologetic as she hooked her arm through Milton's and pulled him gently up from the sofa. She paused behind Rachel and stooped to rasp in her ear. "Don't bother waiting up for me."

"We won't, Gran," Rachel assured her. "Have fun!"

The sofa cushion sank slightly as Patrick twisted and waved to the departing couple. Rachel's hand drifted down his back when he leaned to jab the glowing log with the poker, releasing a spray of embers onto the hearth.

"Isn't this beautiful?" Her eyes traveled from the Christmas tree to the bayberry candles gracing the mantel.

"It's just perfect." Patrick settled his arm around her and imparted a tender kiss on her forehead. "All comfy and happy?"

"Blissfully comfy." Rachel rested her head on his shoulder, snuggling deeper into his embrace. "And very, very happy. I'm especially glad Gran and Milton have finally *found* each other after being friends all these years."

When Patrick chuckled, Rachel relished the feel of his chest vibrating beneath her cheek. "Your grandmother and Milton have become quite an item, haven't they? No telling when those two will finally call it a night. If Gran's not careful, she might arrive home as Santa slides down the chimney."

"When you were a kid, did your parents tell you Santa wouldn't come until you were asleep?" Rachel asked, nuzzling her cheek against the soft lamb's wool of his sweater.

"Religiously. That's how Pete and I learned to sleep with one eye open and the other one closed. Not a bad skill for a cop, come to think of it. I'm really top-heavy with cop skills. Too bad I probably won't need them in my next job," he added, his face suddenly sobering in the flickering light.

Rachel stiffened, suddenly glancing up. "What are you talking about?" she demanded.

"That my police background doesn't seem to translate into the new career I'm trying to forge for myself."

Now thoroughly shaken, Rachel struggled to sit up straight and look him in the eye. "You can't just abandon detective work, Patrick!" she protested.

Patrick shook his head and smiled wearily. "Please! I'm hearing that line from enough people without your echoing it, too."

Rachel was in no mood to be sidetracked by humor. "I'm serious. I will not have you turn your back on the successful career you've built for yourself just for my sake."

"Who said anything about my making the change for you?" Patrick ruffled her hair with mock roughness. "Trust me, Rachel. This idea has been brewing in my head for a long time. I was sniffing out new career opportunities long before we were engaged—long before I thought you would ever speak to me again, for that matter. Helping Milton run the camp last summer gave me a chance to explore some options I'd never considered before. I like working with kids who need a push in the right direction, the youngsters who fall through the cracks."

"You're good at it, too," Rachel conceded, although she was still not entirely convinced that she had not figured in his decision.

"I think so, too," Patrick agreed modestly. "I just need a chance to prove it to potential employers."

"You already have proof. Look at the marvelous job you did at the camp," Rachel pointed out, now thoroughly involved in Patrick's newly revealed endeavor.

"I had hoped codirecting Camp Onoconohee would count for something, but so far, every youth-worker position I've investigated requires at least a master's degree in social work." His big hand glided across her cheek, deftly pulling her back to the comfortable niche of his shoulder. "So far my résumé hasn't attracted one serious nibble. So, you see, my new career is still off somewhere in the realm of pipe dreams. I hate to tell you, but you may be doomed to marry a lifer cop, after all."

"That doesn't sound all so terrible." Rachel was glad she could honestly make that statement.

Patrick gave her a grateful hug. "If we must discuss careers tonight, then please let it be yours and not mine. Somehow, I find your comanaging Heathervale Farm more suitable Christmas Eve conversation than my setting up sting operations with Arnie."

Rachel nodded her agreement. "The only drawback I can see is my going back to Boston next month. But I do have to tie up the loose ends with Marquette Brothers. They've been too generous for me to leave them in the lurch. I owe them my help until they fill my position. Still, it's going to be hard, being separated from you for two whole months."

"Boston isn't off somewhere in another galaxy. We'll manage to see each other as often as we can." He jostled her shoulders lightly. "Besides, if I can't persuade you to come home on weekends, I'm sure Gran will have the desired effect by appealing to your sense of duty. She's going to feel as if she's temporarily lost her right hand without you."

"It's funny. I never thought that much about my job when I took leave from Marquette. But I'm already worrying about Heathervale, and I haven't even left yet."

"Just be thankful you'll be coming back." Patrick's lips teased her ear invitingly.

"We do have a lot of things to be thankful for this Christmas. Has Al shown any more signs of regaining consciousness?" Although Rachel was certain Patrick would have shared word of any improvements in his partner's condition, she posed the question on the outside chance that he had been saving good news for their quiet time together.

"He continues to respond to touch, and the doctors believe he's aware of things going on around him. But no one can be sure how long the road back will be." A tender expression suffused Patrick's face, heightened by the reflected glow of the wood fire. "Kitty has put up a little tree in his hospital room as a way of letting him share the baby's first Christmas. Who knows? Maybe next Christmas, he'll be home."

"Maybe sooner," Rachel whispered her wish against the well-muscled cushion of his shoulder.

"Maybe." She felt Patrick's cheek rest against her head.

"We should also be thankful that Milton has found the funds to run the camp next year," Rachel put in.

"And that Milton and Gran have found each other," Patrick contributed. "But we've already talked about *that*."

"How about Patrick and Rachel finding each other?"

Patrick stretched his legs, sticking his feet as close to the fire as he could manage, and smiled. "That's something I'll be thankful for every Christmas for the rest of my life."

Rachel snuggled a little closer to him. "Imagine all the Thanksgivings and Christmases and anniversaries we'll celebrate together. Next year, we'll decorate our first Christmas tree in our own home. And when we have children, can't you visualize them tearing into their booty on Christmas morning?"

Patrick feigned a groan. "Does this mean I have to learn to set up an electric train without making any noise?"

"Uh-huh." Rachel nodded contentedly. "We have so much to look forward to."

"The present doesn't look all that bad to me, either."

Patrick enfolded her in his arms, pulling her gently back across his lap. She closed her eyes as his lips caressed her neck, then the pulse point in the cleft of her throat. She turned her mouth to meet his, cradling his face with her hands. As long as she lived, she knew her fingers would never tire of exploring the contours of that pleasantly rugged face. In the past month familiarity had deepened the intimacy between them, but had dulled none of the excitement.

Tonight, as their bodies wove together in the ritual of lovemaking, their hearts and minds joined in a spiritual union, the celebration of the true love that transcends physical bounds. In their moment of shared ecstasy, the common laws of physics were suspended, the lines distinguishing one's being from the other's blurred. For a time, made all the sweeter by its brevity, the barriers separating their individual feelings and thoughts and desires vanished and they were one.

Basking in the warm afterglow of their passion, they lay in each other's arms and watched the fire simmer to a bed of fiery coals. Rachel at last pushed herself onto one elbow, but only to stroke Patrick's hair lightly, curving the short curls over her finger.

"You know what would be nice?" she murmured.

"If it involves you, a million and one things come to mind."

A languid smile spread across Rachel's face. "How about a delicious warm bath?"

"I said, 'if it involves you,'" he reminded her, tracing her smile with the tip of his finger.

Rachel arrested the teasing finger with a kiss. "Of course it does! Come on." She stood up and took him by the hand, leading him up the stairs.

Inside the yellow-tiled bathroom, they filled the deep, old-fashioned tub with steamy hot water. With promises that Arnie Nordstrom need never know, Rachel persuaded Patrick to let her lace the water with a generous sprinkling of bath salts. They both giggled as she selected canisters and boxes from the wicker cabinet. Soon the close atmosphere was redolent with the blended fragrance of sandalwood and apples and bitter lemon.

Their physical contact was playful now, each taking turns scrubbing backs and massaging feet. As she lolled in the fragrant water, Rachel felt as if all her senses had been satisfied to the maximum.

The phone rang while she was lathering her hair with strawberry-scented shampoo.

"I'll get it," Patrick volunteered. Climbing out of the tub, he knotted a towel around his waist and hurried downstairs.

When he picked up the phone, he smiled, expecting to hear Gran Chase tell him that she wouldn't be home until the wee hours, but not to worry. He was surprised when an unfamiliar, clipped female voice greeted him.

"Hello? You must be Patrick!"

That she knew who he was only added to the mystery. "Yes, I am," he acknowledged, a little uncertainly.

"Patrick, this is Janet Chase. Rachel's mother," she added to dispel any lingering confusion about her identity. "Sorry if I startled you, but I got Rachel's note announcing your engagement, and when you answered just now I sort of put two and two together. Congratulations!"

"Thank you. Uh, I know you want to talk with Rachel. If you can hold on, I'll get her. She was washing her hair when you called, but if you can give her a few minutes..."

"Oh, don't bother her," Janet Chase interposed hastily. "My flight has just been called anyway. I'm in the Helsinki airport. Some place to spend Christmas, eh?" When she laughed, Patrick thought he detected the faintest shadow of loneliness in the quick, brittle voice. With the finesse of one practiced in concealing embarrassing emotions, Janet quickly picked up the conversation. "I'm sure you two are having a splendid holiday at Heathervale. And I do want to wish you both a very Merry Christmas."

"Merry Christmas to you, too. I'll look forward to meeting you at our wedding in June."

"That would be grand." She paused, and Patrick sensed that, for once, Janet Chase had no idea what she should say. A loudspeaker warbling in the background came to her rescue. "Uh-oh, last call for Copenhagen. That's me. Gotta go. Give Rachel my best, okay?"

"I will," Patrick promised the phone that clicked in his ear. Although he couldn't put his finger on the exact reason, the brief conversation had left him oddly dissatisfied, like a meal gobbled in haste and only partly digested. The discomfited feeling followed him as he walked back upstairs.

Rachel met him on the landing, dressed in a terry-cloth bathrobe with a towel wrapped turban-fashion around her head. "Who was that?" she asked. She loosened the towel and began to blot her pale blond hair with it.

"Your mother. She phoned from the Helsinki airport."

Rachel greeted the news with a short laugh. "Someday Mother is going to earn a mention in the *Guinness Book of World Records* for using a pay phone in every airport in the world."

"She wanted to wish us a Merry Christmas." Patrick followed Rachel down the hall to her bedroom. He leaned in the doorway, bracing both hands on the frame, and watched her rummage through the drawers of her dressing table.

"Well, I hope you wished her a merry one back." Rachel frowned in the mirror, trying to ease a tangle from her hair.

"I did. I also encouraged her to come to the wedding."

Rachel shook her head, giving him a tight smile as she unwound the cord looped around the blow dryer's handle. "Unless the world stops dead still on its axis that day, *something* will come up to prevent Mother from being here. Most people only have to make sure their parents make the right flight connections from Kalamazoo or wherever. But with Mother, you have to worry about things like military coups and earthquakes. Trust me. If anything newsworthy enough to be photographed happens on June 6, Mother is going to be there and not here.''

When she abruptly switched on the blow dryer, Patrick suspected Rachel was just as eager as Janet Chase had been to cover her emotions.

IF RACHEL AND PATRICK'S engagement had been contracted in the midst of the winter's harshest snow storms, the balmy weather fate bestowed on their wedding day more than compensated. Perhaps it was her imagination, but Rachel was convinced that Heathervale's fields had never been more bounteous, its centuries-old trees more verdant or its gardens more blessed with an abundance of fragrant, colorful blossoms.

As if nature had not done a splendid enough job, Gran Chase had converted the front room of the house into a veritable arbor for the occasion. Snowy clusters of lilac, baby's breath and lily of the valley spilled from vases in lacy profusion, while pots of waxy gardenias lent their sweet perfume to the fresh summer air. Garlands of moss-green velvet ribbon, interspersed with delicate dried nosegays, framed the mantel and wove through the bannister.

That Rachel even managed a glimpse of the lavishly decorated house prior to the wedding was nothing short of a miracle. A traditionalist to the core, Gran did her best to keep the bride clear of the wedding preparations until the last minute. When Rachel appeared on the stairs just an hour before the ceremony was scheduled to begin, her grandmother hastened to shoo her back to her room.

"I hope you're not intending to get married in *that*."
Gran cast a disdainful look at Rachel's extra-large T-shirt
and tattered jeans.

Rachel pretended to compare the grass-stained jeans with
the gracefully woven garlands. "The knees of these pants do
sort of pick up the moss color, don't you agree?"

Gran clapped her hands together as if she were herding a
gaggle of wayward geese back to their rightful domain.
"There will be plenty of time for clowning about after
you're married. Right now, it's time you did your duty. A
wedding is rather like an opera, Rachel, and the bride is the
diva. Remember, your audience will be depending on you.
Don't let them down."

As Rachel obediently followed her grandmother back to
her room, she suspected that Gran relished the role of im-
presario far more than she did that of star. Gran's face
glowed with the radiance normally reserved for brides as she
helped her granddaughter dress for the occasion. Still, if
Rachel could ever permit herself a flight of fancy, then this
was certainly the time. Turning in front of Gran's antique
wardrobe mirror, she luxuriated in the cool brush of bias-cut
satin against her legs. The dress was the stuff that dreams
were made of, a creamy flow of candlelight silk enriched
with satin-stitch embroidery. A demure tiara of pearls and
satin rosebuds completed the dreamlike image.

That this was no dream was brought home to her when
Gran cracked the door an inch to peer into the hall. The
sound of voices, many of them, chatting and laughing and
whispering in anticipation, rose from the ground floor and
filtered into Rachel's room. They had come to share a joy-
ous and solemn occasion with her and Patrick, the celebration of their union as husband and wife. For some reason,
the thought suddenly made Rachel feel very inadequate.

Gathering up the long skirts into two nervous fistfuls of fabric, Rachel paced back to the mirror. "We should have eloped," she muttered to the blanched reflection in the oval glass. "We could have had a nice, quiet ceremony in Nantucket with no one making such a fuss over us. For heaven's sake, I hope I don't trip over my skirt on the stairs. It shouldn't be this complicated, getting married. And I shouldn't be going through this all alone. Patrick and I should be together. I want Patrick."

"You'll have him soon enough, dear." Gran ignored her mumbling as she pried Rachel's fingers loose from the skirts and smoothed out the wrinkles. Taking her granddaughter by the hand, she led her to the door. "You're simply beautiful, darling! I'm very, very proud of you!" Rising on tiptoe, she brushed Rachel's cheek with a motherly kiss before hurrying downstairs.

Rachel drew a deep breath as she waited for the first notes of "The Wedding March." When the familiar music filtered up the stairs, she walked to the landing. Gran was waiting below in the hall, arm in arm with Milton, but her smile telegraphed her support to Rachel over the distance.

Through the fragile strains of the chamber ensemble's wedding processional, Rachel could hear the faint beating of her own heart. When she reached the bottom of the stairs, Milton stepped forward to take her arm. As they began their slow, measured walk to the waiting minister, she gazed around her at the faces of the friends and relatives assembled to honor the love she and Patrick shared.

The Morrissey clan was clustered at the end of the hall, Patrick's mother smiling through her tears, his father misty eyed but stoic, Maureen with an arm around both of them. Rachel was pleased when she recalled several faces from the family reunion, as well as a host she did not. Her own contingent from Boston formed a phalanx along the far wall, old college chums as well as the friends she had made during her days at Marquette Brothers. When she spotted Richard, standing arm in arm with Maddie Cusack, a smile flickered across his face, at once a sign of truce and of his blessing.

As Milton escorted Rachel into the front room, she continued to pick familiar faces out of the crowd: Jody Marshall, looking very grown-up in a green voile tea-length gown; Trip Barton, sporting a new moustache and an uncharacteristically serious expression; Arnie Nordstrom, doing his best not to look as out of place in the flower-filled room as he obviously felt. But the sight that touched her most was that of Kitty Ruiz standing beside her husband's wheelchair. As Rachel and Milton approached the waiting minister, Kitty stooped to whisper to the thin-faced man seated in the wheelchair. When Al slowly nodded, Rachel felt an enormous lump swell in her throat.

Her thoughts of Al and Kitty, of all the good friends and loved ones gathered in Heathervale's blossom-scented front room vanished in the single instant she glimpsed Patrick waiting for her with Peter at his side. As they repeated the simple vows after Reverend Baker, their eyes locked in a vision that excluded everyone but each other. Countless couples had used the same words to pledge their devotion to each other, but to Rachel, the promise to love, to honor and to cherish for a lifetime seemed as personal as if it had been composed for them alone. Their gaze never wavered as they exchanged rings and listened to Reverend Baker pronounce them husband and wife. The reverential hush was broken only when the minister gave his permission for the kiss. When Rachel's and Patrick's lips met, the wedding guests murmured their approval and the chamber ensemble broke into the recessional march. Solemn formality suddenly vanished as the newlyweds emerged into the hall and the guests swarmed around them.

"There now, dear. You didn't have to go through it all alone, did you?" Gran squeezed her arm so tightly, Rachel almost winced, and she could see that her grandmother was doing her level best to keep from crying.

"No, Gran, I didn't." Rachel blinked her own perilously brimming eyes as she threw her arms around her grandmother and gave her a grateful hug.

She released her hold as Patrick gently tugged at her elbow. Turning, she found herself face-to-face with a flush-faced Arnie Nordstrom. Although she didn't know him personally, in the past Rachel had regarded the police lieutenant as an adversary, a rival bent on keeping Patrick mired in a dangerous profession. Now, however, this stocky, embarrassed-looking man seemed anything but threatening as he racked his brain for something to say.

"Congrats, Morrissey." Arnie's plump hand pumped Patrick's. "Mrs. Morrissey." He nervously nodded to Rachel. When she held out her hand, he gave it an uncertain look.

"Thank you, Lieutenant Nordstrom," Rachel prompted with a smile. When Arnie took her hand, his palm was damp with perspiration.

Arnie was relieved of any further pressure to make light conversation as the crowd parted to make way for Al's wheelchair. Turning to Patrick, Rachel looped her arm around his waist and smiled at the Ruizes.

"I'm so happy for you," Kitty began, her small fingers tight with emotion on the back of the wheelchair. "We both are—" She broke off as Al's hand stirred on the arm of the chair.

"Con-grat-u-la-tions." Al shaped the word carefully, putting a volume of heartfelt feeling into each syllable.

Rachel bit her trembling lip as she watched Patrick reach out to his old friend and partner. When the two hands—one tanned and sinewy, the other pale, but driven by an unquenchable will—joined in a shake, she was powerless to hold back her tears. She was still dabbing at her eyes when the haphazard receiving line finally broke up and everyone headed for the sumptuous buffet Gran had laid out in the dining room.

"It's okay, Rachel. Brides are supposed to cry." Jody offered her consolation along with a tissue, as they followed the party down the hall.

Rachel paused in front of the hall mirror to blot smeared mascara from her cheeks. She smiled at the freckled face reflected next to her own. "I'm going to remind you of that in a few years."

Jody made a horrified face. "With the guys I know? Forget it! You got the last good one."

Not the last, but certainly one of the best, Rachel thought as she crumpled the smudged tissue. She turned, bent on finding at least one of the wastebaskets Gran had hidden for the occasion, when she spotted a woman standing in the front door. For a moment, Rachel could only stare at the phantom apparition that so closely resembled her own mother.

"You make a lovely bride, sweetie. But I always knew you would." Lingering on the threshold, Janet Chase shifted her purse awkwardly from one hand to the other.

Rachel snatched up her long skirt and rushed to the door. She pulled up short of her mother. "I didn't know you were here, Mother. How did I miss you in the crowd?"

Still clasping her clutch purse like an unseasoned debutante, her mother let her gaze drift back to the front lawn. "You didn't overlook me, Rachel. I—I didn't make it in time for the ceremony," she confessed. "Damned plane out of Rotterdam was delayed because of fog, and you know how it is getting out of Kennedy under any circumstances. When I got to Hartford, I jumped into a rental car, but they'll only go so fast.'' She broke off and blew out a heavy sigh. ''Here I go making excuses again, just like I always do. Someday, I guess I'll learn to just say I'm sorry and be done with it.''

''You don't have to say you're sorry, Mother,'' Rachel offered. *And I'm so happy you're here.* She swallowed, trying to ease the words out of her throat, but they refused to budge.

''You're a dear.'' Rachel's mother looked as if she wanted to say more but was unsure where to begin. ''Well, I got to see my baby all grown up and married. Now I suppose I ought to meet my new son-in-law and then be on my way.''

''No!'' Rachel was startled by the vehemence of her own protest.

Janet Chase blinked in surprise. ''What do you mean?''

''I mean you just can't drop in here, congratulate me and then run out again. You just can't!'' Rachel licked her lips, trying to bridle her urgent thoughts and marshall them into some coherent form. ''We need to talk.''

Her mother was silent for a long, painful moment. ''You're right,'' she at last conceded in a voice utterly devoid of its usual brisk confidence.

Glancing over her shoulder to make sure that the wedding party was still safely occupied in the dining room, Rachel took her mother's arm and guided her out of the house. Only when they reached the garden did she trust herself to speak.

''I'm really glad you came today, Mother.'' Rachel paused to clear her throat. ''And I don't for the life of me understand why it's so damned hard to say so. But it is. I guess I've conditioned myself over the years to hide my feelings for you. You always seem to be so busy, forever on the run. I haven't ever felt as if I could compete with all the important, exciting things in your life, and I suppose I started pretending I didn't want to."

"Oh, for God's sake, Rachel!" her mother interrupted with a hint of her old impatience. "Compared to you, all this other drivel in my life is meaningless."

Rachel blinked at her, too stunned to respond. "I-I don't understand," she at last managed to stammer.

Janet Chase's strong, capable hands balled into a tight knot. "You're not the only one in this relationship who's conditioned herself to hide feelings. Maybe if I hadn't been such a lousy mother..."

"Don't say that!" Rachel interjected, but her mother waved her into silence.

"To put it bluntly, I never felt up to the task of raising the precious child your father and I had been given. Oh, sure I read Dr. Spock and a dozen other experts, and I suppose I was competent enough, technically speaking. But I never had that...that extra something your father had. He was a natural parent, and I wasn't." A heartbreakingly sad smile trembled on her lips. "You were always 'Daddy's special little girl.' God knows, I didn't begrudge him your love, but I knew I was outclassed from the start. After we lost your father, I hoped for a while that we could become close. But I soon realized that Gran was all the parent you really needed."

"But I did need you too, Mother! Desperately."

Janet Chase stared at her daughter in disbelief. "But I thought...I mean you were always here...I had no idea. Oh, God, Rachel! What a fool I am sometimes!" She shook her head wearily.

"You're not a fool, Mother, just human, like me. I guess if either of us had risked speaking up, we could have saved ourselves a lot of pain. But let's not talk about what should have been." Rachel pressed her lips together for a second before going on. "Just know that I love you, Mother. And my wedding day simply wouldn't have been complete without you here to share it."

Her mother opened her hands, then clasped them again briefly before throwing her arms around Rachel. Hugging her daughter to her, she allowed herself the tears she had held dammed for so many years. "I love you, too, Rachel. With all my heart."

Epilogue

"I'm going to make a cyclist of you yet!" Panting, Patrick stuck out a foot to brake the heavy balloon-wheeled bicycle alongside Rachel's. "Are you sure you haven't been doing any training on the sly since our outing with the campers last summer?"

"Positive," Rachel assured him, releasing her hold on the handlebars to clamp one hand over her heart. "And before you start making plans for the Grand Prix, let me remind you that Bermuda is blessed with a flat coastline, ideally suited to trainer-wheel types such as myself."

Patrick leaned the bike to one side, allowing himself to slip an arm around Rachel's waist. His eyes swept the azure cove, sparkling in the morning sun below the terraced bike path. "It's certainly the perfect spot for a honeymoon. Milton and Gran make wonderful vacation scouts, don't they? We ought to think of a way to repay them."

"Maybe we'll have to take a trip to some exotic locale and then recommend it for their honeymoon," Rachel suggested.

Patrick considered the idea for a moment. "I suppose we need to get them engaged first."

Rachel laughed. "I wouldn't be surprised if our leaving them alone in Scarborough for these two weeks didn't do the trick!"

"Maybe we should extend our honeymoon for an extra week, just for good measure." His lips tickled her earlobe playfully.

Rachel wrinkled her nose, relishing the teasing kiss. "I could probably talk Gran into letting me have a few more days off from the farm, but something tells me Arnie would be a little harder to persuade."

Patrick groaned. "He's not exactly what you'd call a born romantic, is he? You know, he seemed surprised when I told him to count me out on a big operation he was setting up this month. I had to explain the quaint custom of the honeymoon to him, but I still don't think he could quite grasp why two people who have just gotten married would want to sneak off by themselves for a couple of weeks."

Rachel braced the bike with her knees, freeing her arms to give Patrick a quick hug. "Well, however skeptical Arnie might be of marital rites, you're safely out of his reach here. No one but Gran and Milton have the name of our hotel, and torture couldn't wrest a confession from either of them."

"Speaking of slow torture, that's what this ride is going to turn into if I don't get some breakfast pretty soon. I'm all for a good, brisk bout of exercise in the morning, but this is supposed to be a vacation." Patrick pressed a hand against his lean stomach to still its hungry rumblings.

Rachel straightened the bike and gave herself a hearty push off. "Race you back to the hotel!" she called over her shoulder. As she rounded the curve winding down to the resort bungalows, she glanced back to see Patrick's feet furiously fumbling with the pedals in a vain attempt to launch a rapid takeoff. She made a point of dismounting to greet him with folded arms when he finally coasted to a halt by the hotel's bike racks.

"That wasn't fair! You got a head start." Patrick's exertion-flushed face lent weight to his protest.

"Bike racing is a cutthroat sport, my dear," Rachel reminded him blithely.

"Yeah? Well, remind me never to go scuba diving with you," Patrick retorted dryly. "What shall we do for breakfast? Hit the dining room or have room service bring something to our bungalow?"

Rachel raised her hand shyly. "One vote for room service."

"It's unanimous then."

Lapping his arm over her shoulders, Patrick led the way up the path to a pale pink stucco bungalow. He unlatched the wooden door, ushering them into the cool whitewashed room. While Rachel opened the double doors onto the patio and arranged cushions on the terrace chairs, Patrick phoned room service to order a full English breakfast. They had just showered and changed into fresh shorts and polo shirts when the waiter tapped at the door. Rachel's mouth watered as she watched him arrange a platter of eggs and mixed grill on the patio table.

As soon as they were seated, Rachel reached for the tumbler of chilled tomato juice. "Shall we make a toast?"

"Why not? We've made one before every other meal we've shared during our honeymoon. I think we've toasted ourselves with everything from soda to tea, with some champagne here and there, just to keep it official."

"Well, for our tomato-juice toast I'd like to drink to Gran and Milton, first, for finding the Bridgewater Bungalow Resort for us." She lifted the glass. "And, second, for keeping it a secret." She nicked the rim of his glass lightly before taking a sip.

"I'll certainly drink to that." Patrick tipped his glass, tasting the thick, tart juice. He settled back into the comfortable patio chair, cradling the glass in his hands as he surveyed the tranquil bay stretching out to the horizon.

Rachel was passing the toast when the telephone buzzed. "Who on earth can that be?"

Patrick frowned over the dollop of orange marmalade he had just spooned onto his plate. "I don't know. Room service, maybe? The waiter could have forgotten something."

Rachel scanned the crowded table. "Only if breakfast includes the kitchen sink. Did you order a boat for this afternoon?"

"Uh-uh. You don't suppose something might have happened back home?"

An unwelcome tightness seized Rachel's throat, effectively blocking the progress of the toast she had just nibbled. "Oh, surely not!"

Inside the bungalow, the telephone kept up its persistent buzz. They both cast a reluctant glance through the open doors.

"Well, there's one way to find out who it is," Patrick conceded at length.

Rachel sighed as she pushed herself up from the table. "Stay put. I'll get it," she volunteered. When she grabbed the receiver, it seemed to vibrate with urgency in her hand. "Hello?"

"Mrs. Morrissey?" The speaker was gruff and no-nonsense, a cross between a football coach and an IRS investigator, but there was something vaguely familiar about the curt voice. "This is Lieutenant Nordstrom."

"Lieutenant Nordstrom." Rachel slowly breathed out the name into the phone.

"Yeah. Listen, I'm sorry to disturb you during your, uh, honeymoon. But I need to talk with Morrissey, I mean, Patrick. Is he around?"

Rachel glanced back at her husband of less than two weeks, comfortably lounging on the sun-baked terrace and for a split second, she was tempted to lie. Before she could think of a suitable story, however, her conscience got the best of her. Fabricating excuses was no way to begin life as a cop's wife. Better to let Arnie have his say and get the damage over with.

"Just a minute, please, and I'll get him." Rachel laid the phone on the credenza and walked to the patio door. "It's for you, Patrick."

"Who is it?" Patrick asked on his way through the door.

Rachel hung back, waiting until he had the phone securely in hand. "It's Arnie."

"Arnie!" Patrick almost shouted and then quickly cupped his hand over the receiver. "What the hell does he want? And how did he find out where we were?"

Rachel nodded helplessly toward the phone. "Maybe you ought to ask him."

Patrick's eyes were blazing blue flames as he lifted the phone to his ear. "All right, Arnie. This had better be good." He tugged angrily at the phone cord. "Uh-huh. Yeah, well it was supposed to be hard to get in touch with me. That's why we asked Mrs. Chase not to tell anyone where we were. What did you do to get it out of her? Threaten to sic the Health Department on her for not wearing a hair net in her kitchen?" Shaking his head, he gave Rachel an exasperated frown. "Oh. When?" Patrick looked surprised as he blinked at the pastel watercolor hanging over the credenza. "How did you hear about that? You did?" Patrick propped a hip against the credenza, a peculiarly sober expression spreading over his face. "Gee, that's really great! I mean, thanks. Really. Okay. Bye." After he had hung up the receiver, he continued to stare blankly for a few seconds.

Rachel was weaving from one foot to the other, scarcely able to contain her curiosity. "What on earth was that all about?"

"Arnie recommended me for a job as public relations officer for the police department's Youth at Risk program."

Now it was Rachel's turn to gape in amazement. "He what? You never told me there was a position like that opening up."

"I never knew there was. Until just now. That was why he wanted me to hang around this month, to talk with the powers that be. But he's assured me that everything's in the bag. The program director is an old buddy of his. Apparently, Arnie's recommendation is a seal of approval as far as this guy is concerned."

"So you're still a cop, but you're going to be working with young people, as well," Rachel marveled. "Just like that," she snapped her fingers in the air, "with one phone call?"

Patrick nodded. "Isn't it unbelievable?"

"Yes. I mean, *no!* I mean…" Rachel fumbled for words. "What *do* I mean?"

Patrick crossed the room, took her by the hand and led her back out onto the patio. With the warmth and brilliance of the morning sun flooding the small balcony, he ceremoniously picked up their glasses of tomato juice and gave them the hard, critical look of a wine connoisseur.

"Hmm, just the right color." Giving her one glass, he closed his eyes and sniffed the fragrance from the other. "Ah, yes, a bouquet fit for a king." He looked at Rachel out of the corner of his eye and winked. "It was a very good year."

"Yes," she said sternly, following his lead and assuming the tone of mock propriety. They clicked glasses in a final toast. "A very good year, indeed."

HARLEQUIN
American Romance®

COMING NEXT MONTH

#373 HEARTS AT RISK by Libby Hall

Reporting for an underground newspaper, Jennifer Wright champions
counterculture causes—and fears love's dangers. Test pilot Lij Brannigan explores
the limits of speed and performance in experimental jets—and struggles with his
own demons. And on the day man takes his first step on the moon, the
antiestablishment journalist and the fearless top gun enter an unknown world—
one that mingles age-old desire and space-age conflict. Don't miss the next
A CENTURY OF AMERICAN ROMANCE book!

#374 LAZARUS RISING by Anne Stuart

Though Katharine Lafferty was engaged to be married, her heart was still in
mourning. When Katharine had been nineteen and a college coed, Danny
McCandless had been twenty-four and a cool-headed criminal. In her innocence,
Katharine never thought that Danny might be bad for her. Now, ten years later, the
shock of Danny's death lingered—but it was nothing compared with the rude
shock of seeing him again.

#375 DAY DREAMER by Karen Toller Whittenburg

At first Jessica Day thought she had just imagined him. But soon she realized that
she could never have imagined anything half so strange and wonderful as Professor
Kale Warner and his oddball tale of stolen research and cloak-and-dagger antics.
And, even as Jessie was drawn into Kale's adventure, she wondered if someday
she'd be left with only unbelievable daydreams of a man she could never forget.

#376 MAGIC HOUR by Leigh Anne Williams

Oscar-winning director Sandy Baker wanted no partners on or off the set. But
Victoria Moore couldn't help getting involved—her first and most
autobiographical novel was being brought to the screen. Delving beneath the
written word, the charismatic filmmaker uncovered Victoria's private sorrows and
secrets. And despite the risks to her career and heart, Victoria couldn't suppress a
burning need to know this man, this stranger, who understood her like a lover.

Take 4 bestselling love stories FREE

Plus get a FREE surprise gift!

Harlequin Superromance ®

A powerful restaurant conglomerate that draws the best and brightest to its executive ranks. Now almost eighty years old, Vanessa Hamilton, the founder of Hamilton House, must choose a successor.
Who will it be?

Matt Logan: He's always been the company man, the quintessential team player. But tragedy in his daughter's life and a passionate love affair made him make some hard choices....

Paula Steele: Thoroughly accomplished, with a sharp mind, perfect breeding and looks to die for, Paula thrives on challenges and wants to have it all . . . but is this right for her?

Grady O'Connor: Working for Hamilton House was his salvation after Vietnam. The war had messed him up but good and had killed his storybook marriage. He's been given a second chance—only he doesn't know what the hell he's supposed to do with it....

Harlequin Superromance invites you to enjoy Barbara Kaye's dramatic and emotionally resonant miniseries about mature men and women making life-changing decisions. Don't miss:

- CHOICE OF A LIFETIME—a July 1990 release.
- CHALLENGE OF A LIFETIME
  —a December 1990 release.
- CHANCE OF A LIFETIME—an April 1991 release.

Harlequin Superromance®

THEY'RE A BREED APART

The men and women of the Canadian prairies are slow to give their friendship or their love. On the prairies, such gifts can never be recalled. Friendships between families last for generations. And love, once lit, burns hot and pure and bright for a lifetime.

In honor of this special breed of men and women, Harlequin Superromance® presents:

SAGEBRUSH AND SUNSHINE
(Available in October)

and

MAGIC AND MOONBEAMS
(Available in December)

two books by Margot Dalton, featuring the Lyndons and the Burmans, prairie families joined for generations by friendship, then nearly torn apart by love.

Look for SUNSHINE in October and MOONBEAMS in December, coming to you from Harlequin.

MAG-C1R